'Co
gre
fast

'[M
his
it .
Rya

'Po
cas
illu

'Ca
of t

'Co
and
way

'He

'Th
it's
vis

'It's a great read – it has the feeling of an epic film'
Mairead Ronan, *Today FM*

For more information on Marita Conlon-McKenna and her
books, see her website at www.maritaconlonmckenna.com

The Hungry Road

Marita Conlon-McKenna

TRANSWORLD IRELAND

TRANSWORLD IRELAND PUBLISHERS
Penguin Random House Ireland,
Morrison Chambers,
32 Nassau Street, Dublin 2, Ireland
www.transworldireland.ie

Transworld Ireland is part of the Penguin Random House group of companies
whose addresses can be found at global.penguinrandomhouse.com

First published in the UK and Ireland in 2020
by Transworld Ireland
an imprint of Transworld Publishers
Transworld Ireland paperback edition published 2021

A CIP catalogue record for this book
is available from the British Library.

ISBN 9781848271982

Typeset in 11/14.5 pt Ehrhardt MT by Jouve (UK), Milton Keynes
Printed and bound in Great Britain by Clays Ltd, Elcograf S.p.A.

The authorized representative in the EEA is Penguin Random House Ireland,
Morrison Chambers, 32 Nassau Street, Dublin D02 YH68

Penguin Random House is committed to a sustainable
future for our business, our readers and our planet. This book
is made from Forest Stewardship Council® certified paper.

For my family

Part One

Chapter 1

Skibbereen, County Cork, Ireland
June 1843

FROM EVERY FIELD AND FARM, LANE AND STREET, VILLAGE AND townland in West Cork, the people came. Some in groups, some alone, they walked in heavy boots or barefoot to witness their great hero, Daniel O'Connell, speak at the Monster Repeal Meeting in Skibbereen.

Mary Sullivan was among them, for she was determined to see the Great Liberator, who had done so much for Ireland and her people. She had been anxious about leaving her children, but her kind neighbour Brigid had offered to mind them.

Band music filled the stilly June air as she, her husband John, his brother Pat and uncle Flor neared the market town. The crowded streets of Skibbereen were bedecked with welcome flags and brightly coloured bunting, and every store, stall and merchant was busy. Mary laughed, caught up in the heady excitement and gaiety of it all.

Filled with anticipation, they joined the slow, winding snake of men and women of all ages as they pushed forward towards Curragh Hill, where their champion would address them.

Since sunrise, Father John Fitzpatrick had been watching the crowds arriving in Skibbereen. The people were like pilgrims travelling from afar, arriving in carts and coaches. Some were staying in the town's hotels and boarding houses, and many had walked miles to get there.

The numbers were huge – thousands and thousands – far greater than he and his fellow priests had hoped for when they sent out word to the people of Carbery that all were welcome to attend a meeting where the great Daniel O'Connell would speak of repealing the hated Act of Union, which had merged the parliaments of Great Britain and Ireland. He gave a silent prayer to the Lord to grant them a fine dry day for their endeavours.

After he returned home from saying mass, Father Fitzpatrick checked that his housekeeper, Bridey, had the spare room ready. He had informed her that a guest would be staying with him in the parish house that evening. The brass bed was made up with their finest linen, the wardrobe and chest of drawers were freshly polished with beeswax, the glass in the window was sparkling.

'I suppose they are going to the big meeting too?' Bridey asked the priest as he came downstairs. 'Will the two of you be eating here afterwards?'

'No, Bridey, don't trouble yourself. We're attending the Repeal Banquet in the Temperance Hall tonight. But I'm sure my guest would enjoy a good breakfast with some of your soda bread tomorrow morning before he sets off on his travels.'

'Father, I've never seen such a palaver in the town. But don't worry, I'll be up early to cook a few fresh eggs for the good father too.'

He laughed at her assumption that it was a man of the cloth who was coming to stay. He felt disingenuous, keeping the identity of his guest from her, but Bridey couldn't be trusted not to brag and boast around the town.

Father Fitzpatrick had had to admit to being rather surprised that Daniel O'Connell had rejected the Repeal committee's offer to take a room in the comfort of the nearby Becher Arms Hotel and requested to stay with him instead. Perhaps the great man preferred the privacy and quiet of a simple priest's home to more luxurious surroundings where he would be approached constantly by admirers. He would do his utmost to ensure Daniel O'Connell found rest and peace here in the parish house if that was what he desired.

Satisfied that everything was in order, Father Fitzpatrick left to join the large welcome procession of parishioners, carpenters, shoemakers, weavers, other tradesmen and musical bands getting ready to escort O'Connell and his carriage to the packed meeting place.

Dr Daniel Donovan was finishing his rounds of the Skibbereen Union Workhouse when the young midwife came running after him.

'The matron ordered me to fetch you,' she called, out of breath.

With O'Connell's visit to the town later that day, Dan was pressed for time, but he knew well that the matron would not request he attend unless she was in need of medical assistance.

The young mother-to-be in need of attention looked no more than eighteen years old; a pretty girl with thick dark hair that clung to her head with sweat.

'I am fearful for her and the child,' the middle-aged matron confided.

'I am here to help you,' he tried to reassure the girl. Her brown eyes were filled with fear, and she was too exhausted to take notice of him, let alone deliver a child.

As he examined her, it became clear that the baby was breech. Instead of presenting head down, one of the unborn child's tiny feet was beginning to appear first. Difficult and risky in any case, breech deliveries often resulted in the loss of mother and child.

Dan thought back to his medical school days in Edinburgh when his professor would lecture him and his fellow students on such cases. He would drive home the vital importance of judicious and decisive assistance with such problematic births to try to ensure both lives were saved.

O'Connell would have to wait, for the mother was near collapse and he needed to deliver the baby immediately. Dan ordered the two women to help him hold the mother as he attempted to extract the baby as swiftly as he could.

'I know you are tired—'

'Her name is Maggie Hayes,' interjected the matron.

'Maggie, let me help your baby.'

A foot, a leg, a thigh, the buttocks . . . Somehow he managed to hold the child's lower limbs steady and guide them as they emerged. Then, holding its body firmly, he quickly proceeded to ease the baby's neck and small head downwards, trying to ensure he did not damage the neck or spine. The infant was blue and still. Dan untangled and cut the cord quickly, willing the boy to take his first breath.

The silence was ominous as he caught the little fellow and held him up, clearing the mucus and blood from his face. Suddenly the baby stirred and moved his hands before giving a low, faint cry. Dan held and rubbed the child, relieved as the infant began to give a stronger cry, his lungs filling with air and his colour improving.

'You have a fine son,' he told Maggie, placing the baby into her waiting arms, 'but you must rest awhile.'

He nodded to the matron who was tending to her, before glancing at his fob watch and realizing how late he was.

Maggie smiled weakly.

'I am naming him William after my late father and Daniel for the Liberator who is in town this very day, his birth day,' she said proudly, kissing the baby's head.

'A day all of us will remember,' Dan acknowledged as he took his leave.

'I'm sorry for delaying you,' apologized the matron as she escorted him to the door, 'but thank you for your assistance.'

'You did the right thing,' he assured her, 'for both the mother and baby are healthy.'

'There is no mention of a father,' Matron sighed. 'The girl will have to stay here and nurse and mind the child.'

'At least they are both in your good care, Matron,' Dan said as he climbed up into his horse and trap, and set off home with great haste.

Henrietta Donovan was growing anxious, for her husband had promised to return for the meeting in plenty of time. Seeing such crowds, she fretted that they wouldn't get there soon enough. What could possibly be delaying Dan on such an important day? Suddenly, she heard his rapid footsteps on the stair.

'Where were you?' she scolded lightly. 'I was getting worried that—'

'Hush,' he soothed. 'I'm here now, just let me change my shirt and jacket. I was delayed in the Union, assisting a difficult birth. Fortunately, both mother and child are well.'

'Thank the Lord for that.'

She knew there was no point in rebuking Dan, for his patients would always come first. Her husband, the physician for the recently opened Skibbereen Union Workhouse and the town's dispensary, was possessed of a kind nature and an utter dedication to the care of the sick.

As they set off in the horse and trap, Dan took his wife's hand.

'You look pretty, my dear, in that new lace dress,' he offered.

Henrietta was delighted, for she had taken great care in curling her dark brown hair and applying a very slight touch of rouge to her lips, as well as purchasing a new dress for the occasion. She was gladdened by his compliment as Dan never usually noticed fashion!

The crowds had thinned as they made their way through town. Skibbereen's bars and taverns were all closed, for O'Connell was an outspoken advocate for the Temperance movement and did not want his Monster Meetings marred by the raucous behaviour of a few drunks.

Before long, Dan and Henrietta joined the line of horse-drawn vehicles pulling up at the enormous meeting place.

Henrietta's heart pounded with the reverberation of the drums as she and Dan were escorted to a position near the large podium. All around them were townspeople and tradesmen, tenants and labourers, united in the hope that O'Connell would help restore an Irish parliament to Dublin that would govern the Irish people fairly.

'Did we ever think that we would see this day?' laughed Daniel McCarthy, the wealthy brewer, unable to disguise the pride and emotion in his voice. 'The most famous man alive and, thanks to our own good efforts, here he is in Skibbereen.'

'We knew the people would come.' Dan gazed around him at the huge crowds. 'For O'Connell speaks of what is in every man's heart.'

'And woman's,' Henrietta reminded her husband, squeezing his arm.

There was a flurry of movement as carriages and a procession of people bearing tall, billowing banners began to approach the enormous gathering. As the band struck up loudly in the distance, she was overcome with a frisson of excitement.

Chapter 2

GAZING OUT ACROSS THE FLOWING RIVER ILEN, MARY SULLIVAN was overwhelmed by the sight of tens of thousands of people gathered together on Curragh Hill. The sea of O'Connell's supporters shimmered in a haze before her.

'Keep a hold of my hand,' urged John as he propelled her forward.

A regiment of soldiers stood to the side at the ready, observant and unflinching, as the couple manoeuvred their way through the waves of bodies towards the large wooden podium positioned at one end of the field.

A massive roar of welcome broke from the near seventy-thousand-strong crowd as three marching bands, followed by four stagecoaches bearing Daniel O'Connell and his entourage, arrived in the grounds. As the bands played a loud triumphant march, a procession of priests, parishioners and local tradesmen led the coaches up the field to cheers and applause. There was such a din that Mary worried how the drivers would control the horses.

The coaches finally came to a stop and the tall, heavy-set figure of Daniel O'Connell in his black cape stepped out and up on to the podium. He was an imposing figure, with a broad face and a head of dark curls. His eyes roved appreciatively over the huge crowd.

A hush fell as a man with pride in his voice welcomed the Liberator to Skibbereen, citing O'Connell's achievement in securing Catholic emancipation and his fight now to repeal the despised Act of Union.

The crowd began to cheer wildly as O'Connell threw off his cape with a confident swagger. In grand style he stepped forward and flung open his arms, greeting his supporters warmly in a clear, booming voice. There came a roar of approval as he began to speak in Gaelic, and laughter at the bewilderment of the large force of British military and constabulary that had surrounded the field. The redcoats were left scratching their heads, wondering what he was saying.

'I am honoured to be your representative in Parliament,' O'Connell continued, his eyes shining, 'even though it is a Parliament packed against me.'

The cheers echoed through the still summer's day as he spoke of the achievement of Catholic emancipation, which had finally given Catholics the right to hold important offices and serve as members of the British parliament.

O'Connell's voice filled with emotion as he looked down at the crowd.

'I may have been at the head of the battle, but victory could not have been won without you, the people, behind me.'

11

A profound silence fell as he outlined his new Repeal campaign to regain Irish freedom and self-government with the return of an Irish parliament to Dublin.

'It is the right of every Irish man over twenty years of age to have a house and to vote.'

O'Connell's voice carried loud and clear across the field, filling the spectators' parched hearts with the hope of change. They latched on to his words, all tiredness and soreness in their feet and legs forgotten. The prospect of freedom hung in the air, blowing tantalizingly among them, along with the cherished hope of regaining the right to own the roof over their head and the land on which they raised their crops. Many were ready to rally to his call and take up arms to fight if need be!

However, O'Connell soon made his opposition to violence clear.

'This battle will be fought in Parliament peacefully and legally, with justice and equality as our swords. Good people, I call on you to support the Repeal movement, for we intend to grow it. Lastly, I ask you all to give three cheers for Queen Victoria, who rules the empire. The Queen!'

John and Pat remained stubbornly silent, their eyes cast down as the cheers echoed across the fields and hills.

'Hurrah! Queen Victoria! Hurrah!'

As O'Connell brought his speech to a close, he thanked the crowd for travelling so far – from all over Cork, Kerry and Tipperary – before bidding them farewell. The band struck up again loudly and, in only a few short minutes, the coaches and horses departed the field to more cheers as the Liberator's carriage passed.

As the crowds began to disperse slowly, Mary felt strangely bereft.

'He has the men, so why doesn't he organize us instead of sending us home with only words?' Pat remarked angrily as the coaches disappeared from view. 'Words won't win back our cottages and our land.'

'Hush, or you'll get us all into trouble,' cautioned Flor, noticing a soldier standing nearby.

'Will we all go into town for a pint of porter to mark the day?' suggested Pat. 'Hopefully one or two public houses will be open.'

Mary had no interest in joining the men in one of the town's noisy hostelries. Instead, she decided to call on her sister, who lived in the crowded, rundown lanes of Bridgetown on the far edge of Skibbereen.

'I'll meet you in Kathleen's later,' promised John, 'and we'll walk home together.'

Chapter 3

AS THE PEOPLE STREAMED BACK INTO SKIBBEREEN, MANY OF THE shops and stalls had re-opened. Mary paused as she passed Honora Barry's dressmaking shop where she had worked as a seamstress before her marriage. It was still closed but Miss Barry had wisely placed a pretty sprigged-cotton dress in the window to attract customers.

She continued on her way and turned in to the narrow streets of Bridgetown, with its rows of small low cottages and cabins built almost on top of each other. Children played in the dirt and a group of women in shawls chatted loudly about the handsome Liberator.

The Caseys' cottage was down the end of a lane. Outside, her nephews and niece – Michael, Jude and Sarah – were busy with a piece of old rope they had found, and some sticks and a plank of wood.

'We're making a boat to float on the river,' boasted eleven-year-old Michael as Mary ruffled his thick curly hair.

Kathleen welcomed her younger sister warmly as she stepped inside.

'You were up at the Liberator like Joe and the rest of them?' she asked. 'I'd a mind to go myself but Lizzie is teething and she'd have roared the place down.'

Mary could see the baby's hot red cheeks and felt an immediate sympathy for her once-beautiful sister, who now looked worn out. Things were hard for Kathleen as her husband, Joseph Casey, who had charmed her with his handsome looks, grand talk and promises to make a fortune, was a simple labourer who went from one job to another. He had been employed on building the large Union workhouse, but had had little work since then.

Mary did not know how Kathleen could bear such circumstances. The small, one-roomed cottage with its half-door was in the worst part of town. It was cramped and gloomy. The three older children slept in a low space under the thatch roof, while Kathleen and Joseph slept on a pallet bed placed against one wall, with Lizzie in a makeshift crib nearby.

Kathleen flung more turf on the fire and brewed some leaves for tea while Mary told her excitedly about O'Connell and his stirring words.

'I've no use for politicking.' Kathleen shrugged. 'What have all these members of parliament ever done for the likes of us?'

She called the children in and insisted that Mary share their family meal of spuds and buttermilk.

'There will be better eating in a few weeks,' she apologized as they dipped the old, greyish spuds in salt and mustard. 'Once Joe gets harvest work.'

*

By the time John called to collect Mary it had grown dark and Kathleen was putting the children down to sleep. After saying their goodbyes, Mary and John took the road for home together.

The stars shone high above them and John reached for her hand.

'That was the grandest day ever.' Mary's heart was full of hope from the Liberator's words. 'One I will always remember.'

'Aye, so many people gathered together,' John agreed. 'But it will all come to nothing if no one listens to us!'

'Daniel O'Connell will win them over.'

'I fear no matter what he promises, it's the landowners of England who will decide our fate.'

Even in the darkness Mary could sense her husband's doubt.

'Believe me, they will fight tooth and nail to stop Repeal,' he warned her.

'But we will win!' She'd no intention of letting John dampen her enthusiasm.

He reached down impulsively and kissed her. His lips tasted of porter, and as she responded he pulled her even closer to him, holding her so near that she could hear the steady beat of his heart. She ran her hand along his face tenderly, her fingers touching the stubble of his cheek and jaw.

'*Mo ghrá*.' He gave in, kissing her again, this time gently. 'I pray that you are right.'

They walked along the starlit road until they neared the familiar potato fields with the tall willow trees and scraggy hedges.

'One day this will be ours,' she affirmed as they walked

towards the low thatched cottage where their children slept. 'Every root, stalk and blade of grass, and every bit of earth beneath our feet will belong to us.'

'Sullivans' fields,' John shouted, spinning her round and round in the darkness. 'Sullivans' fields.'

Chapter 4

THOUGH THE HOUR WAS LATE ON THEIR RETURN FROM THE DINNER in the town's large Temperance Hall, Father John Fitzpatrick sat talking with his guest by the fireside.

A huge crowd had attended the Repeal Banquet and people had milled around, keen to be introduced to the great man. After dinner, a toast had been proposed to O'Connell and Repeal, which had nearly raised the roof.

One young Irelander had declared boldly his determination to shed his blood for Repeal, even if it was on the scaffold. O'Connell had told young John Shea Lawlor that rather than die for Ireland, he would rather live for Ireland, for one living repealer is worth a churchyard full of dead ones! It had been inspiring to listen to the great orator.

'You must be tired after such a successful day,' Father John ventured as they sat back in their chairs. 'And then to have to go and meet and talk to so many people again tonight.'

'Father, that is what is expected of me in every town the

length and breadth of the country.' O'Connell yawned as he stretched out his legs in front of the fireplace. 'But it does help to raise contributions and funds for the movement.'

Father John could see his guest was weary. The man's eyes were heavy and his face was slightly flushed. He looked every bit of his near seventy years of age.

O'Connell chose that moment to confide in the priest that although he was often surrounded by crowds, he was lonely. He had his sons and grandchildren, but he desperately missed his late wife, Mary, and her conversation and company.

'You of all men must understand. Here you are with a large parish yet come home at night to sit at a lonely hearth?'

Father John did indeed know all too well. Answering the call to the priesthood meant that he would always remain a man alone with no wife or child of his own.

The two men continued to chat easily. O'Connell sighed heavily as he reeled off a list of places that he was still to visit to speak at before the largest Monster Meeting of all.

'It will be in October, in Clontarf in Dublin. I hope that you will join us, Father John, for there will be Repeal supporters coming from all over the country.'

'I and a few of the Skibbereen committee will certainly try to attend,' the priest promised.

'We need to demonstrate – to Peel and to Parliament – the massive support our movement enjoys, and force them to respond to the demands and will of the Irish people,' said O'Connell with fervour.

'Such a large-scale event in Dublin will certainly attract their attention.'

'I fear the authorities and Dublin Castle are already opposed to it. No doubt the military will be out in full force,' O'Connell confided. 'But I believe that Clontarf, the place where the great Brian Boru vanquished the Vikings, will be the place where we may gain our own victory. We will have such numbers that they will have no alternative but to grant us Repeal and the return of an Irish parliament to Dublin.'

The next morning, Father John was glad to see that his guest looked more refreshed after a good night's sleep. Bridey almost scalded herself with hot tea when she recognized the Liberator sitting at the dining table.

'I'm sure Mr O'Connell would enjoy some of your bread and an egg or two before he sets off on his travels,' said Father John with a smile.

Ever the gentleman, O'Connell complimented the blushing housekeeper on her soda bread and begged her for a few slices more before he left.

'Father John, until we meet again in Dublin,' Daniel O'Connell said, shaking the priest's hand and thanking him warmly for his kindness and hospitality.

As the priest watched O'Connell's carriage drive down North Street, he could not help but wonder how much longer the Liberator could continue his fight for Ireland and her people. Surely the time was coming for a new, younger generation to take up the mantle and battle for the change Ireland needed so desperately.

Chapter 5

Creagh, County Cork
October 1843

AS MARY TIDIED HER SMALL VEGETABLE PATCH, SHE COULD FEEL the warm autumn sun on her back. John teased her about growing cabbages, turnips and onions, saying it would be far better to plant potatoes there, but her mother had always grown a few vegetables and she wanted to do the same.

When she had married John Sullivan, Mary had moved out of Skibbereen to the holding near Creagh that John shared with his father, Cornelius. The old man had welcomed his new daughter-in-law and had insisted she and John take the room he had shared with John's late mother, Anne. He had also been glad, she suspected, to have a woman around again to clean the place and cook the meals.

Little by little, Mary had made some changes. She had convinced John to mend the cottage's thatch roof and wash its walls with lime, and to build a wooden pen for the pig to stop it from wandering about and destroying the place. Encouraged, she had even persuaded him to make a small hen-house to hold their hens.

'With all these improvements, we will have the landlord down on us looking for more rent,' John had said, worried.

'They are only small things,' Mary had assured him. 'Things any bride would want.'

Old Corney Sullivan's eyes had filled with tears when he held his first grandchild, Cornelius John Sullivan, in his arms. He was a wonderful grandfather, who loved young Con – and his little sister, Nora, who followed soon after – dearly.

Following his father's death, John had been heartbroken. The only consolation was that his parents were finally reunited, buried together in the nearby graveyard.

Soon after, John had gone to Henry Marmion, the land agent for their landlord, Sir William Wrixon Becher, and asked to take over his father's holding. The tenancy was agreed but the rent was increased.

'A young man like you should be well able to work harder and earn more than the old man ever did,' Mr Marmion had told him as he gazed about the Sullivans' well-ordered fields and cottage.

Mary had felt guilty that her husband's fears had been well-founded and that her few improvements had somehow caused the increase.

'This is no fault of yours, Mary,' John had reassured her. 'That man has been waiting many a day for my father to die so he could do this and try to squeeze even more money and work from us.'

In the years that followed, Mary and John had worked hard, raising Con, Nora and their third child, little Tim, and tending their holding of one and a half acres. They now fattened two pigs – one for the market and one for themselves – and kept a few sheep. She even had twelve hens, and supplemented the family's small income by selling some of their eggs.

Looking up from her work weeding the vegetable patch, Mary laughed as she watched the children play with Patch, their black-and-white collie. Eight-year-old Con was throwing a stick for him to fetch, but the dog began to bark as he spotted John and Pat returning from town in Pat's small, horse-drawn wooden cart.

'There is bad news,' John called as he climbed down. 'O'Connell's Monster Meeting in Dublin was cancelled.'

'The Lord Lieutenant had the military and the police surround the city,' said Pat angrily. 'They even had warships at the ready in Dublin Bay to attack the crowds. They are all afraid of O'Connell and the millions who follow him!'

'O'Connell had no choice but to call it off, for many might have been injured or killed,' John explained as he lifted a sack of oats from the cart.

'There is talk that O'Connell himself will be arrested! Parliament and the authorities detest him and the Repeal movement.'

'The Liberator will fight on,' Mary insisted.

'Then he should have fought earlier when he had the chance,' Pat said sarcastically, urging the horse on as he headed across the fields to his own small dwelling.

Later that night, as she and John sat by the fire, Mary's thoughts were with the proud, strong man who had stood on Curragh Hill and promised to champion the cause of poor tenants like them.

John stared into the glowing turf. 'O'Connell may well be arrested, but he has shown us that we have the numbers. Pat and his Young Irelander friends are right. The time is coming that we should forget politics and fight properly for what is ours.'

Mary loved her husband dearly but was suddenly afraid of what he might become involved in.

'John, we have the children and the farm. Promise me that you will not—'

'Hush,' he said, placing his finger on her lips. 'I cannot make a promise I may not be able to keep.'

Even in the dull firelight she could see that he would brook no more discussion on the matter.

Chapter 6

Skibbereen
September 1844

'GRAND DAY, FATHER!' BEAMED TIM MCCARTHY DOWNING.

Father John Fitzpatrick had stopped in front of the large site on North Street where he hoped in time to build a much-needed new school for the town.

'Like myself, you must be delighted to see Daniel O'Connell released from prison and a free man again,' the local solicitor ventured.

'Indeed I am, Mr McCarthy Downing, for his imprisonment was a travesty.'

The priest, along with most people, had been deeply troubled by O'Connell's arrest the previous year on charges of conspiracy. Following the ban of last autumn's Monster Repeal Meeting in Clontarf, the great man had been treated like a common criminal. Along with his son, John, and five followers, he'd been sentenced to a year in Richmond Prison.

Father John had written to his former house guest, and his

heart had lifted on hearing that O'Connell was in good spirits. He received news that he was being treated fairly, and his family and friends were permitted to visit him. Then, earlier that month, the House of Lords had thankfully deemed the trial unfair and O'Connell was released.

'By all accounts, he's had a hero's welcome in Dublin, with over two hundred thousand supporters coming out to cheer him. It must have been a fine sight to see,' laughed Tim McCarthy Downing. 'The Liberator transported through the streets of Dublin in that gilded carriage drawn by six horses!'

'It is only what the man deserves,' the priest acknowledged.

'How are the plans for the new school here going?' enquired McCarthy Downing.

'I'm afraid there are still funds to be raised and a great deal of paperwork and planning details to be worked out before we begin,' Father Fitzpatrick admitted honestly, 'but we will persist until we get our school.'

'If there is any assistance I can give, please call on me, Father,' the solicitor offered.

'I may well take you up on that, Mr McCarthy Downing.'

The construction of St Fachtna's School had been a long-cherished hope of Father John's. In his eyes, the children of Skibbereen deserved a good education and to attend a school where they would learn to read and write. In his mind, it was the only way to a fairer society.

'Father Fitzpatrick, if you are free on Sunday would you care to join us for lunch?'

'That is most kind of you,' he said, accepting the offer, for McCarthy Downing was a generous man and a most considerate host with a beautiful home. 'I shall look forward to it.'

26

'We can celebrate O'Connell's release,' the other man said with a smile, and took his leave.

There was indeed much to celebrate, but the priest's delight at Daniel O'Connell's freedom was tempered somewhat upon hearing that some considered the Liberator's health to have deteriorated during his incarceration, and there was the suggestion that he was a changed man. Father John prayed that Ireland's great leader would be restored in strength of mind and body before long and, with his usual courage and conviction, would soon take up the fight for Repeal once again.

Chapter 7

Creagh
August 1845

ALL AROUND MARY, THE WHITE POTATO BLOSSOM FLUTTERED IN the fields. The pale flowers crowned each lazy bed of the crop, for the drills were nearly ready to be dug. The air was heavy and warm. Patch lumbered over to sit near her feet, panting with the strange, intense heat of the day. Mary pulled up her streels of light-brown hair as it was so warm, and closed her eyes momentarily as Con, Nora and Tim played together, while ten-month-old Annie slept in her crib inside the cottage. She was roused from her moment of stillness by Nora, whose freckled face was flushed from running.

'Ma, it's too hot for us. Can we get some water?'

The hens clucked around Mary as she walked to the well and filled the bucket with cold, clear water. She dipped the can into it again and again as she and the children drank their fill and splashed water on their faces and arms to cool down. Each time she refilled the bucket and tipped it into the hens' dish, Patch lapped up the spilt liquid.

Within half an hour the heat of the day was gone, for the sun had disappeared behind a dark heavy cloud. Without warning, rain began to lash down and she called to the children to join her inside as they ran to escape the torrential downfall. As the heavy raindrops beat the ground and the straw roof, she worried how their plants would tolerate such a deluge.

It was the second time this week that the strange rain had come.

'Mam, there's a fierce bad smell outside,' announced Nora. ''Tis everywhere.'

Curious, Mary stood up immediately and, with Annie in her arms, went to investigate.

As she looked around, she could neither see nor smell anything except for the peaty scent of smoke from the fire. She was about to go back inside when she glanced towards their fields. Her attention was caught by the strange, sudden wilting of the tall potato stalks, which seemed to have blackened and collapsed. Row after row of their potato plants were stricken.

'Take your sister!' she ordered Nora as she made her way to the drills.

Within seconds, Mary too was assailed by a sickening stench – rotten and putrid. She had never smelt the like of it and was filled with apprehension. Taking the spade, she began to dig. As she reached with her fingers, she lifted a clump of shapeless blackened potatoes that resembled nothing she had seen before: the vegetables were a stinking mess in her hands.

Worried, she called for the boys to come and help her.

'Ugh!' grimaced Con, covering his nose with his hand.

'Run and fetch your father!' she urged. 'He's down in the lower woods with Flor, cutting logs. Tell him he's needed here!'

Her eldest son took off while she and seven-year-old Tim dug a few more plants.

'Mam, these are bad,' complained Tim, for the ones he lifted were marked with signs of some strange disease.

Before long, John returned from the woods with Con. Uncle Flor, out of breath, followed behind them with Smokey, the old donkey, and the little cart. John grabbed the shovel from Mary immediately, cleaving deep as he dug into one drill after another, checking the potatoes.

'God's truth, I've never seen the like of it,' he said with worry as he scrutinized the potatoes, his fingers touching the oozing softness of the blackened tubers.

'I'm away to our place,' declared Flor, his eyes filled with concern.

'Any potatoes you find that are white and hard, throw them in the bucket,' John told the boys as he turned the earth, searching the ridges desperately for any potatoes that could be saved from the pestilence that had fallen on their crop.

Mary could see in the neighbouring field that the Flynns' crop appeared to be in the same sorry state as their own. How could potato plants have turned so quickly from growing strong and healthy one minute to this state?

Over in the small field, the drills seemed a bit better and John dug quickly, the lug of the spade turning up clumps of firm white potatoes that seemed untouched, unlike the other tubers.

'Con, bring the buckets for me to fill!' he called out.

30

Side by side, the family worked together, examining every smooth round shape closely in the hope of finding healthy and edible potatoes. In the surrounding fields, Pat, Flor, his wife Molly and their neighbours were digging and kneeling in the earth, backs bent, doing the same.

When he came to some of the drills at the far end of the field, John gave a shout of triumph. Despite having black spots dotted on their leaves, the potatoes seemed firm and healthy. The family filled four or five buckets with them, then John layered those that bore no sign of disease carefully in the potato pit where they would be kept until they were needed.

Annie began to cry hungrily, and Mary sat down on the stone wall to feed her.

'Are ye all destroyed too?' asked their neighbour Nell Flynn, coming towards them. Her hair fell around her face in dirty streels, and her skirt, blouse and feet were covered in mud. 'There is divil a bit to eat in our patcheen of a field. I've never seen the like in all my years. What did we do to deserve this?'

Mary knew how hard things were for the Flynns, who lived with their three sons in a tiny cabin near the end of the lane. They had only a bare quarter-acre to feed them. Nell's husband, Tom, with his bad hip, was unable to do the same heavy work as the other men, and he and Nell constantly borrowed and begged off their neighbours.

'Nell, will you have some tea?' Mary offered her. 'It's too hot to be sitting here.'

The older woman followed Mary, who was glad to get away from the sight of the rotting stalks, into the cottage.

'The boys will go hungry for we've nothing to give them,' Nell complained as she sipped her tea noisily.

'They'll not go hungry tonight for you'll take a few eggs and a half of soda bread home with you,' Mary found herself offering, for she was used to Nell and her ways.

'But you might have need for them yourself,' Nell wheedled, looking around her.

'I have more flour in the barrel and my hens are good layers,' Mary insisted as Nell left, trying not to give in to the rising panic she felt at the loss of most of their potato crop.

John stayed outside, searching their fields for any more healthy-looking potatoes, as Mary prepared their evening meal. The children were quiet, their eyes big in their heads, as she served up a pot of the first crop of new potatoes with some salt. To her mind there was a slight taint to them.

'I think they taste grand,' said ten-year-old Con, who always made the best of things, as he helped himself to more.

'What are we going to do, Mammy, when the taties are all gone?' ventured Nora.

'Your daddy and I and all of you will be fine,' she assured them, trying to hide her worry and fear. 'We have three sacks and some in the pit. We have plenty of flour in the barrel and vegetables, pigs and sheep to sell at the market. We'll not go hungry, for your father will always get work.'

The children were gone to bed when John finally crossed the door, his black hair wet with sweat. Mary flung her arms around him and made him sit by the fire. She dished up the new potatoes with a mug of buttermilk, which he ate hungrily.

'At least we've three good sacks and some in the pit to feed us,' she said, serving him a few more.

32

'Near two-thirds. The best part of our crop is gone,' he said forlornly.

'It's not the end of the world,' she replied quietly. 'We've lost part of the crop before.'

'Nothing like this!' he said bitterly. 'It is like some quare disease that has fallen on them. Denis Leary says it is everywhere across the Mizen and that the pestilence came in the mist and the clouds and the rain.'

She thought of her brothers' fields in Goleen, and wondered if they too were badly affected.

'I don't know what we will do, Mary,' he said in despair, 'for we still have to find the rent money.'

'We can sell the animals,' she said reassuringly.

'Aye,' he agreed with a yawn. 'Besides, without potatoes we have nothing left to feed the pigs with.'

They were both worn out and so made ready for bed. John finally gave in to exhaustion and fell asleep beside her, but thoughts crowded Mary's mind. She stared up at the dirty thatch, wondering how, with so much of their crop gone, they would manage during the hungry months to come.

Chapter 8

Skibbereen
September 1845

AS DAN DONOVAN WAS DOING HIS DAILY ROUNDS OF THE SKIBBEREEN Union Workhouse, the master stopped him outside the small infirmary for the sick. A tall, imposing man with bushy eyebrows and whiskers, Mr Falvey appeared a rather intimidating figure, but Dan found him to be meticulous in his duties with a great concern for the fair treatment of those who entered the Union.

'Doctor, we've had a large increase in the number of admissions these past few days,' the master explained. 'No doubt the potato failure has contributed to it.'

'With so little to eat, some will have no recourse but to enter here,' Dan acknowledged. 'I fear that it will likely get worse, so the Union must prepare, Mr Falvey, for this increase in our numbers to continue.'

The Skibbereen Union Workhouse had opened only three years ago and housed far fewer inmates than it was built to hold, for local people had a huge fear of crossing its threshold. Who could blame them, for it provided little comfort and operated under the same strict rules as other workhouses built across the country and throughout England and Wales. Men, women and children who entered were all separated and housed in different wings, and had little contact with each other.

Dan Donovan's role as physician was to ensure the inmates remained healthy, that they were cared for medically, if necessary, and that there was no outbreak of contagion or disease among them. He did his best to ameliorate their conditions, treating them in the same way he did all his patients, for the Union was the last resort of the sick, the homeless and the mentally ill, who had no family or friends to care for them.

'Then we are in agreement.' The master nodded seriously as Dan continued on his way to the women's ward.

There, he met with an elderly woman who begged him for help. Not for herself, but for her husband who was in the men's ward.

'He's blind, doctor. These past years I've minded him all this time, but with the potatoes gone how am I going to feed and keep the two of us?' she sobbed.

'Mrs Reilly, I promise that he will be fed and looked after here,' he assured her. 'You both will.'

The relief on her tired, wrinkled face was visible.

'Can I see him?' she begged. 'Tomás and I have never been parted and he will be afraid, for he knows nothing – only our small cabin and patch.'

'In time your husband will get used to being here, but I will arrange with the master that you can visit him.'

Continuing on his rounds, Dan's next stop was the men's

ward to see Mrs Reilly's husband, Tomás. He found the poor man deeply upset, his hands clasped over his head and clearly terrified by his new surroundings.

'I talked to your wife and will arrange that you are allowed to see her,' Dan promised the elderly man, taking hold of his hands.

As he examined Mr Reilly, he could see the man was malnourished but otherwise well cared for by his wife. Both eyes showed cataracts, their lenses a dense milky white, but the right eye was slightly better than the left.

'I lost the sight near ten years ago,' Tomás sighed heavily. 'I prayed that it would come back but it never has.'

Disorders of the eye had always fascinated Dan and he had studied ophthalmology in Scotland. He had considered practising as an oculist, but instead had become a general physician. However, he still maintained a keen interest in researching and treating eye conditions, and had developed quite a reputation in that area. Patients came from all over to consult him and he wondered if there was any way to restore even a little of Tomás's vision.

Moving on to the children's nursery, he examined two sisters who had been found by neighbours. The little girls were unwashed, uncared for and clearly malnourished.

'The eldest girl told us her mother died and their father went away,' declared the nurse angrily. 'He left them like two unwanted puppies.'

Dan examined the children gently, for they were both terrified. Their matted hair was riddled with lice and scabies.

'I'm Dr Dan,' he told them kindly, 'and the nurse is going to wash you both. She's going to cut and comb your hair, and put a special lotion and ointment on your skin that will take away the terrible itch. I promise it will help you both to feel better.'

'Do we have to stay here, sir?' the older child asked tearfully.

'Yes, I think it is for the best,' he ventured, not trusting himself to say more. 'You will be safe here.'

It angered him deeply how people treated their children, with no regard for their feelings.

As he was leaving the ward, young Will Hayes ran over to greet him.

'Dan . . . Dan,' the boy called, gripping the doctor's leg.

Dan lifted up the two-year-old in the air. Will was a fine, sturdy fellow with straw-coloured hair and piercing blue eyes, and only a year younger than Dan's youngest son. Whenever he saw the little boy on his rounds, he made a point of talking and playing with him, for being a workhouse child was no easy thing.

Will's mother had absconded from the Union after six months, leaving her illegitimate child to be raised in the workhouse. His childhood would be one of hardship and work, with little affection shown to him. At twelve or thirteen, the boy would likely be apprenticed out to some local farmer or tradesman. Dan hoped that some day, far from the Union, little Will would find the love and happiness he deserved.

Riding back towards Skibbereen that evening, Dan stopped his horse and trap to survey the blighted fields all around him. Most of Carbery district had been affected by the murrain, with more than a good half of the crop ruined. Even the few acres he had purchased in Poundlick, where he grew mostly oats and barley, had seen heavy losses of potatoes.

He had ridden out there after church on Sunday to discover that most of the crop belonging to his tenants had been destroyed, leaving them fearful. They were decent men with families and he had assured them that, for the time being, he was prepared to forgo the rent payment, due to the circumstances in which they found themselves. As he told them, he had seen the gratitude and relief in their eyes.

Looking around him at the stinking, blackened potato stalks, he hoped that many of the local landowners were prepared to do the same for their tenants.

Chapter 9

October 1845

HENRIETTA DONOVAN AND HER CHILDREN STROLLED HAPPILY around the crowded Carbery Agriculture Society Show, admiring the prize-winning livestock on display.

Her eldest boys, Henry and Jerrie, and daughters Ellen, Fanny and Harriet were beside themselves with excitement at seeing all the animals. The big bulls that blew steam from their nostrils; the grunting, smelly pigs; the sheep; the flocks of fowl that squawked and quacked; and the gentle plough horses that let the children pat them. There were ploughs for sale and new items of farm equipment on display, and a tea tent for the ladies to enjoy. Henrietta took great pleasure at browsing the stalls with their rounds of creamy cheese and prize-winning displays of fruit preserves and pickles, to which she was partial.

The children ran around the showground, stopping to watch some small piglets squirming over each other in a pen, and pleaded for Dan to buy them one.

'Please, Dada,' begged Ellen. 'Can you buy us the middle one with the black tip on his ear?'

'Little pigs soon become big smelly ones.' Dan laughed before distracting them with a visit to the toffee-apple man.

Later that evening, Dan attended the Agriculture Society Dinner and Henrietta stayed awake until he arrived home at eleven, to see how he had enjoyed it.

'You should have heard them, Henrietta,' he fumed, unable to hide his annoyance. 'All the big landowners talked about was the progress and improvements being made in agriculture that could help them increase their tillage or livestock.'

'That is a good thing, surely?' Henrietta asked, confused.

'These men are blinkered!' he cried. 'The loss of the potato means little to them. How can they not see the devastation it is having on their tenants, who cannot feed their families?'

'Perhaps some of their lands have not been affected,' Henrietta suggested gently as she brushed her hair.

'I have travelled the six parishes in the county and the potatoes are destroyed most everywhere,' Dan explained forcefully. 'Attempts to store undamaged potatoes are proving hopeless. Reverend Traill from Schull and his landowner friend Mr Thomas Somerville have both devised some exacting new storage methods, using special pits to preserve whatever is left of the crop, but I doubt them.'

'Reverend Traill is a most intelligent man?' she ventured.

'Their method is useless! It makes no matter if the potatoes are stored in pits or in cabins or in outhouses, for I suspect they will likely carry the hidden disease that has caused this devastation. I've read reports that it is the same in England

and Scotland, and on parts of the continent. Fortunately, these places do not have millions of poor people who depend on the crop like we do.'

'What will happen?' Henrietta asked, suddenly fearful.

'Unless they are helped, the people will go hungry,' Dan said as he undressed. 'It may even lead to famine.'

'Oh, Dan, don't say such a terrible thing!'

'I only speak the truth, but thank heaven that Henry Marmion, Mr Welply, and Mr Clerke from the bank have good sense. They suggested that we have a duty to buy corn to protect the county from famine and each pledged one hundred pounds. But I fear no matter what we try to do, it will not be enough as most have no means of buying food.'

Henrietta grew anxious thinking of their children and the new baby, dark-haired little Margaret, who lay asleep in the crib near her parents' bed.

'I'm sorry, my dear, I did not mean to distress you at this late hour, but I am distracted by it and we have always shared our concerns and worries.'

'Dan, I am here by your side always,' she assured him. 'I am glad that you told the tenants on our lands in Poundlick that you would not take rent from them while they are under such duress.'

'It was the least I could do.'

'My love, you are generous-hearted but are you sure that you can afford it?'

'I will not touch any money that should be used to buy grain for these men's families,' he insisted. 'They are good tenants and will no doubt repay me with their labours when I need it.'

As they kissed goodnight, Henrietta thanked heaven that she had followed her heart ten years ago and married the serious-minded young medical man with the long narrow face, intelligent eyes and quick wit who had swept her off her feet. She loved Dan dearly.

Chapter 10

Creagh

MARY HAD WATCHED AS JOHN AND PAT LOADED THE TWO SQUEALING pigs into the cart to sell at the busy market in Skibbereen.

'I didn't even get a fair price for them,' John had complained bitterly on his return.

Three weeks later he sold their few sheep to O'Driscoll's butchers on North Street.

'We should have got far more for them, but at least we have money in our pockets,' he pronounced firmly.

Mary was relieved that John had managed to collect money for the rent in this way, but worried all the same, for there was very little remaining from the sale of their livestock to keep them.

On his next visit, Henry Marmion, accompanied by his under-agent George Hogan, made his position clear to all the tenants of Sir William Wrixon Becher.

'Potatoes or no potatoes, the rent is still to be paid,' he declared.

'But we have nothing to give you,' pleaded Nell Flynn. 'Would you have us take the food from our children's mouths to give to a man who has never known a day's hunger or hardship in his life?'

'Mrs Flynn, there are no exceptions to the rule,' George Hogan replied coldly. 'Those who do not like it know well what the result will be.'

Mary thanked heaven that, unlike Nell, she and John at least had their rent, though little else to feed their family with during the coming winter months.

'Everyone has bad years,' John consoled her, 'but we'll manage to get through the long lean months until we have next summer's potato crop.'

As the days grew shorter, Mary and the children foraged and scoured the hedgerows and shoreline. Early in the morning, she combed the fields for mushrooms, and gathered nettles and herbs. She even paid a secret visit to the orchard at Creagh House, for the house was empty, where she filled her apron and shawl with damaged windfall apples.

John worked all the hours that he was able, doing whatever rough labouring jobs he could get, but there was little enough work to be had with so many other men trying to keep their families fed.

The Sullivans' last sack of potatoes grew emptier by the day and Mary fed the children turnips and eggs. Now, even the poor hens were laying less for she had no meal to feed them.

All around her, the neighbours were beginning to sell their possessions to purchase food and pay their rent. Mary looked around her small cottage to see if she had anything worth selling or pawning.

There was her bristle brush, with its silver handle, that John had bought her when they were courting; a rough brush and a simple comb would suffice now. She studied the pair of fine, soft leather shoes that she rarely wore any more, for they were not sturdy enough to use on the farm. They could certainly go. Then there was John's mother's heavy, black woollen shawl with the tassels. It was far too big for Mary to wear, but it had sentimental value, as did the blue-and-white china jug and plate that had also been his mother's.

She opened the chest where her wedding dress lay carefully folded in the hope that, one day, one of her daughters would wear it. She wasn't ready to part with it yet and closed the lid firmly.

Pat offered to give her a lift into town as he had some business there. He made no comment on the fact that she intended to sell some of his late mother's things. As she climbed down from the cart they arranged to meet later.

Mary swiftly joined the queue of people outside Hegarty's pawn shop, waiting their turn to have their possessions assessed. The women around her carried shawls and dresses, blankets and shirts. Men carried wooden stools, cradles, frock coats and fishing tackle, their eyes downcast as they stood in line. All were ready to sell each and every item in order to buy oats, flour and grain with which to feed their families.

She watched the people ahead of her enter the shop, only to leave with disappointment etched on their faces as they counted the money in their hands before entering the provisions store next door, which was also owned by Denis Hegarty and run by his son.

'Bad cess to you,' an old man in a stained coat and hat

shouted angrily as he left. 'Thieving off the poor in their misfortune!'

Mary tried to remain composed as she moved up the line and entered the busy pawn shop. A good-looking woman ahead of her held a blue satin hat trimmed with fine feathers, which she wanted to sell.

'Dublin-bought!' the woman claimed, tossing her hair.

'Fine feathers, but who is to wear them here, my dear?' sneered Mr Hegarty.

'Then what about this?' she asked, producing a golden locket which she dangled in front of him.

The shop owner studied it carefully, weighing it in the palm of his hand as the two of them haggled over the price.

'I could take it to Cork or Dublin,' she argued, her cheeks reddening.

Mary could see that, under her good coat, the woman's shoes were broken down and her dress well worn.

'That is your right, if you want to travel so far,' the pawn-broker said coldly. 'But my offer is eight shillings. That, of course, will include the hat.'

The woman nodded reluctantly. Stretching out her hand, she grabbed the money and pushed past Mary in her rush to escape the place.

Putting a smile on her face, Mary stepped forward, as if her business with Mr Hegarty was an ordinary, everyday matter. She did not want him to sense her nervousness.

'What have you got today, Mrs—'

'Sullivan,' she interjected, placing the shawl on the counter before her. 'A heavy woollen shawl, in perfect condition.'

He said nothing as he lifted up the item and inspected it.

'It was my late mother-in-law's. I would wear it myself but she was of a much taller and broader physique than me.'

She could sense Hegarty's eyes run over her neat, trim figure.

'Hmm,' he muttered, fingering the garment. 'I already have a store room of shawls.'

'But this is of far better quality than most,' Mary insisted, holding her ground. 'I also have a pair of fine leather shoes that are barely worn. I live out in the countryside now but used to work in the town.'

Hegarty feigned disinterest, but he knew the shoes were well made and would appeal to the ladies in the town.

Mary produced the jug and bowl next before finally placing the pretty silver-inlaid bristle hairbrush in front of him with a flourish. Denis Hegarty began to tally some figures, scratching them on a scrap of paper with a pencil he took from behind his ear.

'I can give you twelve shillings for the lot,' he said in his nasal tone. 'Though I'll likely be stuck with them, for who wants to buy such items these days?'

She flushed, for the amount being offered was far less than she had hoped for. Two women pushed and shoved behind her, awaiting their turn.

'I expected that the brush and shoes would be worth more?'

'That is all they are worth to me, Mrs Sullivan,' Hegarty said, the shillings already in his outstretched hand. 'Take it or leave it!'

He gestured for the next customer to come forward.

'Thank you, Mr Hegarty,' Mary said politely, taking the pawn tickets and coins in her palm.

There was enough to buy some grain and oats to sustain her

family for a few weeks, but she would not give Denis Hegarty the satisfaction of spending it in his provisions store next door. He'd had enough of her business for one day, and she would go elsewhere for her purchases.

Skibbereen was crowded with people like herself trying to purchase food for their families, but despite their numbers the normal commerce of the town continued, with people still going about their business and visiting the bank and hotels, solicitors and tradesmen.

Out of force of habit, Mary stopped outside Honora Barry's and found herself pushing open the door and entering the dressmaker's shop where she had worked years before. Honora was busy with a customer so Mary stood quietly and watched the older woman narrow the fine pleats on the front bodice of a pretty satin dress. She then proceeded to pin up the cuffs of the gown as the sleeves needed shortening very slightly.

Before her marriage to Jeremiah Collins, Mary's mother had been a seamstress in a big house in Bantry. She used to work by the fireside in the evenings, when Mary and her siblings were children, taking up hems, making and mending garments. She had taught both her daughters how to sew, but Kathleen had no patience for it, injuring herself with the needle and scissors. Mary, on the other hand, enjoyed it and began to make clothes herself from scraps of material.

Her skill with the needle had led to her being hired as an apprentice seamstress at the age of sixteen by Honora Barry in her shop in Skibbereen. The hours were long but Mary soon learned how to cut patterns, sew satins, silks and lace, and make dresses, skirts and jackets. It was at the shop that she had met John Sullivan, the tall, dark-haired young man with the rather hesitant smile and a solitary dimple in his lower left cheek, who constantly seemed to need torn jackets, shirts and trousers mending.

It had taken months for him to finally summon the courage to ask if he could visit her at her parents' cottage on her Sunday off.

Within five months she had fallen in love with John, who, with his kind heart and steady way, declared he could not live without her. She had accepted his marriage proposal happily and that summer made her wedding dress. Honora had given her advice along the way and admired the beautiful garment Mary had designed and hand-sewn herself. A married woman, Mary left the shop to look after her husband and growing family.

Mary smiled as she watched her former employer fit the customer's satin gown expertly.

'The bodice and neckline are ideal for someone with your fine figure,' Miss Barry complimented.

'Will my dress be ready in time?' the dark-haired young woman fretted. 'We are visiting Dublin and attending a few balls.'

'Certainly, for it will take only two days to make these slight alterations,' the older woman promised, tapping the pincushion that was tied to her wrist.

'I'll be with you in a few minutes, Mary,' acknowledged Honora Barry as she escorted her customer to the discreet changing room to help her out of the gown.

The stylish young woman re-emerged soon after in a beautiful fitted coat with a velvet-trimmed collar and cuffs. Miss Barry accompanied her to the shop door before turning to her visitor.

'Motherhood suits you, Mary, for you look as pretty as ever,' she told her, before enquiring after John and the children.

Mary nodded. 'They are all well. Though we lost most of our crop and have had to sell our animals.'

'The government needs to step in and do something about giving assistance,' pronounced the dressmaker in sympathy.

'Miss Barry, I came to ask whether you have any spare work – alterations, repairs or mending – that I could do?'

Mary worried that she was being presumptuous, but could see that Miss Barry was considering her offer, knowing well that Mary was one of the finest seamstresses she had ever employed.

'I need the work,' Mary admitted, 'and could do it for a reasonable rate.'

'Normally I wouldn't have any spare work,' the dressmaker said, arching her grey eyebrows, 'but Catherine left me high and dry just last week. She's moved to Cork City where she and her betrothed are getting married next month. Her position is free, but with the way things are at present I do not intend taking on another employee for the workroom. There is, however, still work to be done.'

'Please, Miss Barry, give me the chance. I won't let you down.'

Honora Barry smiled. 'Mary, if there is one thing I know it is that you are a good, reliable worker. So perhaps such an arrangement might suit us both for the present.'

'Oh, that would be grand, Miss Barry. When will I start?'

'Well, you can start today, for I have this bundle of men's clothing that needs repairing. It's just sitting up in the workroom, and Jane and I are far too busy to attend to it at present. Would you be able to have it done and returned by next week?'

'Yes,' Mary promised.

The bag of mending was heavy and she was glad that Pat was still in town with his cart so she could get a lift home, for she still needed to go and purchase some oats and flour.

'Well, isn't that a piece of luck, getting some work?' congratulated her brother-in-law as they drove home. 'Though there is little enough for me except hauling and carting stuff.'

Mary knew how hard it was for Pat of late. A few times a week he came to the cottage to eat. They didn't have much but she could not begrudge him a share of what was in the pot, for when he could he provided them with a rabbit or hare, or even a fish to eat.

Passing Oldcourt, the small harbour and inlet overlooking the sea and the river, Pat and Mary watched two ships that had journeyed from Liverpool to West Cork's fishing port of Baltimore and then upriver, carrying grain bound for McCarthy's brewery. Men worked tirelessly unloading the stores of grain on to four smaller boats and barges that would transport it to the quays and the brewery's piers.

'O'Connell and his committee in Dublin called on the Lord Lieutenant and the authorities to stop the export of food and corn, and to halt brewing and distilling so that the grain can be used to feed the people,' Pat said in despair. 'But they refuse to do it.'

'How can they use grain for porter when people can't even afford to buy it?' Mary protested.

'Some day they'll pay for making the like of us scratch and scrape for food,' Pat said coldly, urging the horse homewards.

Chapter 11

November 1845

WHEN THE DAYS GREW SHORT, JOHN SULLIVAN DISCOVERED THAT the few potatoes he had stored in the potato pit had all rotted.

'Bad cess, every single one of them has turned black,' he told his wife, disgusted. 'Even the smell of them would make you sick.'

Mary could not understand how such a thing could happen to saved healthy potatoes lifted from the ground, but the same thing had happened to all their neighbours'. Everyone was at their wits' end, for they still had the winter to endure and the long months of spring and summer ahead of them before the next potato harvest.

Mary sat darning and patching, and repairing hems and tears late into the night until her fingers grew tired and her eyes became heavy with sleep. The money she earned from Honora Barry was scarcely enough to buy a bag of meal each week and the odd jug of buttermilk or piece of smoked fish, but if she was frugal, she and her family would survive these hard times.

A few weeks later, with not a bag of oats or grain in the place, Mary decided without a second thought to take her wedding dress and a lace blouse to sell at Hegarty's. A sack of flour was now more valuable to her than any item of clothing.

She still had her hens but she suspected someone was stealing their eggs, for whenever she or John went to check on them, a few would be missing. She told the children to keep an eye on the birds and watch for anyone who was lurking around their field and hen-house.

To her dismay, it wasn't long before one of her good-laying hens disappeared too.

'Maybe a fox or dog or cat got her,' consoled John.

'It was no hungry animal,' she retorted. 'There is no sign of a feather even, so I know well 'tis a thief who took her and stole the food from under our noses.'

'Hush,' he said, trying to calm her. 'If it were a hungry person who was desperate, we cannot begrudge them.'

'Well, you may say that when all the hens I have kept are gone and we don't have even an egg for the children to eat or a hen for the pot, while others feast on them!' she said, angered by her husband's reaction.

She warned Con and Nora to be on the lookout for the culprit.

'Mark my words, they will come back again.'

'Mammy, I saw Paddy Flynn searching one of the nests under the bush,' Con confided in her. 'You know, the hen with the

53

white speckles, and I think he took her egg. I tried to talk to him but he just ran away home.'

'Never fear, pet. I'll keep my eye on him and his brothers.'

Annoyance burned inside her that Nell Flynn, to whom they had always been good, would use them in such a fashion.

'They have little enough, God help them,' soothed John, 'and my mother was always fond of her.'

'Well, 'tis not your mother she'll be dealing with if they steal any more of my eggs!'

At night Mary listened, and during the day she watched. Then, one evening when she was about to lie down, Mary heard the hens squawking. She rushed outside in the darkness to find a figure just about to lift another protesting bird away from her roost.

'Who is that?' she called. 'Is that you, Nell, or one of your thieving family trying to rob us?'

Mary lunged at the figure and caught them by the shoulder. As she made them drop the hen and pushed them towards the cottage, they let out a sob.

In the gloom of the fire, Nell stood there, defiant.

'You have nine fat hens and my family have nothing,' she declared.

'At the rate you are going, soon I will have no hens,' Mary retorted angrily. 'They will all have found their way into your pot. What am I to feed my family with then?'

'It's just a hen,' Nell wheedled. 'A stupid old hen.'

'It's my hen and she's a fine layer.'

'There is not a pick of food in the place or even a few leaves

54

for the tea!' Nell sobbed. 'And we have Hogan threatening to put us out for we have no rent. Poor Tom is addled with it.'

Mary felt guilty immediately, but she had her own family to think of.

'Nellie, don't let me catch you near our hens!' she warned.

'It won't happen again,' her neighbour promised.

'I am sorry for your troubles,' she offered as she watched the forlorn figure of Nell in her black shawl walk slowly back across the fields.

Overcome with pity for her neighbour, the next morning Mary sent Con over to Nell's with two turnips and a screw of tea leaves.

Chapter 12

Skibbereen
December 1845

'THEY SAY THAT A THIRD OF THE CROP IS LOST IN SOME PLACES,'
Tim McCarthy Downing explained to the huge crowd at the
packed public meeting in Skibbereen Courthouse to discuss
the potato failure. 'But here it is far worse than in other parts
of the county, with half or even two-thirds of the crop gone.
Given such circumstances and the situation we face, I suggest
that we set up a fund to make provision for famine in the coming months.'

There was instant approval for raising such a fund.

Dan's heart gladdened to see landlords, labourers, farmers,
and both Protestant and Catholic clergymen coming together.
They all knew that the state of affairs was grave.

Sir Robert Peel, the prime minister, had been forced to resign
over the repeal of the Corn Laws, which would have permitted
the import of duty-free grain. Peel at least had the decency to
order a larger shipment of Indian corn from America to Ireland,

and had appointed a Relief Commission for Ireland under Randolph Routh to distribute it.

Only a month ago, Daniel O'Connell and the Mansion House Committee in Dublin had made an appeal to the Queen herself, informing her of the situation across the country and the effect it was having on her poor subjects. Queen Victoria's reply had been to advise her Irish subjects that they were in her care constantly. To Dan's mind, that care was certainly not adequate!

'I propose that we appeal to the government for public works,' Reverend Robert Traill said, getting to his feet to address the meeting.

'Hear! Hear!'

'I have written to the heads of government in both England and Ireland concerning the scarcity, and also to all the landlords in my parish, requesting that they let their tenants keep their grain, in order to spare seed potatoes for planting next year's crop,' he continued. 'And I suggest to all the clergy present here that they do the same.'

Father John Fitzpatrick and the other church men present nodded heartily in agreement. Perhaps the landlords would listen to them!

'With regards to Reverend Traill's suggestion of public works, I propose that we apply to the government for assistance for the deepening of the river Ilen, which is badly needed, and for the construction of a military barracks,' Henry Townsend added. 'For these works would be productive and good for the town.'

Next, a young tradesman in the crowd stood up bravely.

'Property has its duties as well as its rights,' he reminded them, looking directly at the landowners and influential people present. 'I am speaking for the humblest, and I ask that land-lords make a reduction on rents, for people cannot pay them.'

There came shouts of approval and applause, but a few regarded him stony-faced.

Dan admired the man's courage in speaking out at such a gathering, and hoped that his words would have some effect.

'Now I turn to medical matters,' Dan said, serious. 'There have been a few small outbreaks of scarlet fever and smallpox in the district. I recommend that a section of the fever hospital be isolated for such cases. Unfortunately, further building at Skibbereen workhouse has ceased due to lack of payment by the Board of Works. However, this work must be done, for the people are in a poor state facing into the winter. Scarlet fever is spreading from the west and smallpox from the east!'

He could see the alarm in the eyes of all gathered at the mention of such contagion.

'Of course, Dr Donovan,' Tim McCarthy Downing responded. 'You must take whatever steps you believe are necessary.'

As the meeting came to an end, Thomas Somerville of Castletownsend asked anyone present who was willing to set up and organize a relief committee in Skibbereen to remain behind. As a doctor, Dan felt it was his duty and volunteered immediately to become involved.

There was much work to be done if they were to alleviate the growing distress of the people of the district during the hard winter months ahead, for the many who had no income or food, Dan believed, now faced the very real threat of starvation.

Chapter 13

Creagh
July 1846

JOHN HAD PLANTED OUT THE SEED POTATOES IN MARCH, THE DAY
after St Patrick's Day.

'Mary, will you give up your old vegetable patch?' he'd
pleaded, 'so I can set more seed potatoes?'

'No, I need it for the vegetables!' she had refused stubbornly,
for after last year she intended to grow even more cabbages and
turnips.

The winter had been the worst since they had married, for
they had little to eat except what they foraged or what Mary
could purchase with the money she made. She'd killed the last
of their hens over three weeks ago as the bird was better in her
family's bellies than in her neighbours'.

They had cleared their two fields of any last trace of the
diseased potato crop. They had raked up and burned the stalks
and debris, and turned the soil, before John dug fresh new
drills for planting. He and Pat had carted heavy loads of

iodine-rich seaweed to their fields from the rocky shoreline, and spread it over the beds to fertilize them and feed the plants. They hoped that it would give them a better yield of potatoes.

She and John were like two broody hens with a clutch of eggs as they watched over this year's new crop. They inspected their plants nervously for any sign of blight or leaf damage, but were relieved as the months passed and the drills grew tall and strong.

'This will be the best harvest ever,' boasted Flor, sitting on the wall across from his cottage. He sucked at his clay pipe as he and grey-haired Molly surveyed the potato plants all around them. 'It will be a fine crop to make up for last year.'

'They say it promises to be good, but we must not take the crop for granted,' John warned, unable to shake off the nagging fear that the blight would return.

'Brother, you are worrying over nothing,' teased Pat. 'For it is clear to all eyes that this year's potatoes are thriving.'

Looking out across the fields at the pale pink-and-white potato blossom which blew and danced like a wave, Mary was reassured that their potato pits and sacks soon would be full again with this year's harvest. Once their crop was stored for the year ahead, it would not be long before the hard times were behind them.

John and Pat were busy getting in the barley and wheat crop for their landlord.

'The grain stores will be full,' John remarked as they sat around the fire, sharing a pot of gruel and griddle cakes.

'Though most of this year's crop is bound for Liverpool, Leeds and London.'

'Why must we feed the factories and workers of Britain,' pondered Pat, 'when all we have is gruel to keep us until our own crop comes in?'

'It has always been the way.' John shrugged. 'But it's the wrong way.'

'I'm telling you, it's time that things change.' Pat's eyes flashed angrily. 'We can no longer be like an old dog lying under its master's table, waiting for scraps. The time is coming for the hound to rise up and bite.'

'Will you hush up with your talk, Patrick?' Mary warned, noticing that young Con and Nora were glued to his words. 'Do you want to bring trouble down on this house and our children?'

'No!' He lapsed into silence and ate his gruel.

Con's eyes shone as he looked admiringly at his uncle and Mary thanked heaven that at least her son was too young to be involved with Pat and his group of Young Irelander friends.

Pat disappeared in a huff as soon as he had finished eating.

'Why did you chase him out of the place?' rebuked John later. 'You know it's lonely for him, being on his own.'

'He should have thought about that four years ago when he broke off his engagement to Frances McCarthy and chased after Julia Carmody.'

'Unfortunately, a man is ruled by his heart not his head.'

'I'm not sure that I would call it his heart!' Mary teased. 'He threw Frances over, with her father's ten acres of land and a cottage, for that black-haired beguiler he paraded around the town with.'

'Julia was not the woman for him,' John admitted. 'She'd not live on Pat's *scrapeen* of land.'

'Well, Frances is happy now, and her husband has charge of the land since her father took ill last year and died. I hear she is due a second child soon.'

'It upsets him thinking of what he lost.'

'Maybe Pat will find another girl.'

She felt a surge of pity for her handsome brother-in-law. With his long dark eyelashes, deep-brown eyes and easy smile, he had a certain way with women, but still lived alone in a small cabin and spent many of his nights drinking porter or talking politics and rebellion in the local *síbín* with another few wild men like himself.

'He will be a lucky man if he finds himself a girl as beautiful and kind-hearted as the one I found.'

Mary laughed. She had forgotten what a charmer her husband could be!

Dusk had fallen, and together they listened to the unexpected rain which had begun to patter on the thatch roof. John ran outside to look at the drills and returned soaked to the skin but happy.

'Will you stop your worrying?' Mary urged him as she pulled off his sodden shirt and made him sit by the glowing turf. 'The potatoes are grand, just grand.'

Chapter 14

August 1846

MARY WOKE TO THE AWFUL CLOYING SMELL OF LAST SUMMER.
Dread filled her heart, for John was already racing outside,
pulling on his britches as he went. Gripped with fear, she ran
after him across the fields, for she could see the potato stalks
drooping, their leaves already spotted with black.

Her mouth dry and heart pounding, she knelt down and
began to dig frantically with her hands to unearth the potatoes. Her fingers closed around what seemed like three or four
large, healthy ones, but as she lifted them out of the soil Mary
could feel their flesh was already putrid and foul. She tried
another plant, and another. It was useless. Every clump she
touched was marked with disease. The potatoes in their mud-
stained skins were already decaying, rotting in her hand.

As she shook off the clay, she could see the lumper potatoes
were black in parts, soft and oozing, the stench so pervasive
that it made her queasy. She looked over at her husband,
despair already written on his face.

'Look at them!' he shouted, back bent digging in the earth with his shovel as he tried desperately to save their potatoes from the deadly blight that had spread through their crop overnight. 'They're destroyed.'

How could this happen again, she asked herself, when John had been more than vigilant and had tended their crop with such care!

The children had been woken by the commotion and ran outside. Con, Nora and Tim's faces went white with shock as their father, streaked with mud and the stinking sludge, shouted at them to help dig and lift the potatoes from the ground.

'Help us to save them!' John ordered loudly.

Nora began to cry at the memory of it all.

'Any good potato, even if it is very small but is firm and hard,' he said, softening his tone, 'throw it in the bucket.'

Little Annie, terrified by the smell and strangeness of it all, clung tightly to her mother as Mary took in the disaster around her, for every field as far as she could see was the same.

Con went on his knees in the dirt, digging at the plants to see what could be saved. Somehow, like a thief in the night, the pestilence had returned to poison their crop. John, meanwhile, had crossed to their other field. From the slump of his shoulders, Mary could tell that it too had been affected.

'Rotten! Every one of them!' he shouted despairingly as he checked each line of drills.

Nora worked beside her mother. Her little hands and face were spattered with the filthy slime. Tim went down the rows, checking the fetid piles for any healthy potato they might have overlooked, and Annie trailed behind him with a little bucket. Mary continued to pull at plants, lifting the potatoes. The stench around them had worsened and hung heavy in the air, over their fields, and the acres and acres of land. It clung to her hair and skin, and was so bad that she could taste it.

Surely to God, somewhere here there must be a few of their crop untouched by the murrain; a few that they could harvest and use!

Someone was crying, and it was a terrible sound in the stillness.

The family worked for hours. Mary's nails were broken, and her fingers were red and sore. Every plant, stalk and drill was checked, and the few hard lumpers that were found were put carefully in the tin bucket.

The children were caked in mud, going from row to row with their heads and backs bent, like blackbirds searching the festering stalks and clumps for a small, firm pearly potato.

Mary's back ached, but she couldn't give up.

In the distance she could see Pat, digging his patch. She prayed that he had been luckier than they had. Flor and Molly were moving from drill to drill, carefully doing the same. In the fields all about her, Denis and Brigid and their children, and Nell, Tom and their sons were all digging frantically, searching their drills in vain. Every holding as far as the eye could see was already ravaged by the fast-spreading murrain.

Mary went inside and returned with two cans of water and some leftover griddle cake, which she shared between her family.

'John, you must take a rest,' she begged, passing him the can of water. She had never seen him in such a state. Soaked in sweat and covered in mud.

'I cannot stop.'

He took a few gulps of water and threw the rest over his face and head.

Con, also sweating and filthy, stood shoulder to shoulder with his father, trying to help him. Nora looked as if she were about to collapse, and usually carefree Tim was grim-faced as he searched through every clutch of potatoes, desperate to find a few that they could eat.

'Da, I got four,' he proclaimed proudly, carrying them carefully to the near-empty tin bucket.

Mary tried not to give in to the mounting panic she was feeling at the devastation of their two fields and the complete loss of their crop this time.

John, agitated, continued with his shovel. Digging, digging and digging . . .

Eventually, Mary sat down and told the exhausted children to rest.

At last, John too put his shovel down and looked out over their fields. There was nothing more they could do.

The children were scared, their eyes full of fear. As they huddled together, Mary vowed that she would not let her children go hungry . . .

Part Two

Chapter 15

MARY STARED OUT AT HER FAMILY'S DEVASTATED LAND AND THE stinking acres all around them, unable to believe that such a calamity had befallen them again.

In the bright morning sunlight things looked worse. The foul stench still hung in the air, and the drills were filled with the rotting mass of stalks and potatoes where they had dug and laboured the previous day. How in God's name would they survive this?

All night John had thrashed and turned beside her in the bed, restless yet exhausted. The children still lay asleep, curled up in their rough blankets like little mice.

Tears welled in Mary's eyes as she surveyed everything the blight had taken from them. This time it had left them with nothing . . . Nothing to eat, sell, or pay their rent with. A deep fear at what lay ahead gripped her heart. She and John no longer had a purse of hidden money, nor even a penny or a shilling to call their own. Everything had depended on them raising this new potato crop.

She watched the smoke begin to curl from her neighbours' chimneys as people began to rise and process the full extent of the catastrophe wreaked upon them. From what she could see, nobody had escaped the destruction of their crop.

John came outside to join her, gathering his thoughts as he assessed the damage.

'If it is all across the county, I don't know what we can do, for we are all ruined.'

'We will manage somehow,' she said, resting against him. 'We are both strong and good workers. That has to count for something.'

'It will count for nothing when the landlord sends his men for the rent, or when the children cry with hunger pains in their bellies.'

'Don't say such a thing!'

'It is the truth.' John sounded utterly forlorn.

In all the years she had loved him and slept beside him and borne his children, Mary had never heard such despair in his voice. Her husband was the one who usually rallied her when she felt low or worried, or was tired out from the children.

'John Sullivan, I will not have you speak like that! We will do what we need to survive. I will not have us put out of this cottage and off the land, or see our children go hungry.'

His blue eyes held hers and she could tell he sensed her fury.

'You are right. We must act quickly and make ready for the hungry months ahead. The Sullivans have always fought for this place, and I'll not be the one to give it up to Wrixon Becher or anyone else!'

Relief washed over Mary and she took his rough hand in hers.

'Aren't we are a grand pair?' John said, leaning over and kissing her gently, as if they hadn't a care in the world.

She felt overwhelmed with emotion momentarily. They both knew well that this time, with no animals or possessions to sell, terrible times lay ahead, but at least they were together.

Brigid Leary called down to her, red-eyed and weary.

'The children are so upset that I'm awake half the night,' she confided. 'Denis was weeping like a boy over the potatoes. I've never seen him like that before.'

Mary hugged her, glad of their friendship, as they shared their fears and worries.

'I don't know what Denis and I will do, for we haven't a penny to our name. If he doesn't get work, there is no saying what will happen to us.'

'He and John will both find something,' Mary encouraged her, not wanting to see Brigid more upset.

Around midday Pat came over. He looked rough and dishevelled, and clearly had been drinking.

'Drowning my sorrows, like most of the men in the district,' he admitted, gulping down two cans of cold water and pleading for half a griddle cake to set him right.

'You are a saint of a woman,' he thanked Mary as he ate quickly.

Mary said little in return but resolved there would be no more food for him under their roof when he was still in the throes of drink. A man who wasted his money on porter would not be welcome at her table any longer, for she had the children to think of.

'I was down in the *síbín* last night. The pestilence is through

71

the district. Not a field or a farm in the whole of Carbery is untouched. I tell you, there was a good crowd of us, all destroyed after yesterday. Not a man among us will be able to pay the gale rent when Marmion comes looking for it.'

'We've not a penny either,' John admitted angrily. 'I have to get work.'

'First thing in the morning we'll take the horse and cart and set off to search,' Pat agreed. 'Two strong men with a cart must have some chance of paid labour.'

Mary hoped that her brother-in-law was right.

She was intent on travelling to town tomorrow to ask Honora Barry – nay, beg her – if she had any more sewing or mending for her. Every penny she earned would be needed to help feed the family. She had no intention of sitting by idly and watching her children weaken and starve.

The Sullivan children were fretful and anxious. They could sense how bad things were and Annie clung to her mother like a little shadow. Mary did her best to reassure them that all would be well. She could not destroy their innocence and let them know the seriousness of their situation and the distress they might face.

'Stop mooning around like a load of sick lambs. Let's go up the fields and hunt for early blackberries,' she coaxed, despite the strange heavy weariness and fear that assailed her, for she was desperate to distract them. 'Now, grab a tin bucket and some cans, and we'll be off!'

No matter the scrapes and scratches from the thorns and brambles, the children enjoyed themselves. Patch barked with excitement as he ran among them. Little Annie opened her mouth like a baby bird to eat the fruits, getting used to the sweet but tart taste, her face stained with blackberry juice.

'I wish we had blackberries to eat all year round.' Tim grinned, his tin overflowing with plump berries.

Back home, the smell of the pestilence lingered everywhere, awful in its intensity. Mary went to boil the few remaining potatoes but they had already turned grey and sludgy in the bottom of the bucket. Nausea washed over her as she threw them out.

As she fetched a few turnips from her patch, she thanked heaven that they looked healthy and seemed not to have been affected by the murrain. At least she had something to put in the pot and feed the children with in the hungry days ahead.

Chapter 16

Poundlick, County Cork

AS HE RODE AROUND THE DISTRICT VISITING THE UNION AND HIS patients, Dan grew accustomed to the sulphuric smell of rotting potatoes that emanated from field after field. It lingered heavily in the warm air and was nauseating.

The signs of destruction were everywhere. He could see where tenants had tried to dig and pull the rotting crop from the rows of potato drills with their wilted blackened stalks and leaves. They had hoped to save some of the crop only to discover the putrid potatoes that broke apart in their hands and on their spades. Such was their atrocious state they could not be used even to feed an animal.

From Ballydehob to Skeaghanore, Caheragh to Roscarbery, Glandore to Union Hall, Creagh to Baltimore, everywhere he rode it was a terrible sight to see. Most of the tenants grew nothing else in their small fields – no barley, no corn, not even turnips. Looking across the acres and acres of destroyed potato fields, he worried how the people would manage to feed themselves, let alone pay their rent, which was now due.

Dan had then ridden out to Poundlick to inspect his own lands. Every single potato field there had been affected, and he could see fear and desperation written in the wary eyes of his tenants. His acres of barley had flourished and were due to be harvested, but in the small potato fields beside each cabin and cottage lay the rotting detritus of the crop upon which his tenants depended.

'Dr Donovan, you can see yourself that all is lost to us,' admitted Tim Driscoll – one of the tenant farmers – approaching Dan as he got down from his horse. 'The murrain has destroyed us, for we have nothing.'

'I can see that, Mr Driscoll,' the doctor said, looking at the neatly kept holding where five small, stick-thin children gazed out at him nervously.

'I'm afraid, sir, that I cannot keep my promise to pay the rent due to you at this time,' the farmer said, his gaze clear and unwavering, man to man, one father to another.

Tim Driscoll was a good worker, who took pride in his holding and was not one to shirk his responsibility. Dan had respect for the already gaunt-looking man. How could he possibly insist that this fellow pay his long-overdue rent when he had a wife and children to care for!

It was the same for the rest of his tenants – the McCarthys, the Lynches and the Murphys – who all had large families to feed. The half-year rent was due, but looking at the ravaged fields around him and knowing the men and women who tilled and tended this land, Dan could not put any extra demand on them this time. He knew well there was not a penny to pay him. These people lived hand to mouth at the best of times.

This trouble was no fault of theirs, so the only decent thing he could do to ease their burden was to forgo his rent again this year. It would affect his finances badly, which no doubt would displease his bank manager, but Dan would not impose such penury on his tenants or threaten to evict them.

'The barley has done well this year, but given the failure of the potato crop and your need to sustain and feed your families, there will be no rent collected here,' he reassured them.

Men shook his hands warmly with relief and gratitude.

'You're a gentleman, Dr Donovan,' pronounced Michael McCarthy, his eyes filled with tears. 'God bless you.'

The men would help to harvest his barley and he would make sure that each received a large bag of grain in return for their work.

As he bade them farewell, he turned his horse and set off for Skibbereen, for he had an important meeting that evening with the relief committee.

Chapter 17

Skibbereen

'I'VE NEVER SEEN SUCH PANIC AND FEAR, FOR THE PEOPLE ARE already weak and starving,' Dan said, enraged, at the urgent meeting being held in the Union workhouse. 'Can the bureaucratic fools in London and Dublin not see that with nearly the entire Irish potato crop devastated, hunger is surely staring us in the face?'

'We have done our best to buy oatmeal and Indian corn from the Cork depot for the needy,' their designated chairman Thomas Somerville admitted as the committee members voiced their concerns. 'But without government assistance, I too fear we are facing impending disaster.'

'The potato crop is all but destroyed,' declared Father John Fitzpatrick, his voice racked with emotion, 'and hungry hordes of labourers travel the streets and countryside with poverty depicted on their countenance. Relief is urgently needed, and I deplore the many landlords who have not subscribed, and those who have given only stingily!'

'There are landlords here who get rental of two thousand pounds a year from Skibbereen and have only given a measly two hundred pounds in relief,' denounced Tim McCarthy Downing. 'That is less than they would spend at the races in Cheltenham! I appeal to those same landlords to reduce rents.'

'The government has sanctioned public works for Skibbereen, which will employ the destitute, but unfortunately, little work has commenced,' Michael Galwey, the local magistrate and a cousin of Dan's, complained.

'The men desperately need work,' added Reverend Fitzpatrick. 'I did my best to ensure that men from Bridgetown and Windmill Lane and the district were employed as labourers building the new school, but now, with the school finally finished, unfortunately there is no further work for those poor souls.'

'Without employment, the whole fabric of society may dissolve,' worried landlord Lionel Fleming.

'How are the people to buy food?' Father Fitzpatrick interjected. 'Are there any plans by the government to supply food and meal to the needy?'

'Unfortunately not,' said Thomas Somerville. 'The government food depots are instructed to remain closed until the end of the year, even though food supplies are already scarce in the town.'

'Gentlemen, we do not have months, or even weeks, to solve this!' Dan warned. 'If the authorities do not take action immediately to feed these people, there will be terrible consequences. I have already seen outbreaks of cholera, which I suspect were caused by eating rotten potatoes.'

He could see dismay written on the faces of the good men of the town.

'Over six hundred people have already been admitted to the workhouse, and we have doubled the number of patients in the fever hospital,' he informed them. 'Though they are very sick, some must sleep three to a bed. It is intolerable! Unless there is some sort of intervention, these numbers will continue to grow.'

'Doctor, we are all in agreement with you,' reassured Thomas Somerville. 'We have already written letters of appeal with regards to the crisis, to little avail. So I suggest instead that we send a delegation from here to meet the new Lord Lieutenant, Lord Bessborough, in Dublin to inform him of the alarming state of Skibbereen district and to request relief, to save it from anarchy.'

'What if the Lord Lieutenant does nothing?' Dan demanded.

'Then the delegation will go on to London, if necessary,' Somerville replied firmly, 'to meet the prime minister, Lord John Russell, and appeal to him for relief!'

There was unanimous approval for such action to be taken, though Dan worried that it would have little effect.

'Thank the Lord the public works are finally going to open,' declared a delighted Michael Galwey the following week, on hearing that the prime minister had introduced the new Labour Act, which would employ people on public works relief schemes. 'It's exactly what we hoped for.'

'We must apply immediately to the Board of Works' presentment sessions and put forward proposals for new roads, piers and harbours that will benefit the district,' urged Thomas Somerville.

*

When the relief committee discovered that many of the most useful and beneficial proposals had been rejected, Dan and his fellow committee members were perplexed.

'A road to a bit of a village? Building a new wall across from an empty field? It makes no sense!'

'Work is work,' Michael Galwey consoled. 'At least the men will be paid and able to buy food.'

Chapter 18

September 1846

FATHER FITZPATRICK WALKED PROUDLY AROUND THE RECENTLY opened St Fachtna's School on North Street. For the past two years he had put much work and effort into its planning, organization and construction.

Now the school was finished, it did his heart good to see the rows of new pupils, girls and boys. However, some were ragged and gaunt, poorly nourished with scabs around their lips. It was a sight different from that which he had expected – rows of healthy, energetic pupils – but, despite the calamity that raged around them, he could see a spark in the children's eyes that showed they were still eager and ready to learn.

The large girls' classroom upstairs was already half full, there were only a few places left in the boys' one downstairs, and the numbers were growing in the two smaller infant classes. The parents of Skibbereen, despite their troubles, were determined that their children would enjoy an education that few of them ever had.

As he listened to the young sing-song voices reciting the alphabet with their teacher, he gave thanks that these children had the opportunity to fill their hearts and minds with learning. Education had been the way forward for him. He had attended a small school for boys in Fermoy, run by his older brother James, a priest. With an aching thirst for knowledge and learning, he had decided to follow in his brother's footsteps and later study for the priesthood. A choice he had never regretted.

Bidding the children farewell, he returned home to discover a man in broken-down boots and a stained top coat that flapped about his bony legs waiting patiently for him.

'Come inside,' he offered, leading Jeremiah O'Driscoll into the dining room.

He asked Bridey to provide them both with a cup of tea, and gestured for Mr O'Driscoll to sit down. He listened considerately as the man outlined the dire circumstances in which he found himself: yet another rent demand from his landlord, Reverend Stephen Fitzgerald Townsend.

'I cannot read or write, Father,' the man admitted, embarrassed. 'So I am begging for your help to intercede on my behalf and write a letter from me to Reverend Fitzgerald Townsend, pleading for leniency.'

Father Fitzpatrick sighed, for he had heard this story from many tenants, repeated over and over again. So many were illiterate! Hopefully the new school would help to change things.

'I have done my best, Father. Last year I sold all we possess to pay rent, but now there is nothing left, and my wife and children are suffering distress, and the hunger—' The man's voice broke. 'I appealed to Reverend Fitzgerald Townsend's agent, but he insists that the rent must be paid or we will lose our holding and be put off it.'

Father John had grown up as part of a large family. His had been a relatively humble background, for he'd been raised on a smallholding and knew well the concerns of tenants such as Jeremiah O'Driscoll.

It had been almost eleven years since he'd been appointed parish priest here and he had already written officially to every landlord in the district – Lord Carbery and Reverend Stephen Fitzgerald Townsend, who owned nearly half the town and townlands between them, along with R. H. Becher and Sir William Wrixon Becher. He'd pleaded for leniency for their tenants and asked that rents be forgone during this time of affliction, citing the deplorable condition of the people, but all to no avail.

However, if writing a letter was the only hope this poor man had, Father John would not deny him the opportunity to state his case in yet another appeal to Reverend Stephen Fitzgerald Townsend, one of the largest and wealthiest landowners in Carbery district.

This so-called man of the church was another oppressive absentee landlord, who lived in England. He had demonstrated not a bit of interest or care for his tenants and their families in Ireland, and their deprived circumstances, but perhaps this time might be different.

'My father, my grandfather and great-grandfather were all tenants of the family,' Jeremiah O'Driscoll explained. 'We have always paid what is due, and I give my word to Reverend Fitzgerald Townsend that once things improve and our crops have returned, I will pay him the rent.'

Father John Fitzpatrick could see the man's sincerity and concentrated on writing down his words exactly, listing carefully all the relevant details.

Bridey appeared with a tray with the tea and two cups, and Jeremiah O'Driscoll stared as she poured their drinks.

'Is my meal ready yet?' Father John enquired.

'Aye, Father, I have it kept warm for you.'

'Then you can serve it now, Bridey. Please bring two plates, for Mr O'Driscoll and I will share my repast.'

He could see by his housekeeper's disgruntled expression that she did not approve, but she returned and served them with two plates of bacon, cabbage and mashed turnip.

Father John watched with satisfaction as his guest ate slowly, savouring every mouthful. Afterwards, he insisted that the man take the remaining bacon and vegetables home to his wife and children. Then he presented to Mr O'Driscoll the letter he had written for him to make his mark.

'I will send it to England tomorrow by post and shall contact you if I get a reply,' he promised.

The man nodded, full of hope that his letter writing would bear fruit as he bade the priest goodnight.

Father John yawned, for he had lost count of the number of similar letters he had written.

'I keep warning you, Father, not to let those people through the door, but you pay not a bit of heed to me,' Bridey sighed heavily, her plump face flushed as she tidied away the plates.

'I know you have only my interests at heart, Bridey, but Mr O'Driscoll is one of my parishioners,' he reminded her gently, as she flounced out of the room.

Chapter 19

Creagh

'THE TICKETS ARE BEING ISSUED FOR THE NEW RELIEF WORKS,'
Denis Leary had told John when he called in to the Sullivans'
cottage to share the news with his neighbour. 'You and Pat and
Flor should sign on, for everyone needs the work!'

The following day, Pat had taken the three of them in the
horse and cart to register their names in the hope that they
would get on the scheme. John and Pat returned with their
tickets, but poor Flor was upset because an official had judged
him too old for heavy labouring.

'There is more strength in me than in most men!' he complained bitterly.

A few days later Mary watched as John made ready to leave for
his job on the new roadworks.

'The pay is said to be poor,' she said with worry, 'and the
work very hard.'

'Will you whisht, Mary! Hard work never killed a man,' he

said quietly, pulling on his brown jacket and worn leather boots. 'And 'tis better surely for me to earn the few pennies we need every day than to sit home and watch you and the children go hungry?'

'Of course.' She smiled and reached out to bid him well.

He set out to join a few of the neighbours who were walking to the works along with Pat, Denis and Tom Flynn. They had all been surprised when Tom, who complained of a bad hip, had been issued a ticket for the new scheme, but Flor had been refused.

Mary was filled with hope that now John was working, the huge burden of feeding and keeping their family would ease a little. At last there would be meal and oats for the pot, and perhaps a little bread to keep the starvation and hunger off them. The whole family was weak and badly in need of nourishment, and every penny he earned would give them a little more strength.

'Oh, you're soaked to the skin,' she fussed, when John returned that evening. She took off his jacket and shirt, and put them near the fire to dry.

'I'm fine,' he protested as she made him rest easy and warm himself in a blanket, huddled close to the turf fire.

'Where are you working?'

'Over beyond Oldcourt.'

'Are they putting a new road there?'

'Aye, some kind of road down near the harbour.' He shook his head heavily. 'They have us digging out the ground for it, while some are set to breaking stones.'

'At least you will earn some money.'

'Eight pence a day,' he said bitterly. 'That is all they are paying us, and the like of Tom Flynn get even less. All the Board of Works wants is for us to be employed doing some sort of heavy work. One man told me that the works schemes are designed to occupy the like of us building roads and walls to nowhere!'

'Why would they do such a thing?' Mary puzzled as she warmed up the yellow meal for him.

John was all done in, too tired to talk. He went to bed early, and fell into a heavy sleep, snoring as he lay against her.

Every day, John would set off early in the morning with his head down and only a cut of bread or a few spoons of gruel inside him. He would return home exhausted, saying little to Mary about the works. She would serve him an evening meal of stew with wild onion, turnip and cabbage, for there was little left to forage these days.

'We do the work they ask, yet they still haven't paid us,' John grumbled. 'Not a penny for any of the men. How can we keep on working and get nothing in return? A poor young fellow collapsed beside me this morning. He told me his belly was empty these past two days. A man cannot work on that!'

'What will happen?'

'We complained to the foreman but he cares not a toss for us. He just said that we had to wait for our wages.'

Mary grew alarmed that John was labouring for no reward. Digging, lifting, and the breaking of stones and laying them was backbreaking work. She could see it in the stiffness that had developed in his shoulders and arms, and in the taut look on his face, which betrayed how difficult the job truly was.

The following week, he finally got paid. The paltry few shillings he earned was used immediately to purchase a bag of meal and oats.

'Pat has gone to Maguire's,' he sighed.

'Well, I'm glad that you didn't join him there, drinking porter,' Mary said sharply.

'He has no wife or chicks to feed,' her husband said defensively, 'and deserves a few pints for all his hard work.'

Two days later Mary found it hard to stifle her annoyance and anger with Pat. He was back at their table, sitting across from them and eating their hard-earned food, as most of his wages were gone. She served him only a small portion of the soup, for no matter what John said, she had no intention of letting him steal the food from her children's mouths.

'This is no life for man,' he said, eating some of the bread she had made to go with the cabbage soup. 'I'll not stick this, for it's no life at all.'

Chapter 20

Skibbereen

AS DAN DONOVAN RODE THROUGH THE FALLING LEAVES, HE SLOWED down his horse. Some distance away was a large group of men bearing shovels and spades that glinted in the autumn sunlight as the men marched along the road. There were hundreds and hundreds of them, a dishevelled rag bag, poorly clad and poorly fed. Stalwart men now emaciated, likely employed on the new public roadworks near Caheragh.

For the most part they looked too undernourished to lift a pick or shovel and be set to hard physical labour. Dan had protested at the treatment of these men, advising the authorities to feed them and allow them to return to strength before employing them, but they refused to listen.

Lately, Dan had heard of the failure to pay the men the subsistence money they were due. No doubt this half-starved mob was making its way to town en masse in some form of protest.

Dan feared what would happen when this massive army of nearly a thousand men reached Skibbereen, where they would face the armed military forces. Skibbereen had asked for food supplies but instead they had been sent more soldiers, who were now stationed in the town to protect the district's food stores.

There was little time and so Dan rode on quickly to forewarn Major Parker, the head of the Board of Works, about the workers.

'There are near a thousand of them,' he warned. 'I presume that they are in search of food or money. You must appease them, Major, or else there will be violence this day on the streets of Skibbereen.'

Dan could sense that the major was reluctant to believe him. Immediately, he turned his horse quickly and went to warn some of the townspeople, before heading home to alert his own family.

'My dear,' he told his wife, 'you must stay inside with the doors locked and make sure that the children do not go outside.'

'What is happening?' Henrietta cried, alarmed.

'Hundreds of men from the roadworks are marching into town, no doubt to protest to the head of the Board of Works, and I fear they will not be deterred in their purpose.'

'Promise me that you will be careful, Dan,' she cautioned, 'for you have done these people no wrong.'

As he headed back into town, Dan passed the courthouse. There he met his cousin, magistrate Michael Galwey, who had been attending court, and told him of the situation.

Confirming Dan's suspicions, within a short time hundreds and hundreds of angry workers poured into Skibbereen, protesting that they could not afford to buy food for their families as they were owed their pay by the Board of Public Works.

Terrified merchants, shopkeepers and the bank staff all rushed to close their doors, but many of the townspeople were sympathetic to the workers' plight.

The men kept coming, like some pale spectral army, and the intensity of their demands and anger seemed to grow and grow. Seventy soldiers, with their guns ready and loaded, awaited them in front of the town's new school.

'We are famished!' the men chanted again and again, clanging their shovels and spades on the ground.

'We have no food! Our wives and children are starving! We work and get not a penny in payment! Not even a piece of food!' they yelled, shouting out their grievances to the passers-by. 'The hunger is on us!'

'We'll have our money!' a grey-haired man shouted to the crowd, raising his shovel high in the air as the mob surged towards the bank.

The soldiers began to surround them, bayonets at the ready, but they were far outnumbered and would surely come under attack before long.

Dan pulled aside one of the soldiers.

'Go and tell Mr Hughes at the depot that he must distribute some food to them,' he told him. He abhorred the unfair treatment of these men and believed that they were justified in their actions.

'I'll speak to them,' offered Michael Galwey. 'Perhaps they will listen to me.'

He stood up in front of the school and the men came to a halt.

'As the local magistrate, I inform you that this riot is

unlawful. You must all return to Caheragh and not disturb this town or, I warn you, the military here will be forced to use their weapons and take action against you.'

'We may as well be shot as starved!' they shouted back loudly. 'We have not eaten a morsel for twenty-four hours!'

Michael Galwey raised his voice and ordered the seventy soldiers to prepare to fire. The town fell silent. There were only slight mutters of dissent as the rioters took a few steps back.

The grim-faced soldiers held firm.

Afraid of the army that now faced them, with their guns raised and ready to fire, the protesters stopped. A voice declared loudly that there would be no trouble.

'Return to work and I promise that the money due to each of you will be distributed in a matter of days,' urged Michael Galwey.

At that point, Mr Hughes from the food depot appeared.

'Open the food store immediately, Mr Hughes,' the magistrate ordered, 'and issue these men with a quantity of biscuits. Three cheers for the Queen and plenty of employment tomorrow!'

A few half-hearted cheers rose from the crowd of workers, but most kept their heads down and said nothing. Their riot defeated, the exhausted men sat quietly and devoured hungrily the biscuits they were eventually served.

Dan had to assuage his own anger. How could the Board of Works not understand how desperate the men were for the eight pennies a day they were being paid? For them, it was the difference between life and death. He wished they had fought harder for their demands. They had strength in numbers and should have refused to leave the town till they were paid.

But Dan could see it everywhere: hunger and disease were slowly killing the people's spirit and their ability to fight for any kind of justice.

Chapter 21

HENRIETTA DONOVAN WAS MOVED AND UPSET BY THE GROUPS OF paupers who loitered constantly near her front door in the hope of seeing her husband. It had been the same scene every day since the hunger had come.

The hungry and sick were everywhere, flooding into town looking for work and food. They sought assistance from Dan as the Union's physician: a ticket for a visit to the dispensary with a sick child or wife, or for Dan to visit them in person; a ticket to be employed on the public roadworks; or a pass to be admitted to the Union workhouse. Desperate people during this desperate time!

Henrietta worried as she watched her husband set off every morning, dressed in his usual frock coat and tall black hat, sporting his neat side whiskers, his countenance filled with concern for the care of his patients. She and the children scarcely saw him, as Dan worked longer and longer hours, returning home later and later every day.

She had tried to persuade him to move away from the area for the sake of their family. He was a renowned oculist who not only had papers published regularly in *The Lancet* and other medical journals, but also had patients travel to consult him on his medical expertise in the area of eye diseases. They came from as far away as Dublin and Galway as well as from overseas.

'Dan, we could leave here and you could practise as an oculist in Dublin or Edinburgh, such is your reputation,' she cajoled. 'Or you could take up a position in one of the big city hospitals, for you are a skilled surgeon.'

'Hetty, I have a rewarding position here,' he reminded her. 'And I have no intention of leaving it . . .'

At night, despite his tiredness, Dan sat at his desk for hours, writing his 'Diary of a Dispensary Doctor' and reporting truthfully on the state of affairs in the town and district. His accounts were now being published in the *Southern Reporter* and in other newspapers further afield. Henrietta was so proud of him and dearly hoped that his words would shame the authorities into providing the relief needed.

'Why does Dada not care for us any more?' puzzled Fanny, her brown eyes serious. She wore a tight little frown on her brow as she wondered what they had all done to upset him so.

'Your dada does love you all so much,' Henrietta tried to reassure her children. 'It is just that he is kept very busy looking after the sick.'

'And there are sick people everywhere,' Ellen pronounced knowledgeably.

'Yes, I'm afraid so,' her mother agreed.

'That is why we cannot go out to play like before?'

'Your father would prefer you to stay at home or play in the garden for the moment, until things improve.'

'When will that be?' Fanny pressed.

'Soon,' she tried to reassure them. 'Soon.'

She too found it suffocating to spend so much time confined to their home, trying to teach the children and amuse them. Glad to escape the confines of New Street, she welcomed invitations to visit Dan's relations. Visiting their country houses for afternoon tea or a walk in the nearby woods always cheered her. There, she could watch the children run and play and laugh and chase around like children should. For the most part, the youngsters of Skibbereen were now silent and quiet, all childhood fun and games for many banished by the hunger.

Of late, Dan had taken to entering their home via the back scullery door. He had requested that Henrietta or their maid, Sally, leave a clean shirt, waistcoat, top coat and pair of shoes there for him to change into, following his visits to the decrepit cabins and cottages of his patients, which had become dens of effluent and human waste. She would watch as he removed his soiled and often foul-scented clothing meticulously, and washed and scrubbed his arms to the elbow in the scullery sink before re-dressing. A handsome man, he had always been a fastidious dresser, and took care of his appearance, with his starched white shirt and tailored top coat with its brass buttons and lined lapels.

On his return home, she felt Dan deserved the reward of a good meal after his work and endeavours throughout the day. He was partial to beef and so she tried to ensure it was served a few times a week. There were no potatoes for the present, but turnips, pastry, boiled onions and dumplings pleased him, followed by a pudding.

That evening there was beef and vegetable pie served with

96

turnip, then an apple and raisin pudding, a favourite of his. Dan enjoyed the meal, but left the pudding untouched, and pushed the bowl away.

'Is it not to your taste?' she queried.

'I fear that I do not have the stomach for it. Perhaps one of the children will take it.'

She passed the bowl to their eldest son, Henry, a growing boy who was certainly partial to pudding. It concerned Henrietta that her husband's lack of appetite was perhaps a sign of some kind of illness.

'Are you feeling unwell, Dan?' she asked him in the drawing room, after the children were all in bed.

She was fearful that he might be developing a fever, like so many others in the town.

'I am not ill,' he reassured her, as if reading her mind. 'It is just that I cannot countenance enjoying such a rich table while all around us the people are starving. It is abhorrent to me.'

'What do you want me to do?' she demanded, upset by him. 'Empty our larder and pantry, and put the food and provision out on the street for the beggars to eat? Though I must remind you that we have a large family of our own that needs feeding . . . Our own flesh and blood, our children to care for.'

She could not hide her anger, for it was Dan who, despite her pleas to move away, insisted on remaining in Skibbereen so that he could minister to his patients and the people who thronged into the town.

'My dear,' he soothed. 'I do not intend to upset you. There is no better mother who cares more for her family than you. It is just that, given the present circumstances that pertain in the district, it would be better if no pudding or cake were served with meals under this roof. I believe the food should be kept plain and nourishing with no lavish, rich or luxury ingredients. Good meals simply served for the family.'

Immediately, Henrietta felt contrite. She was ashamed that she herself had not thought of such a matter, given the scenes she witnessed daily on her own doorstep. She was in agreement with him.

'Very well. I will instruct Sally and, if you wish, I will ensure that no more puddings and cakes will be served for the present,' she promised, knowing full well that Dan would miss such delicacies more than the rest of the household. 'No treacle pudding or slices of the ginger cake that you favour.'

She leaned over and kissed the worry line on his forehead that seemed to be there almost permanently these days, then his cheek and then his lips.

'Sometimes I think that you are far too good for your own good,' she teased him gently, 'but I wouldn't have it any other way.'

'I know how hard it must be for you and the children with my work and the constant demands on my time.'

'Dan, you are a doctor. I knew that when I married you and accepted what being a doctor's wife means.'

'But what is happening here is beyond any expectation!' He sighed heavily.

Tears welled in her eyes unbidden as she remembered the early days of their marriage when they lived near the coastal village of Union Hall. Much happier times!

'Hetty, you are an angel to put up with me,' Dan said as he pulled her gently on to his lap. Tenderly, he wiped the tears from her eyes. 'My own beloved angel.'

Chapter 22

Creagh

MARY WAS GROWING WORRIED FOR JOHN'S HEALTH. WORKING ON the roads was taking a toll on him, sapping his strength, energy and spirit.

'They work us like slaves,' he admitted as he hunched over the fire, bone weary and exhausted.

'Well, I am no slave,' declared Pat angrily as he sipped a warming mug of tea she'd made with leftover tea leaves. 'They want to break us all – every man, woman and child – but I'll not let them break me. I'll leave this poisoned place and make a life somewhere else. I'll not die laying stones at the side of a road.'

'Ah, brother, how could you go? Where would you find the money?'

'I'll find it somehow,' he declared testily, refusing to be drawn any further.

Mary studied her brother-in-law and could see he was intent on it. He did not have the same ties to the land as she and John; his was only a smallholding, barely enough to support a family. He had no sweetheart or wife, or child to bind him here. Why would he stay amid such calamity when a better life beckoned him across the sea?

As Mary and John readied for bed that evening, John sighed.

'Patrick and his old talk of leaving! He'll never leave this place.'

'Don't be so sure. I think he means it,' she said, tracing the curve of her husband's bony shoulder. 'For there is nothing to keep him here any more.'

Every second or third day Pat called to the cottage, joining them to share whatever little they had. Shamefaced, he would sometimes bring something at least to add to the pot. Mary was caught by surprise one evening when, with a flourish, he produced a big bag of meal and a large hare that he had somehow managed to catch.

'How this wily old fellow has managed to escape all this time.' He grinned and passed the skinned and cleaned hare to Mary. 'But today was not his lucky day. I got him fair and square lying in the ferns.'

'You are good to share him with us,' she thanked him appreciatively as she transferred the hare to cook slowly in the pot.

Of late, her brother-in-law had surprised them on several occasions with bags of meal, a small round of cheese, a box of salted herrings, a sack of oats, and now this!

'Don't ask where he gets it from,' warned John. 'It's better that we know nothing of where he and his wild boys get these goods.'

After they finished their feast, the children cleaned their bowls and licked their fingers. In the corner, Patch chewed hungrily at a bone and everyone sat around the warmth of the turf, talking. Pat then brought out a small bottle of *poitín*, which he insisted on sharing with his brother.

'It's grand stuff . . .'

'That will warm your heart and spirit,' Pat joked as the two brothers reminisced about their childhood.

Later, he confided in Mary and John about the cart of grain, bound for shipping to Liverpool, that he and two friends had managed to intercept.

'I promise you, those three bags that we took while the cart-man went for a piss won't be missed until the sacks are unloaded in Liverpool!'

'What if they catch you?' Mary asked, worried.

'They won't.' He shrugged. 'Besides, grain grown here should stay here.'

As the hour grew late, John fell asleep in his chair. Mary walked Pat to the door and thanked him again for the hare and sack of meal.

'John is a lucky man to have found a woman like you. Truth to tell, I envy him.' Pat's hand reached up to touch her face. 'From the day we met, Mary, I wished that I was the one who had saw you first.'

'Hush,' she laughed. 'It's just the drink talking. Sure, you have been in love so many times, and have half the women of the parish mad about you.'

'But they are not you,' he said, emotion showing in his eyes.

'Pat, I am your sister-in-law,' she reminded him firmly. 'I

love your brother with all my heart, and have always done so and always will.'

He stepped back, crestfallen and a little ashamed.

'Away home with you to your own bed,' she urged gently, watching him take the path for home.

There was no sign of Pat Sullivan for two days. Concerned, John went to his cottage, fearful his brother had fallen ill or, worse still, had been caught and arrested. Pat's horse and cart were gone from the smallholding and John carried home the note he had found there.

'I told you he would go away,' Mary said as John read Pat's words aloud.

The brief letter informed John that Pat would be taking the horse and cart, which were rightfully his to sell. He would be using the money to purchase a ticket to sail to Liverpool and then on to New York. He wanted a new life far from the hunger, and crossing the ocean to North America was his chance of a better future.

'I cannot believe that he has just left with not a word to us!' said John.

Mary was not surprised. She knew their last meal together had been a farewell of sorts as Pat had, in his own fashion, said goodbye to all of them. He had said nothing of his plans for he likely did not want them to stop him. She was angry, however, that the cart and the old horse were gone.

'Pat has little enough with the cottage and only a small patch of land,' her husband said in defence of his brother, 'but my father gave him the horse and cart when he died. Although I used them at times, they were always his to sell.'

'Then he was within his rights,' Mary sighed. 'Let's hope that he got a good price for them.'

'I'll miss Pat. It's likely we will never see him again, but I wish my brother good fortune wherever he travels.'

As she passed Pat's empty cottage to hunt for haws, sloes, rosehips and rowan berries, Mary thought of him. She knew in her heart that he had made a wise decision to escape the hunger while he still could. It was a decision she sometimes envied, as she watched John grow weaker and her children turn pale, the flesh beginning to melt from their bones.

Chapter 23

Oldcourt, County Cork
October 1846

DAN WAS OUT NEAR OLDCOURT, RETURNING FROM A VISIT TO A
man, weak with hunger, who had fallen and broken his leg,
when he stopped his horse. The ships, boats and low barges
that plied their trade in the small but busy harbour were load-
ing and unloading their cargo. This was a place where the sea
and river met. Ships and boats arriving from Liverpool and
Newport and Cardiff sailed as far up the river Ilen as they
could before they transferred their goods to smaller row boats
that would transport them upriver to the town.

He watched as large sacks of grain destined for McCarthy's
brewery were moved to two waiting barges ready to sail
upriver. Grain that could have fed hundreds being used
instead to make beer and porter for the busy taverns of Dublin
and Cork! It made no sense to him.

Protesting livestock, squealing pigs and a few sheep arrived
and were loaded quickly into the hold of a large ship ready for

their journey to England. Baskets of cheese and dried fish, and barrels of butter were stacked tightly on to another vessel, destined to feed the factory workers of Liverpool, London and Manchester.

As he stood on the small quay, Dan noticed that one ship, the *Mersey Lady*, had not been reloaded, but the crew were hoisting the sail and making ready to leave.

'Are you casting off?' he called out.

'Aye, sir, we have to catch the tide or we'll be landed here till tonight.'

'But you have no cargo?'

'We delivered a cargo of corn for Swanton's and will return from Newport with another delivery next week.'

'Do you not usually return with a cargo from here?'

'Rarely,' replied the man whom he presumed to be the captain.

'You have an empty hold returning to Liverpool or Wales regularly?' he pressed.

'Aye.' The man nodded. 'Those are Mr Swanton's orders.'

An empty ship leaving Ireland was a lost opportunity. Surely such a vessel could provide passage to a new life in Liverpool, or another one of England's great cities, for those who had lost everything.

'Would you give consideration to taking a few passengers on your return journey from here next time?'

'This is not a passenger ship,' the man retorted gruffly. 'We transport grain from place to place, not people.'

'Even a few people desperate to escape from this ravaged place?'

'I am employed by Mr Swanton,' the captain replied brusquely. 'You would need to discuss the matter with him.'

James Swanton was one of the town's most prosperous busi-nessmen. He owned a large mill and several warehouses, but unlike other local business owners, he had joined the relief committee and might be prepared to assist Dan.

'We are well acquainted.' Dan smiled at the captain. 'Thank you. I will, as you advise, discuss the matter with him and perhaps we can reach some agreement.'

Chapter 24

JAMES SWANTON WAS BUSY IN HIS OFFICE DOWN ON LEVIS QUAY, but greeted Dan warmly.

'Can I help you, doctor?' he asked, curious about the reason for this visit from his fellow committee member.

'I am not here on committee business but with regard to another matter,' Dan replied. 'I was riding to Oldcourt yesterday and I noticed one of your ships had unloaded corn, but was preparing to return to Newport with no cargo. I spoke to her captain.'

'The import of corn, grain and materials from Liverpool and Newport is the backbone of my milling business.' James Swanton leaned forward and fixed the doctor with his gaze. 'Despite this calamity, business must go on.'

'I understand that, Mr Swanton.' Dan had not meant to sound critical in any way, for he needed to get the merchant on his side. 'It is the empty cargo hold that I want to discuss with you.'

'I may be a businessman, Dr Donovan, but while Irish men and women starve I am not prepared to export any food goods from this country on the ship I have hired. Timber and fuel, yes, but no foodstuffs or livestock! I have considered using the hold to transport those who are willing to leave this sorry place but I'm not sure if any would accept such an offer.'

'Believe me, Mr Swanton, they most certainly would,' Dan declared firmly. 'If such an offer was made, would it be possible to use your empty ship to transport those desperate to escape from here with no fare payment?'

'It is not a passenger ship,' Swanton reminded him. 'There would be no comfort for people on such a voyage, but it would at least transport them quickly and with no charge.'

'That is most generous of you.'

'I need to talk to the captain about it, but I will not agree to provide passage to any who are sick or infirm. I don't want to risk the captain and crew falling ill or have them turned back at the docks.'

'I promise that I will medically examine every passenger travelling and ensure they are strong and well,' Dan assured him.

'Then I will find out from the captain how many passengers he can safely accommodate and agree dates for the sailings with him.'

Dan thanked him warmly and they agreed to meet up in a few days' time to organize things further.

James Swanton arranged free passage on his grain ship for a hundred people. Over the course of the long week that followed, Dan approached a number of orphaned young men to see if they were interested in his plan. He also spoke to Helena

Collins, a widow with three boys who had planned to leave Ireland with her husband, and a desperate young couple who had been evicted and were sleeping rough in the fields. All were anxious to escape the hunger and desperate to begin a new life away from the sadness of their homeland.

Many he talked to were utterly destitute, with not even a coat on their back. They could not be sent to Newport or Liverpool in such a state and so, taking their pawn tickets, Dan redeemed them. Using some of the donations he received, he returned much-needed coats and shawls, boots and britches, and dresses to their rightful owners.

As word got around, Dan became inundated with requests from people wanting to take the free passage across the sea but regretfully he could only issue so many tickets.

Two weeks later, Dan returned to Oldcourt with the *Mersey Lady*'s first passengers. The water was choppy and a strong wind was blowing. The young men and women, and few children he had handpicked for this first voyage waited anxiously as the sailors unloaded their cargo on to the waiting barges and the captain shouted orders.

He waited patiently on the quay alongside James Swanton.

The relief committee had agreed to issue two shillings to each passenger just before their departure, for they would need it on their arrival in Liverpool. The waiting passengers had few other possessions with them, only a blanket and some oatcakes that Mr Swanton had donated to them.

'I am very glad to be of assistance.' The miller smiled as he introduced Dan to the ship's captain.

'Once we land these people I cannot provide any further

assistance to them,' the captain explained. 'They must find work themselves or journey on across the Atlantic, but it is not my care what happens to them. The sea ports are filled with starving Irish, who do little to help themselves and plague the taverns and hostelries. Many of them are being returned to your shore.'

'That is understood, Captain, but I promise you that these people are willing to work.'

'Dr Donovan, I will only transport passengers who are strong, healthy and fit for a sea voyage.'

'That is only prudent and I have checked each one personally. Though they are malnourished, they are otherwise healthy,' he assured him. 'Captain, I thank you sincerely for agreeing to help these people.'

'We will sail in less than half an hour,' the captain announced peremptorily. 'We cannot tarry as rough weather is expected.'

The passengers soon began to board the vessel. Dan was filled with sympathy for Mrs Collins, who wept openly as she and her children stepped on the deck of the ship.

'Thank you, Dr Donovan. We will never forget it for you.' Michael and Jane Carmody, filled both with excitement and plans for their future, smiled as they shook his hand.

'Our uncle has a boot factory in the town,' grinned Donal Harrington, who was travelling with his brother Tommy. 'We hope to get work there.'

One of the doctor's own tenants, Michael McCarthy, had welcomed the opportunity to leave Cork with his family. A few of the other passengers were young men from the lanes of Skibbereen who were more than ready to work and escape their lowly background.

One of the crew untied the ship from its mooring and the sails were hoisted as the vessel moved off. Pulling his coat tightly around him as the wind blew, Dan watched from the harbour wall with James Swanton.

'I'm glad that we managed to assist a few souls today to escape from this place of hunger,' James Swanton declared firmly. 'Thank you, doctor, for your help in arranging such matters.'

'I was glad to do it.'

'Next time my grain ship is here, I'll see to it that it will transport a few more of those who you consider suitable for free passage,' he offered as the two men shook hands.

As he turned for home, Dan was already mentally drawing up a list of deserving passengers.

Chapter 25

Skibbereen

DAN STARED AT THE EMACIATED CORPSE OF DENIS MCKENNEDY, A labourer on the relief roadworks. As he prepared his instruments for the post mortem, he remembered his days as an undergraduate in Edinburgh. Many of his fellow medical students were overcome when confronted with a cadaver, but he had never been affected in that way. He was innately curious about the human body, discovering how it worked and why life had been taken from it. The examination of organs, tissue and bone revealed more than any textbook and usually provided proof of cause of death.

'I suppose another man from the works,' nodded Dr Patrick Dore, who was assisting him.

They both found this work difficult of late, for they had to carry out post mortems on some of the unfortunates found dead in the district's fields and ditches, roads and laneways. Men who had once been strong and able and willing to work, but had died of starvation and fever contracted from the poor conditions they were forced to endure.

Recently, Dan had carried out a post mortem on a similar case – Jeremiah Hegarty, another labourer discovered dead by the side of the road. On examination, his intestines had been found to be devoid of food. At the official inquest, Dan had reported that Hegarty had died from lack of nourishment and exposure.

'I see this man died on the seventeenth of October,' noted Dr Dore as he consulted Mr McKennedy's notes. 'His body is in a worse state than most we have examined.'

Dan could see immediately that the corpse was lacking any sign of muscle or fatty tissue. It was one of the most attenuated that he had ever examined. There was no trace of fat anywhere around the abdomen and scarcely a vestige of omentum. All the adipose matter had been absorbed by the body.

'There is no food in the stomach or small intestine,' he remarked as he examined the man's innards, which were blanched and empty. 'And all I can see is what appears to be a small quantity of cabbage mixed with excrement in his bowel.'

The two doctors looked at each other, both moved by the plight of the man before them.

'How did this poor fellow manage to find the strength to work at all?' questioned Dr Dore.

'Apparently, Mr McKennedy had not been paid since the tenth of October,' Dan said angrily. 'It's appalling that another good man was forced to walk miles and do heavy labouring work for a pittance without any sustenance and nourishment. This travesty cannot continue!'

There were few in attendance at the inquest into Denis McKennedy's death held at the courthouse in Skibbereen.

113

The Board of Works tried to lay the blame on a pay clerk, Mr Hungerford, who had made an administrative error, which had resulted in Mr McKennedy not being paid when due.

Dan took up his notes and began to read aloud the detailed record of the autopsy.

'The only sign of any form of food I could find in Mr McKennedy's bowels was some cabbage leaf.'

A woman near the back sobbed loudly and he could sense the embarrassment of the court officials.

'Therefore, following a full autopsy and examination of the body of the deceased, I find that Mr Denis McKennedy died of starvation owing to the gross negligence of the Board of Works.'

There was a stunned silence at his direct accusation of the Board, followed by a murmur of dissent from the officials. He could see the clerk cast his eyes to heaven, but Dan continued, for he was the court-appointed physician carrying out post mortems on such men.

'And this shall be entered in the records,' Dan concluded loudly, determined that the truth be told and written up officially.

Chapter 26

Creagh

AS MARY COOKED THE YELLOW MEAL IN THE POT, SHE TASTED A little of it on the wooden spoon. No matter how hard she tried to soak and grind and cook it, it had a terrible consistency. Nora and Tim both complained that it made them sick. After eating it a few days ago, they had doubled up from sharp pains in their stomachs, but she had cajoled them into eating more of it to give them some nourishment.

On the way from the dressmaker's earlier that day, she had called to see her sister, who had given her a narrow strip of dried-out fatty bacon.

'Use it to feed you and John and the children,' Kathleen had urged. Mary suspected that her sister or her husband, Joe, may have stolen it, but in these desperate times the poor had no other option but to look after their own.

Mary sliced the meat thinly. She would scrape a tiny bit on top of each plate in the hope that it would give the yellow meal some taste as well as a little extra sustenance. Most of it she would give to John, for her husband was fading before her eyes. His muscles were gone, and his arms were long and thin, like those of a boy. To see him lose his strength was enough to make her cry.

Poor old Patch watched her from the door. The collie was a changed animal, for there were no more scraps from the table and she hadn't seen him catch a rabbit in months. God knows what the wretched creature was living on, for they had nothing to give him.

The dog sidled up to her and Mary rubbed his black-and-white coat gently. His fur had begun to fall out, and she could feel his ribs. He was a good dog, who used to love to chase and roll around in the grass, but since the hunger had come all the playfulness had gone from him.

'You poor old thing, you are suffering like us all,' she soothed. The dog rolled over at the kindness of her words to have his scrawny belly rubbed.

'Aww,' she sighed, bending down to tickle him like he was a child.

She called the children and John to come and sit by the turf fire as she spooned out the yellow meal.

'I'll not take it,' protested Tim.

'You'll eat it or you'll feel the strap,' interjected John. 'None of us likes it, but there is nothing else and it will keep the hunger off us.'

'There is a scrapeen of some nice salt bacon that your auntie gave me. It will make it taste a bit better,' she promised them.

Tim looked dubious, his bottom lip stuck out as if he was going to cry. Lifting the bacon off her own helping, she passed the grey-looking strip towards her son's bowl. Though she was hungry, the fatty meat turned her stomach.

As Tim reached to put it into his mouth, Patch sprang up and flung himself at the boy. He grabbed the bacon, growling and biting, as he dragged it literally from the child's mouth.

'No! No!' Mary shrieked as Con, Annie and Nora all began to cry and scream.

Terrified, young Tim dropped his food as he tried to push the snarling dog from him.

John caught Patch with a kick but the dog kept going, crazed with hunger, gobbling at the meal and bacon that was spilt on Tim's clothes and lap. He bared his teeth at John as his master tried to pull him away.

John kicked Patch again, catching the animal's scrawny body. Despite the dog's biting and snapping, John somehow managed to get him to the other side of the room, where Patch hunched, a deep low growling coming from him. Mary grabbed the willow switch brush and forced the collie out the door.

Tim was as white as a ghost. He was bleeding from the corner of his mouth and there was a gash on his lower lip. His right hand bore the imprint of the dog's teeth.

'Why did Patch do that?' sobbed Nora. 'He loves Tim.'

'He's hungry, pet,' Mary explained sadly. 'And when dogs are hungry, they get fierce and dangerous and forget that you love them.'

She lifted Tim on to her lap and told John to get some water. She began to wash her son's lip, face and hands. He was shaking, terrified that the dog would come back and attack him again.

'Dada and I won't let him near you,' she promised. 'He's not coming back in here ever again.'

John disappeared outside.

The children were quiet as they finished the meal. Con was still upset and asked her if he could go outside to see Patch.

'You are all staying here with me till your father returns.'

'We love Patch,' said Nora softly. 'It's not his fault that he's hungry like the rest of us.'

An hour later, John returned. His shoulders were slumped and his eyes red-rimmed. She could tell he was deeply saddened by what he had had to do, but he'd had no choice.

'Where's Patch?' demanded Con. 'What did you do to him?'

'I put the poor creature out of his misery,' he explained haltingly as the children stared wide-eyed at him. 'It was the kindest thing to do.'

'You had no right to do that!' protested Con, upset. 'Patch is our dog and we care for him.'

'We all cared for him,' John explained gently. 'He was a fine dog, but what would you have me do? Let him attack Nora or Annie like he attacked Tim? We have little enough to eat and there is not a scrap to give the dog when we are hungry ourselves. Would you have us watch Patch starve to death?'

'No,' said Tim. 'Dada is right. I wouldn't want Patch here with us, biting and attacking me again.'

'But I'll miss him.' Nora began to cry, sobbing loudly.

Mary tried to steel herself as she looked at the tear-stained faces of her children. Truth to tell, she felt like crying herself, for the dog was part of their lives.

*

Later, as she lay beside John while the children slept, he told her about Patch.

'The poor dog was terrified. He knew that he had overstepped himself and that we could never trust him again. He was licking my hands the way he always does and looking at me with those big eyes of his as if to say sorry. I kept thinking of when he was a puppy.'

'He was always a good dog,' she agreed sadly.

'I took him over near the trees and sat down with him. I got him with two quick blows to the head. I buried him there—' His voice broke as he told her. 'I was always fond of that collie.'

'I know,' Mary soothed, 'but it had to be done.'

'The children are fierce upset, but when things are better next year we'll get them a new pup.'

'John Sullivan, you are the kindest-hearted man I know,' she said, kissing him and pulling him into the warm comfort of her arms.

Chapter 27

Skibbereen

DAN CALLED TO A SICK FAMILY IN CORONEA, MOST OF THEM SIMPLY weak with hunger, and then to a young boy who was suffering from bad seizures in Bridgetown. His last ticket was to visit the Murphys' cabin in Windmill Lane. Julia Murphy was a gentle type of woman, a young widow who had last come to him when her son had fallen and broken his arm. He was one of two children and Dan wondered who in the family was ailing and required a visit from him on this occasion.

'Mrs Murphy?' he called as he knocked lightly on the low door of the small cabin.

A young girl of five or six appeared in filthy rags and held the door for him. In the dim, smoky light of the one room Dan's senses were overwhelmed by the obvious smell of putrefaction.

'Where is your mother?' he asked the child.

'There.'

She pointed nervously at a hunched figure that lay sleeping on the floor among the filthy straw.

'Julia, it's Dr Donovan,' he called softly.

There was no response. As he approached her a voice moaned, and he bent down to look more closely.

'Julia?'

He stopped suddenly, realizing that there was also a boy of about four years old under the blanket, sobbing tearfully. Beside him lay his mother, cold and pale. He moved her gently and checked, but there was no pulse or sign of life. Her body was already beginning to decay. He lifted up the half-starved child.

'It's all right, little man,' he soothed the scared child. 'You are safe.'

The small girl ran over to join her brother.

Neither of them was anything more than bones, their small stomachs swollen. Lord knows when they had last eaten. Dan searched the damp cabin and found no trace of any type of food. How long had poor Julia Murphy gone without eating? No doubt the little she had she had given to her children while she grew weaker.

Overcome with sadness, he stared at the once-beautiful woman who had lain down and died here in her own home. There was no furniture, no comfort, and she and her children had little clothing. Likely she had pawned their every last possession.

Was there no one in the town who might have helped her or her children? If only they had come to the dispensary, he could have at least had them admitted to the Union! Perhaps pride or fear or shame had prevented Julia Murphy from seeking help.

The small boy clung to Dan's neck. Both children needed to be cared for, so he resolved to take them to the workhouse straight away. Following a proper examination, he would make arrangements for the burial of their poor mother.

'What are your names?' he asked the girl.

'I'm Maria and he's Owen,' she said as she stared at the doctor, her eyes sunken in her face.

'Well, Maria and Owen, I have a fine horse and trap, and I am going to take you to a place where you will be fed and looked after as your mother cannot do that any more,' Dan tried to explain.

'Is my mama dead?'

'Yes, I'm afraid so. But she would want the two of you to be well cared for.'

As he took the children by the hand and led them down to where he had tethered his horse, one or two curious neighbours appeared at their doorways.

'Mrs Murphy is unfortunately deceased, so please do not enter there,' he warned. 'On my return I will attend to things.'

As he drove the young Murphys to the workhouse, Dan thought of his own children and prayed that they would never face such sadness. No boy or girl deserved to see their beloved mother meet her end in this terrible way.

Chapter 28

November 1846

'GENTLEMEN, I HAVE SEEN TERRIBLE THINGS RECENTLY,' DAN admitted, trying to control his emotions as he recalled the tragic deaths of poor Julia Murphy and Denis McKennedy. 'Women and children in a weakened and perilous state, hungry men who are not fit to work on the public relief schemes. It is incumbent upon we who sit on the relief committee to find some other means to assist them, for we can no longer stand by and watch our people as they starve and die before our very eyes.'

'Dr Donovan is right,' agreed chairman Thomas Somerville as they sat around the table in the meeting room of the workhouse. 'We can no longer wait for Charles Trevelyan and his cronies in the Treasury to act. We must try to find an affordable solution.'

'Perhaps here could be further utilized for such urgent assistance?' suggested Michael Galwey, looking in Dan's direction.

'I'm sorry, Michael, but the workhouse is already full,' Dan admitted regretfully. 'There is talk of us having to procure more buildings here in town, to house the additional sick and destitute.'

'Then what can we do to help the hungry?' Father Fitzpatrick demanded.

'The roadworks are oversubscribed. The men flocked to them only because they needed to be fed,' interjected Daniel McCarthy. 'Food is what is urgently needed!'

'Then it is our Christian duty to find some way to feed them,' insisted Reverend Richard Boyle Townsend.

'We must provide relief that does not involve hard labour or people agreeing to enter the workhouse,' Dan proposed.

'I agree with the good doctor.' Reverend Townsend nodded, his thin features animated. 'If we provide food for the poor, there must be no conditions. It must be gratuitous relief.'

'Gentlemen, you do realize the enormous task we may be undertaking here?' warned Daniel McCarthy. 'We may have to feed hundreds – nay, thousands – of poor souls a day.'

'The workhouse serves soup or gruel to the inmates mostly every day, along with bread or some rice,' Dan informed them. 'I believe there is great need to provide a similar type of meal once a day for the hungry here in the town. Miss Penn of the Society of Friends told me of large soup kitchens in Manchester and London which the society ran. They kept thousands of poor people alive by serving similar gallons of soup and rice.'

'Providing a soup kitchen here in town to feed the hungry is exactly what is needed.' Reverend Townsend nodded, excited.

'There must be no charge for the soup,' warned Father Fitzpatrick. 'We must provide gratuitous relief, as Reverend Townsend suggested, with no conditions.'

'No charge? But feeding such a large number will be costly,' reminded the town's brewery owner.

'Mr McCarthy, you know well that they have not a penny to purchase food.'

'That I do. God help us, I see them every day, hungering. But how are we to raise the funds ourselves for such a large endeavour?'

'By subscription, rates money and, of course, charitable donations,' Tim McCarthy Downing said slowly and deliberately, looking around the group. 'The money will have to come from that.'

A low mumble passed around the committee.

'A large soup kitchen will cost a tidy sum to operate, what with ingredients and a few cooks or servers. Then there is the business of having to find suitable premises to hold such numbers!' Daniel McCarthy reminded the room.

'I would offer my church grounds, but we have no building large enough to house such a kitchen,' sighed Reverend Townsend. 'My church will fully support it, however, and contribute towards the running cost.'

'I am in a similar position,' nodded Father Fitzpatrick, 'in that we have only the church itself, which is the house of God.'

'What about that property on the river? The new steam mill?' ventured Michael Galwey.

'The steam mill is not yet in use,' suggested Tom Marmion, the land agent for Stephen Fitzgerald Townsend, one of the largest absentee landowners in the district. 'It might be suitable for such a venture.'

'Tom, I cannot see Reverend Fitzgerald Townsend agreeing

for it to be used for such an endeavour when he refuses even to consider forgoing rent payments from his suffering tenants during this calamity.'

'I suspect there is little generosity or charity in the man.' Father Fitzpatrick sighed despondently.

'This matter does not concern Reverend Fitzgerald Townsend,' Tom Marmion responded. 'The property does not belong to him.'

'Then to whom does it belong?' quizzed the chairman. 'Who do we approach?'

'I am the proprietor of the mill.' Tom Marmion's cheeks flushed. He knew full well that he had surprised the assembled gathering. 'I had hoped that it would be busy milling these past few months. However, given the situation, it is not the proper time to open such a venture. That is why I would like to offer it for use temporarily. To serve as a distribution centre, be it for soup or as a food depot, or whatever is considered necessary by the committee.'

'That is most generous of you, Tom,' Father Fitzpatrick offered.

Dan nodded in agreement. Though he suspected that the purchase of land and construction of a new mill must have cost Tom a pretty penny, money likely amassed from the large rents he collected for Reverend Stephen Fitzgerald Townsend and his like.

'You are a good fellow,' cheered Daniel McCarthy. 'The mill would be ideal for such a venture to feed the people. Perhaps the good doctor can enquire at the Union about the composition of a soup or meal to sustain the hungry of the town during this time of crisis. And we will endeavour to purchase large boilers and such like.'

The soup provided by the large Union kitchen to the workhouse inmates was unappetizing but cheaply produced. It provided the necessary sustenance, though to Dan's mind many of them still suffered from poor nutrition.

'I'm sorry not to be able to help further, doctor,' the cook apologized when he consulted her, 'but we are already overstretched here with the huge numbers that must be fed.'

Mrs Hegarty from the Becher Arms offered to assist them, but the soup usually served in her hotel was too rich and expensive for their needs.

'But it is no problem to make a cheaper standard soup,' she advised, 'that will be both filling and nutritious.'

Henrietta and the Donovans' maid, Sally, had both been intrigued when he questioned them on the merits of the good restorative soup that he regularly enjoyed in his own home.

'We use some meat – often left over from another meal – turnips, parsnips, onion and carrot, doctor,' explained Sally. 'We used to have potato but now barley or another form of meal has to suffice.'

Dan made a note of the quantities needed.

'Mary McCarthy and Elizabeth Townsend both told me that their husbands have got a sudden notion for soup and tasting it,' Henrietta teased him as she spooned some oxtail broth into his bowl. 'Abigail Penn kindly provided us with a recipe that the Society of Friends has used successfully to make gallons of soup for the needy.'

Although the provision of adequate nutrition for an adult was the aim of his research, Dan soon realized that taste and texture were also important. The soup they provided must be palatable to those who desperately needed it. Good cuts of meat would be impossible to obtain, but Sally assured him that poorer quality meat, and even offal, was just as good once some sort of seasoning was added during the cooking process.

Dan, along with Father Fitzpatrick and Michael Galwey, Tim McCarthy Downing, Reverend Townsend, Daniel McCarthy and Tom Marmion retired to the Becher Arms. There, Mrs Hegarty, after much consultation and perusing of the recipes of the Union, Miss Penn and others, had agreed to prepare and serve them each a bowl of standard soup that would be nutritious and suitable for serving the large numbers required at a reasonable cost.

Though he felt the meat had become rather stringy, Dan declared that the soup itself, which was thick and similar to a stew in its consistency, was good to taste.

'I like it,' agreed Father Fitzpatrick.

'It's a nourishing meal,' proclaimed Michael Galwey as he spooned the last of it from his bowl.

'A little more barley, perhaps,' suggested Daniel McCarthy, 'will make it more filling.'

'Dr Donovan, it is a good soup to fill a hungry belly,' enthused Reverend Townsend.

Mrs Hegarty and her cook were both proud that they had managed to provide a nourishing basic soup capable of feeding so many.

*

A few days later, escaping the heavy rain, Dan joined the committee at the large, impressive steam mill which stood at the side of the river.

'The first thing we need is to find someone who will agree to organize and manage the soup kitchen. Someone who is available to do it on a full-time basis,' proposed Thomas Somerville. 'We are all busy men. Unless there is someone here, ready to take on such a task . . .'

Dan looked around him. Who among them could give up their own work for such an onerous duty?

'I may know someone,' interjected Reverend Townsend. 'A fine clergyman of my acquaintance who may be available. That is, if he has not already been assigned to a new parish. Reverend Frederick Trench has great strength of character and determination, and I believe he would be the type of man to take on such a challenge as part of his Christian duty. I will write to him immediately to inform him of our plans and see if the position here is of interest to him.'

The chairman nodded in agreement. 'We will await his reply eagerly and, if he is so disposed, arrange to meet him.'

'We will need a huge boiler, and large cooking pots and ladles, and a big preparation area in order to feed such numbers,' warned Daniel McCarthy. 'I am willing to provide a boiler and the like, but we are going to need people to prepare the soup, and then cook and serve it, and clean up and keep order.'

'We will need long tables and benches for people to sit at and eat,' added Tom Marmion. 'I will be happy to provide them.'

'The people should be given a daily ticket to attend the soup kitchen and must show it, otherwise we risk people returning again and again,' suggested their treasurer, bank manager John Clerke.

'Mrs Hegarty from the Becher Arms has kindly offered us a cook and some of her kitchen staff to assist us temporarily. Her business has suffered greatly with all that has happened, for these days there are few visitors willing to stay in the town for more than a day or two,' Thomas Somerville explained.

'I'm sure more ladies from the town will volunteer to help once we open,' added Father Fitzpatrick.

'Then let us waste no more time. Let us plan to open the soup kitchen to the public as soon as it is possible,' declared Reverend Townsend. 'For every day we hesitate, more poor souls are lost.'

Chapter 29

FATHER JOHN FITZPATRICK WAS DEEPLY MOVED BY THE HUGE crowds he observed along Ilen Street as they converged on the mill. Despite the freezing chill of the November day and its biting wind, the gaunt and poorly clad figures all walked with great purpose towards the newly opened soup kitchen to be fed. Gaunt-faced men carried scrawny, stick-like children on their backs.

The grand opening of the soup kitchen had attracted much attention, and many of Skibbereen's traders and merchants were both curious and concerned to see how this kitchen might help alleviate the terrible hunger suffered by so many. Word must have spread quickly, for all through the town, along the river's edge and across the bridge the hungry walked in their hundreds: barefoot mothers and young children; fathers in ragged coats, carrying infants; elderly men bent over sticks and skeletal old women. Their desperation was etched on their faces.

A few in the parish had raised fears that the relief committee's soup kitchen might attract indigents from the surrounding areas, with more beggars and sick crowding into Skibbereen than before. But looking around him, Father Fitzpatrick felt nothing but pride in what the committee had accomplished.

The enticing smell of the soup was carried on the wind. As he made his way to the back entrance of the mill, the priest saw the tall figure of Reverend Trench in full command of the situation as three women stirred the soup in an enormous boiler. Others were serving it from large cooking pots into tin bowls and cups, and whatever rusty mugs and containers the people carried with them. Those who did not have a suitable receptacle for their portion were given a tin bowl, which was rinsed quickly when they had finished eating so that it might be reused.

The serving women's faces were flushed from the heat and effort of their work, unaware that hundreds more people were queuing outside, desperate to be fed.

Following Reverend Frederick Trench's orders, requests for an extra serving were refused.

'Come again tomorrow,' the servers urged. 'The soup pots will be full again then.'

'This is a good day's work we have done here, Father Fitzpatrick.' Reverend Townsend smiled as he approached the parish priest.

'You are right, Reverend Townsend. We have saved lives this day.'

They watched as the long lines of hungry people continued to swell and grow.

'What if they run out of soup?' he asked, worried. 'We can't turn people away.'

'They won't,' reassured Reverend Townsend. 'Reverend Trench assures me that the women have another two huge pots cooking, ready to use when needed.'

'I never imagined that so many were going hungry. We will have to raise additional funds if we are to feed all these people day after day.'

'Reverend Caulfield and I are set to travel to London as part of a delegation from the relief committee to lodge an official appeal to all those in authority with regards to the situation and relief needed here in West Cork.'

'The government must surely intervene, Richard, for things cannot continue in such a vein.'

'We hope to have a meeting with Charles Trevelyan in which we can inform him first hand of the calamity and terrible conditions we witness daily.'

'I pray that you manage to exert some influence on the treasurer and all those in London who can provide assistance here,' Father John offered sincerely, for he had a high regard for the Protestant minister and his devotion to the people of the town.

Chapter 30

MARY WRAPPED UP THE CHILDREN WARMLY, FOR IT WAS BITTERLY cold outside as they prepared to set off on the long walk to Skibbereen.

'Where are we going, Mammy?' asked Nora, curious.

'We are walking all the way into town to get the soup,' she tried to explain.

Kathleen and Honora Barry had both told her of the big soup kitchen that had opened in the mill by the river. Nell and her family had gone there twice already, joining the long lines of people waiting for a portion.

'It's the grandest soup ever,' Nell had declared. 'There was enough even to help fill those hungry boys of mine!'

Brigid had announced shortly after that she too was taking her children into town to take the soup as there was nothing in their cottage for them.

'My heart is scalded with it, Mary, watching them all go hungry!' she had fretted.

So the two friends decided to journey the four miles to town together, their nine children walking along beside them.

After only a mile or two, Annie demanded to be lifted up and carried.

'She has you wrapped around her little finger,' teased Brigid.

They passed close to the roadworks at Oldcourt, near the pier where John and Denis were employed, but caught no sight of their husbands.

Growing tired, the children slowed down . . . for none of them had the strength or energy for walking they had before the hunger came.

'It's only another two miles,' Mary cajoled them, 'and then there is a grand feed of soup waiting for you.'

'I'm tired,' complained Brigid's youngest, wanting to sit down and rest only a half-mile later.

'It's only a little bit further,' promised her mother.

As they neared the town, the road began to get busier. Hundreds of people were all making their way to the soup kitchen. The children huddled close to their mothers for fear of getting lost.

'We need to get a ticket at the dispensary first,' explained Brigid.

They then joined the long line of people all along Bridge Street, making their way slowly towards the mill . . .

Mary had never seen the like of it as they turned on to Ilen Street. Old and young, hungry and weak, all were lined up, some with their tin cups, to enter the soup kitchen. Some were so exhausted and starved that they could barely walk. Their legs and arms were like sticks dressed in rags. Hunger was etched on their thin faces. A man checked their tickets and beckoned them forward.

Inside the mill was hot and steamy and packed. They could see a huge boiler, and two large serving pots, filled with soup. Behind that, a group of women in aprons were cutting and preparing more vegetables to put in the boiler.

The children grew nervous as they neared the server, a red-faced woman who ladled out a half-bowl of soup for each of them. She gave Con and James – Brigid's eldest boy – a larger ration than the younger ones. She then filled Mary's can with a pint of soup and pointed out where they could get a hunk of bread each before sitting down at the long narrow dining tables to eat.

'Can I get some extra to take home for my husband, please?' Mary begged.

'We can't be doing that,' the woman said, shaking her head. 'Or else there wouldn't be a drop of soup left for all the people here.'

Mary took her seat with Brigid and the children, and made sure that Tim and Annie ate.

The soup was salty, made with carrots and turnip, onion, rice, barley and a little beef. She ate it slowly, not wanting to turn her stomach as she had eaten little for the past two days. The bread she would save for John. Brigid's three boys gulped it down quickly, as did Con, while Nora said little but took it spoonful by spoonful, savouring it. There was little conversation around them as everyone concentrated on their meal.

At the table next to theirs, a pale-faced boy of about eight was shaking his head. Despite his mother's pleas he refused to take the soup, telling her he was no longer hungry. The poor woman dipped her finger into the bowl and made him suck it as if he were a baby.

'Suck, my little *peata*,' she crooned. 'Suck, my little lamb child.'

Before long, a bell rang to signal that all those eating must move on and make way for the next group. A tall young woman came over to collect their bowls and spoons for washing, and urged them to leave.

The soup had warmed them and filled their stomachs, and Mary felt better for it.

Con shouted out when he caught a glimpse of his cousin Jude in the distance, lining up on Ilen Street with his mother, Kathleen.

Mary ran over to speak to them.

'Even though it's near on our doorstep, we'll be here a good two hours or more, waiting.' Kathleen shrugged. 'Take your children home before it rains and sure, I'll see you the next day.'

Walking the long miles home took an age, for the younger ones complained. Tim kept saying that his foot hurt, while Brigid's youngest, Sally, claimed the soup had made her stomach sick!

'Aren't they the grand family we have, after them all being fed!' Brigid sighed as the rain began to fall, soaking them all through.

Mary was glad to get home and sit at the warmth of her own fire. Taking out her scissors, needle and thread, she began to fashion a special pocket concealed in the folds of her wide skirt where she would hide her can on their next visit to the soup kitchen. She would use a lid made of thick cloth to contain a half-pint of leftover soup, which she would save for John.

Every day the children complained about the long miles they now walked to Skibbereen, but Mary would hear none of it. The soup would take the worst of the hunger off them. She would not let them starve like others around them or watch the flesh fall from their young bones. So they walked the hungry road . . .

Chapter 31

HENRIETTA WOULD NEVER GET USED TO THE SIGHT OF SO MANY men, women and children waiting patiently at the mill to be fed. Thousands now flocked to the soup kitchen every day, coming from all over West Cork. From Aughadown, Creagh, Kilcoe, Rath, Baltimore, Ballydehob and Union Hall, they swamped the streets, lanes and roads leading to Skibbereen. Some were so weak that they could barely walk.

'Henrietta, I see we are in the same mind coming to visit here.' Elizabeth Townsend, the rector's wife, smiled at her in greeting. 'It is heartening to see that at long last something is being done to help these poor people.'

'But it is so bitterly cold, and most of them have no shoes or coats, or even shawls to keep them warm,' Henrietta sighed, unable to hide her distress.

'Richard says that they have sold or pawned all they possess in order to buy food. They now face the winter with nothing but rags to wear.'

'Poor things, they will surely get severe chills and colds with this weather,' Henrietta said with worry as she looked at a shivering mother, her two little girls and baby boy.

'Perhaps the women among us could do something to get them some old clothes,' suggested Elizabeth. 'An unused dress or shawl for the women, maybe, and trousers, shirts, jackets and dresses for the children to wear. The minute I get home I will look to see if I can find any warm clothing I can pass on to them.'

'I will search our wardrobes and chests too,' Henrietta promised. 'There must surely be something that we have that would prove useful.'

'Do you think the other wives of the committee and people in town might be interested in organizing such a relief collection of clothing and warm items?'

'I do hope so. Most people are kind-hearted and should be willing to give something.'

'Many have been very charitable already,' Elizabeth reminded her gently.

Henrietta felt somewhat guilty, as Elizabeth was a most dedicated and helpful wife to a busy church minister. She, on the other hand, was caught up with running a busy household, taking care of a baby, her young children and the constant stream of patients all anxious to see her husband.

'Henrietta, will you come to the Glebe to have tea with me tomorrow and we can discuss it further?'

Henrietta had never been invited to their home before, but she knew that their husbands were united in their efforts on the relief committee.

'Your children are welcome to come along too,' Elizabeth added.

'They are noisy and rather troublesome,' warned Henrietta.

'I always enjoy having little ones in the rectory,' coaxed Elizabeth.

Henrietta decided the boys would be better at home, but she dressed up the three girls and baby Margaret and took them along to the rectory with her the following day.

Elizabeth welcomed them into her drawing room warmly.

'What pretty daughters you and Dan have!' she said, admiring Fanny and Harriet, who with only a year between them looked almost like twins in their matching pink dresses. 'They are like two little rosebuds.'

'Thank you.' Henrietta knew that it must be difficult for Elizabeth. She and Richard had not been blessed with any family of their own, yet with good grace she had organized many events for the children of the parish over the years, from Bible plays and pageants to the annual Easter party.

Elizabeth rang the bell and her maid, Jane, came along to serve them tea. She also carried a pretty plate of hot buttered scones with jam and a few small slices of cake.

'Cake! Good-ee!' shouted Fanny loudly. 'We are not allowed to eat it at home any more.'

'Dada doesn't like it,' added Harriet sagely.

'It's just with the situation at the moment,' Henrietta tried to explain. 'He feels that we must not be wasteful or indulgent.'

'Don't worry, these days we rarely have such things either,' Elizabeth admitted. 'But having you and the girls come to visit gives me a chance to be hospitable.'

'Well, we very much appreciate the invitation,' Henrietta replied, helping herself to a scone and some jam.

'Besides, it is nice for me to have a little company while my husband is away. He and Reverend Caulfield have travelled to London to appeal for assistance on behalf of this district,' she explained. 'Richard intends to talk to people at the highest level. He is hopeful of an opportunity to meet Charles Trevelyan and convince him of the urgent necessity for government intervention and support for immediate relief efforts.'

'Well, I pray that their mission is successful.'

'All our prayers are with them!'

Henrietta looked enviously around the neat drawing room, which was a haven of peace. There were shelves filled with books, a piano, and Elizabeth's embroidery hoop lay on a side table.

'Do you embroider?' her host asked, following Henrietta's gaze.

'No, I am afraid that I am all fingers and thumbs.'

'At night I find it relaxing to sit by the fire and embroider while Richard writes his sermons or does some parish work.'

The children, curious, had ventured over to the piano.

'Do the girls play?'

'No, I'm afraid we don't have one,' she told her regretfully.

'Richard and I both play a little.' Elizabeth smiled. 'I find that music is good for the soul.'

Elizabeth crossed the room to the instrument and demonstrated to Harriet and Fanny how to play a few notes. She encouraged Harriet to sit at the piano stool and guided her in touching the keys gently to produce a scale. Delighted, the girls played away. Their playing was tuneless but their enjoyment was evident as they ran their fingers up and down the black and white keys.

Jane came into the room with more tea. She was a pretty

little thing, not more than fifteen years old, with fair hair and a pert nose.

'Will I bring more cake, ma'am?'

'Yes, please. Finely cut for my young guests.'

Jane nodded and left the room.

'Although she is young, she is proving to be a fine maid,' Henrietta's host confided. 'And Kate, our cook, is happy to have young Jane here to assist her.'

On her return, the maid offered to take baby Margaret and the children for a while so that the two women could talk in peace about their plan to ask the wives of the committee members and other friends to consider a clothing appeal. The baby settled happily in Jane's arms as she shepherded the other girls down to the kitchen.

'I have already unearthed almost a box of clothes that neither Richard nor I need any longer, which we intend to donate,' Elizabeth began.

'I found two coats – one of mine and one of my husband's – and a boys' jacket, some clothes from our son Daniel that I can give, and I'm sure I have some warm stockings and a dress or two that the girls no longer need, and three pairs of sturdy boots.'

'Well done, Henrietta, for I'm sure that, like many large families, most of the clothes get passed down between the children, much as my own parents did.'

'Mostly, but I still managed to find a few items that hopefully will be useful. And I'm intent on finding more.'

'We have not been idle but must ask others to join us,' Elizabeth said, taking out a sheet of paper and starting to write a list of names that they should each approach.

*

'I have so enjoyed our visit,' thanked Henrietta, as she and the children got ready to leave. It had turned bitterly cold outside so she buttoned up the children's coats and wrapped their scarves around them tightly.

Elizabeth smiled. 'You are welcome here any time.'

'The next time, perhaps you will come and visit me. Though I'm afraid our home will certainly not be as quiet and peaceful as yours.'

'I will look forward to it,' said the rector's wife graciously as she bid goodbye to Henrietta and the children.

'Mama!' called Harriet and Fanny excitedly, as they ran outside. 'Look, it's snowing!'

Snowflakes tumbled from the sky like feathers, whirling and swirling all around them. The children held out their hands to catch them as they walked back to New Street. The falling snow continued all through the long night and by morning had blanketed the streets and lanes, roads and fields and entire countryside with thick, deep, white cover.

Chapter 32

THE FALLEN SNOW LAY DEEP AND HEAVY ON THE GROUND. Henrietta laced up her boots and grabbed her heavy wool coat. She pulled on her hat, gloves and scarf as she set off to brave the elements, for there were some errands she needed to run.

The streets of Skibbereen were icy, and the hungry who were sheltering from the cold in doorways and gateways begged and pulled at every passer-by for food or money. A small group of them were hunkered down near the Donovans' doorway.

'Bit of food, ma'am, for the hungry?' pleaded a stick-thin man with his wife and two boys.

'I'm sorry but I have no food on me,' she apologized, moved by their plight as she eased her way past them gently as they called after her. How these poor families could endure such weather, dressed only in tattered rags with their feet bare, shamed her. Dan was run ragged looking after such people day after day, and always showed such constant care and consideration for them that it made her love and admire him even more.

She had made a list, for she had to purchase some necessary household items. She would dearly love to order a new dress to see her through the winter and Christmas season but Dan, she knew, would not countenance such extravagance, especially in the face of the distress suffered by their fellow man.

As she had sorted through clothes to donate, she had realized that young Dan was in sore need of breeches, shirts and a new warm jacket, for he had outgrown his infant clothes and was becoming quite a little boy! Her husband could not expect her to dress their small son in the worn hand-me-downs of his two brothers.

She also needed desperately to purchase a book. She got bored being at home so much, and longed to read the latest work of Mr Dickens if it were available. She also was in need of writing paper and some ink of her own, for Dan was forever at his desk writing letters. She dearly wanted to correspond with her family and friends, and to hear some good news, if there were any.

Groups of the poor and hungry huddled together everywhere – in the doorway of the bank, outside the Becher Arms, near the brewery – trying to escape the bitter cold. A small boy tugged at her coat like a frightened sparrow. He held out the palm of his hand, too tired even to say a word. His face was covered with a downy layer of hair.

Poor child! She reached into her pocket and produced a penny, which she handed to him in silence, then watched him scurry away, no doubt to spend it immediately.

At the stationer's she collected the new pen that she had ordered for Dan and some writing paper and ink. One part of the shop held newspapers, periodicals and a small display of books, which she browsed. There were a few of Maria Edge-worth's books and she was drawn to the latest work of Charles Dickens, *A Christmas Carol*, which she decided to purchase. It would definitely hold her attention and might even inter-est Dan.

She then moved on to Hayes's drapery on Main Street to purchase clothing for young Daniel: three pairs of breeches, three shirts, a warm navy wool coat, some undergarments and woollen socks.

'A growing boy, Mrs Donovan.' Mr Hayes laughed as he parcelled them up. 'Anything that doesn't fit the young lad, just return them and we'll find something more suitable.'

Normally, Henrietta enjoyed looking around the shops, but it was far too cold to dawdle. She had just turned off Market Lane when she almost tripped over a woman sitting on the icy ground. The woman's legs were outstretched and she held a baby in her arms. Dressed only in a threadbare shift, Henri-etta could see her bare breasts and skinny torso, her shoulder bones and ribs clearly visible. Her legs were like mottled sticks, and her feet were swollen and dirty.

The baby lay crookedly in her arms, when the woman pitched forward suddenly. Overcome with pity, Henrietta rushed to prevent her from falling to the ground and tried to save the small baby that was wrapped in a filthy bit of blanket.

'Are you all right?' she asked, alarmed by the woman's condition.

The woman said nothing but leaned back and tried to straighten herself up.

'I am weak with the hunger,' she whispered.

Henrietta was filled with concern for her and was about to

hand the child back when she realized how still it was. A terrible fear gripped her when she gazed down and saw that the small face was waxy, the skin almost translucent, with a blue sheen around its delicate lips and closed eyes. The child was stone cold, dead, all the life gone from it. No matter what Henrietta did, there was no saving this child.

The mother's hands reached out for her baby and Henrietta passed her the infant. She felt a strange chill inside her own heart and did not know what to say to this poor mother. Was she aware of what had happened?

'You must stay here,' she begged the woman. 'I am going to get some help for you.'

She took off so quickly that she nearly lost her footing on the ice.

All she wanted was to find Dan and get him to help this unfortunate woman and her child. She had no idea what to do but Dan would know. She gasped as she ran home, trying not to cry as she thought of the poor frozen baby.

Dan was sitting at his desk, writing, puzzled by her disturbance.

'Dan, you must come with me quickly. Get your coat and hat!' she pleaded. 'There is a woman on the street with a dead child in her arms. We have to help her.'

In a matter of minutes Dan was making his way with Henrietta to the street where the woman still sat with her eyes closed, one hand outstretched, the child still in her arms.

'I brought my husband,' Henrietta explained.

'I am a doctor,' Dan said gently, kneeling down beside the woman. 'This lady is my wife and she was concerned for your child. May I take a look, please?'

Wordlessly, the woman passed the bundle into Dan's arms.

Dan looked carefully at the lifeless baby before turning his attention to the mother.

'I'm afraid that your baby is very poorly and you yourself are very weak. The best thing I can advise is that you be admitted immediately to the Union workhouse. I am the medical officer there. I will arrange it. Have you any family?'

'No.' She shook her head. 'Everyone died these past weeks.'

'As you are in a weakened state, I will fetch my horse and carriage and bring you myself.'

Tears of relief slid down the woman's exhausted face and Henrietta tried to control her own emotions in the face of her husband's kindness.

'My wife will stay with you for a few minutes while I go and fetch it.'

Henrietta crouched beside the woman, aware that the few people who passed them averted their gaze as they did not want to be accosted or get involved. She unwound her own knitted scarf from her neck and arranged it gently around the woman's shoulders, covering the child.

The day was growing ever colder. On Dan's return she assisted him in helping the woman – who had told her that her name was Catherine Driscoll – and her baby up into the carriage.

'Will I come with you?' Henrietta offered.

'No, my dear, it is better you return home,' Dan said softly. 'I will take care of Mrs Driscoll and ensure that she is admitted and looked after.'

Back at home, Henrietta fed the children and, despite her worry and distraction, prepared them for bed. They said their prayers and she read a story to them from the Bible. The younger ones' preference was for Noah's ark or Daniel in the lion's den. As she hugged their warm bodies, brushed their curling hair and tucked them in their beds, she prayed for God to keep all the children in the town safe and well that night.

'How is Mrs Driscoll?' she probed as Dan ate his meal that evening.

'Poorly, for she has typhus.'

'What about the baby?'

'Nurse Lynch managed to get her to give up the infant. She told her that it was with the rest of her family in heaven.'

'Oh, that poor woman. How could such a terrible thing happen, Dan?'

'Please, my dear, you must not distress yourself.'

'Of course I must distress myself. Witnessing what happened to that mother and her baby is something that I will never forget . . .' She tried to keep the growing sense of hysteria she was feeling from her voice. 'That woman lost her only living child.'

Dan ate his food slowly and meticulously.

'I'm sorry,' she apologized. 'I know this is what you see every day, but Dan, how can you bear it?'

'Henrietta, it is my duty. And besides, I have you and the children to consider.'

As she lay in his arms before sleep, Daniel soothed his wife and tried to calm her fears.

'Everything will be well soon,' he promised, treating her like a child.

Her dreams that night were haunted by Catherine Driscoll and her baby, and she could not put them from her mind, despite her best efforts.

The following day she enquired about Mrs Driscoll's health. Dan said little, only that she was ill in the fever ward. Three days later he broke the news that she had succumbed to typhus and would be buried with her child.

'You mean they will both be in the pit in Abbeystrewry graveyard?' Henrietta demanded angrily.

'Yes, such are the daily burials,' he said quietly. 'But take comfort in the fact that they are both united in the afterlife, away from this torment.'

'It is small comfort, Dan, for I would far prefer to see her happy with her child, walking the streets of Skibbereen with her head held high, than lying in that cold place.'

That afternoon she lay down on their bed and cried, pulling the blankets around her as the snow began to fall again. A deep weariness possessed her, which she could not shake off and so gave in to sleep.

Hours later she awoke from her slumber. She had slept for so long that she had missed tea and putting the children to bed. She chastised herself! How could she do such a thing when she was a strong young woman, with a husband and family who needed her? Dan deserved a better wife, one who was resolute and steady, who could be relied upon and who would be a constant support to him and his work.

She stretched and got up, re-buttoned her dress and fixed her dark wavy hair. She dabbed a little lavender water on her wrists and neck before slipping on her shoes and making her way downstairs to join her husband who was sitting at the fire.

'I told Sally to tend to the children and let you rest,' he said gently.

His kindness near overwhelmed her and she felt close to tears again.

'It's all right, Hetty dearest.' Dan got up and wrapped his arms around her. 'I am here with you, and I promise that you have nothing to fear. I will always guard and protect you and our children.'

She could hear in his voice the care, concern and love that had always been between them. Without a word, Henrietta found herself sitting beside him, her head on his shoulder, watching the flames flicker in the grate.

'I am better now,' she said a long while later.

'Good,' he said, reaching for her. 'For you know that I cannot bear to see you so upset.'

Chapter 33

December 1846

DAN GAZED OUT THE WINDOW OF THE OFFICE BESIDE THE MILL. The crowds below, like pale ghosts, struggled in the snow and icy conditions to reach the soup kitchen.

'God help them, for this is the worst winter in my memory!' Henry Marmion lamented as the relief committee gathered for its regular Monday meeting.

'It is hard to believe that we are already feeding between a thousand and fifteen hundred people a day,' reported John Clerke, the bank manager. 'The costs, as you can imagine, are enormous, and the numbers taking the soup continue to grow. We have decided to issue tickets that are to be used at different times of the day, which will make controlling such large numbers easier. Reverend Trench has also asked us to order two more boilers. Fortunately, we are receiving donations from generous-hearted Englishmen and a few charitable organizations, but we still need to raise far more money if we are to continue . . .'

The rest of the committee nodded in agreement.

'We must congratulate Reverend Townsend on his successful visit to London, which has already borne fruit.' Thomas Somerville smiled. 'The food depot in town has just opened and will remain open three days a week, while all other depots are to remain closed until after Christmas.'

'Reverend Caulfield and I did our best to inform those whom we met of the terrible conditions that prevail here,' Reverend Townsend admitted modestly. 'We had a good hearing with Mr Trevelyan, but he gave us little indication of his thoughts. However, his recent decision to divert a portion of the money due to Ceylon to aid the destitute here instead is most welcome. Apparently, the Queen has also indicated her intention to write a letter of appeal in the coming weeks to raise funds for her starving subjects.'

'We are very appreciative, Reverend,' thanked the chairman. 'You have done much to help the cause of Skibbereen and her people.'

Two days later, as he was about to leave the dispensary, Dan was appalled to see at least three hundred starving men from the roadworks out by Lisheen, marching along the street in the freezing snow, demanding payment for their work. Most were severely emaciated, shivering with the cold and begging like some spectral army.

'Issue them each with a ticket for the soup kitchen,' he ordered the dispensary clerk, as he led the men to the mill where they were admitted immediately and served a pint of warm soup and a large portion of bread.

The local Board of Works commissioner and his man finally

appeared and tried to appease the men with the promise of payment in a few days' time.

'They should hang their heads in shame,' Tim McCarthy Downing sighed as they watched the commissioner try to squirm his way out of responsibility for the men's poor treatment.

'It's the bureaucracy and ineptitude of those running the scheme that is to blame!' Dan raged, unable to hide his anger.

On the recommendation of Dan's cousin Michael Galwey, Nicholas Cummins, a justice of the peace from Cork, had asked if he could accompany Dan on a few visits to his patients. He wanted to assess the true state of affairs in West Cork and, if necessary, report on it.

'Dr Donovan, I have heard stories of terrible deprivation among the people here, which if they were true shame our government and officials,' he explained. 'Yet others say such claims are exaggerated. It behoves those of us in a position of influence to make our own investigation of such matters.'

'I have my rounds to do, Mr Cummins. You are welcome to come with me,' agreed Dan, 'but I must remind you that my duty is to my patients.'

It was clear that Nicholas Cummins was well intentioned, for only the day before he had visited the little village of South Reen.

'I brought loaves of bread for the people but the place seemed deserted. I went into what appeared an empty cabin only to discover six skeletons lying on the floor. I presumed the family were dead, until I heard moaning.' His voice began to shake. 'They were all sick with fever, Dr Donovan, and it was the same in one cabin after another.'

'It is a frightening thing to see,' Dan sympathized, 'but I'm afraid fever is rampant.'

'Then a gang of nearly two hundred starved, crazed creatures appeared, grabbing at me and pulling at my clothes. I tell you, I was lucky to escape them!'

Dan could see Mr Cummins was still deeply shocked by what he had seen.

As they walked around Skibbereen, Dan pointed out the corpse of a girl that had been dragged out of a cabin and into the street by her sick mother. It lay there, half covered with stones.

'She will be buried later in Abbeystrewry,' he reassured the justice of the peace.

They visited cabin after cabin of the sick and dying, finally stopping at one near the town's cavalry station. Dan warned Mr Cummins to stay at the door. Inside, seven people lay together under a cloak, a young man among them already dead, but the others near death and too weak to move.

'I will arrange to transfer the sick to the fever sheds in the workhouse,' Dan said quietly as he came back outside, for he could see his companion was deeply upset.

'I had never imagined such things in a Christian country,' Mr Cummins declared fervently as Dan finished his rounds. 'It's disgraceful and shames us that people are left to suffer like this. But I promise you, doctor, that I will endeavour to alert those in a position of influence to the horrific state of affairs here.'

Much to the surprise of the committee, only a few days before Christmas they received a visit from the Assistant Commissary-General, Mr Inglis.

'He's been sent by Randolph Routh himself to meet with us and to help us organize a plan for the relief of Skibbereen,' explained Thomas Somerville.

Mr Inglis could not hide his dismay at the scenes that greeted him, not only at the soup kitchen but on every street corner and lane. The committee members were more than pleased when, before his departure, he pledged eighty-five pounds towards the running of the soup kitchen, as it was the first government assistance they had received!

Henrietta begged Dan to take Christmas Day off at least and spend it with his family.

'What of my patients?' he protested. 'I can't leave them.'

'You must rest,' she insisted. 'Or you will fall ill!'

They had celebrated the birth of Jesus at a crowded mass, which many of his patients also attended. Excited, the children had fun outside in the snow with some friends and neighbours, before they returned home for their Christmas meal.

Dan stretched out in front of the fire as they played some new board and card games with the children, and read a few chapters of Mr Dickens's wonderful new book.

'Look at this.'

He called Henrietta over to read a long letter that had been published on the front page of *The Times* on Christmas Eve. Nicholas Cummins had kept his word and had written to the Duke of Wellington. He had told in great detail of his harrowing visit to Skibbereen and implored the duke, in the name of the starving thousands, to break the frigid and flimsy chain of etiquette and save the land of his birth, and the paper had published it in full!

'That letter must have caused quite a stir at many a Christmas table,' Henrietta mused. 'For Mr Cummins requested that a copy of it also be given to the Queen.'

Dan smiled and began to re-read the piece. 'This one voice can say more than a thousand.'

Chapter 34

ON HIS RETURN TO WORK IN THE DISPENSARY, DAN WAS CALLED out to Bridgetown immediately, where there had been serious outbreaks of both typhus and dysentery. Nearly every cabin in one lane was affected. In Windmill Lane the police had found the body of a man which had turned green and been left to rot for at least five days. His wife and children – a boy and a girl – lay ill on the filthy floor near him.

'Why didn't you bury him?' he asked the wife gently.

'I have no coffin,' she sobbed.

Seeing her shame at her near-naked state of undress, it was clear that the sick woman wanted to be left to die with her husband.

Dan was torn between anger at her situation and pity for her as he arranged for the children to be moved immediately to the fever hospital.

Back in the dispensary, a large crowd of patients waited to see him, most of whom were suffering from fever and bowel complaints too. They all clamoured for his attention and Dan's heart sank when he saw Mr Hughes, the commissariat officer, arriving to enquire about the latest statistics for disease in the neighbourhood. Could the man not see he was inundated and had no time to give him?

'Mr Hughes, as of this morning there are about eighty-five cases of fever on a single lane in Bridgetown,' he reported succinctly.

The other figures were similarly grim and he could see the anxiety on the other man's face as he listed them.

'Also, Mr Hughes, I must inform you officially that many of the men employed on the public relief schemes are now succumbing to a new classification of sickness which I call "road fever". It is prevalent among the famished and weakened labourers who are engaged in this work at the expense of their own lives.'

'I will note your concerns, Dr Donovan,' Mr Hughes returned coldly.

Dan was barely able to conceal his frustration. Not only did he battle against disease and hunger but also against a wall of hypocrisy and petty administration that had no intention of acting on any of his medical recommendations.

'You must forgive me, but I am due soon at the Union and fever hospital,' he said brusquely, dismissing the official and returning to his duties.

Over Christmas the workhouse had been overwhelmed by new admissions. Both the women's and men's sections were now so crowded that there was hardly a space in which to stand, let alone in which to lie down and rest or sleep. In the fever wards, the sick were forced to share their soiled straw pallets with other patients.

'I'm sorry, Dr Donovan, but what are we to do?' pleaded the matron. 'My staff and I are doing what we can, but there are no blankets or even pallets left.'

He knew the good woman was trying to manage, but having so many patients packed together was no doubt contributing to the spread of disease. He was also concerned for the welfare of the exhausted staff, some of whom clearly were unwell.

'Matron, I will speak with Mr Falvey and inform the Union guardians officially that we urgently need to acquire more buildings in the town in which to place inmates.'

In the children's wing, a number of young children had also been admitted. He examined them and all were malnourished, with a few showing clear symptoms of dysentery too. They should have been placed in the fever ward, instead of there, where they were mingling with the other children.

Young Will Hayes ran over to Dan, who gave the boy a small red ball he'd kept for him. His own children had received a number of toys for Christmas and he had encouraged them to be generous with their gifts.

The three-year-old's eyes lit up, as he was unused to presents and playthings. Dan showed him how to catch the ball and roll it back and throw it himself. The boy laughed as he caught it successfully. It was heartwarming to see him play.

'Now, I must leave you as I have to work,' Dan said ruefully, bending down to his level.

The child reached out to touch him, and Dan lifted him up and spun him around in his arms, the way he did with his own children, before lowering him slowly to the floor.

'Thank you,' Will said, as he ran off to play with his new ball, followed by two other small boys.

On his leaving the workhouse, the waiting crowd outside assailed Dan, begging for his help to admit them.

'Go home,' Dan pleaded with them. 'Take shelter somewhere else. There is no admittance as the workhouse is full, and many inside are sick with fever.'

It made no matter what he said. They refused to budge.

He arrived home to find Henrietta in a terrible state, weeping into her hands.

'Dan,' she said, throwing herself into his arms. 'Poor Margaret Murphy has just died.'

'What happened to her?' He was shocked to hear of their good neighbour's death.

'Her daughter tells me she caught the fever. She sickened soon after visiting me here only a few days ago. It's entirely my fault!'

'My dear, why would you think or say such a thing?'

'Because it is true. While she was here I opened the door to a patient of yours, Mr O'Shea. He wanted help to buy a coffin for his young son. The poor man was clearly ill and distressed, and Margaret, who as you know was always so kind, made him sit down here and consoled him.'

Henrietta broke down again tearfully as Sally, their maid, tried to calm her.

'Margaret's kindness to that poor man has killed her.' His wife sniffed, her eyes and nose red. 'If she had not crossed this door she might still be alive. Her children would still have their good mother, her husband his wife.'

'Hush, my love, we do not know that for sure,' he soothed, kneeling down beside her, taking her hand in his.

'It is so, Dan,' she said bitterly, taking the handkerchief from his hand. 'Margaret came here because we are friends, and then was stricken.'

Henrietta broke down again, inconsolable.

As he held her hand, Dan's mind was racing. He was growing increasingly worried about the safety of his own family. What would happen should Henrietta or any of the children fall ill, as their neighbour had?

If anyone was to blame it was he, for Patrick O'Shea and his son had been his patients. The child had died of typhus and, frantic to find a coffin in which to bury him, his bereaved father had left his own sick bed to come here for assistance, putting Dan's own family at risk.

These past weeks it had been his greatest fear that the fever somehow would spread from the poor and starving to the rest of the town's population. Now, here in his own home, that fear had come to pass . . .

Chapter 35

January 1847

MARY CAREFULLY FOLDED THE SMALL BUNDLE OF CLOTHES SHE had patched and mended, ready to return them to Honora Barry. Of late, the dressmaker had been giving her less and less work but despite that, the good woman often parcelled up a cut of soda bread, a piece of cheese or a salted herring for Mary to take home to the children, insisting that she had more than enough to eat.

The fields around the cottage were blanketed with thick drifts of heavy snow, for it had fallen again these past two days. It was far too deep for Annie and Tim to walk into town, but despite the fierce weather, John was still working every day.

Taking down her heavy shawl, Mary wrapped it around her shoulders and told Con and Nora to stay inside in the warm and mind their younger siblings.

By the time she reached Honora's shop, her fingers and feet were frozen with the cold. The window looked dusty and the same dress that had been in the window a few weeks earlier was still there. She rang the bell but no one answered. She tried to push the door but it was locked. Peering through the glass, she saw the dressmaker inside, sewing, her head bent in concentration. Mary knocked briskly on the window pane until she got her attention.

'I have to be careful these days,' Honora apologized as she opened the door. 'The town is full of beggars.'

Mary blushed as she followed Honora inside, for by all appearances she herself was no better. The older lady gestured for her to sit down as Mary passed her the small bit of mending she had done.

'Your usual good work, Mary,' she thanked, examining it briefly.

Mary could tell she was distracted and upset.

'I'm so sorry, but I won't be able to give you any more work, for I have little enough of it myself these days.'

Mary was gutted with disappointment but had suspected as much as Jane had stopped working there in November and returned home to Bantry.

'Will you have a cup of tea with me?' the dressmaker offered.

Mary nodded, for a warming drink would hopefully take the chill out of her.

'Business is bad these past months,' Honora admitted as they sat in the back room and she poured the tea. 'The good ladies who used to come to me for their style are fearful of being seen to be extravagant or frivolous in these hardest of times. So, any repair or alteration work for my customers I will now do myself.'

'I understand.' Mary nodded, trying to remain calm and not give in to the fear and sense of foreboding that gripped at her heart.

'I should have moved to Dublin or Cork last year,' the dress-maker said ruefully. 'Closed up my shop and gone like many others. But alas, now it is too late for that.'

She paid Mary a shilling – a bit more than she owed her – taking the money from the tin box that was kept in a drawer in the dresser, and also gave her a half loaf of oaten bread.

''Tis too big for a woman on her own,' she said with a smile as they said their farewells. 'Hopefully we will both soon see better times.'

Back on the street, Mary felt faint and so went to the dispensary to get a ticket for that day's soup kitchen. Clutching the piece of paper, she made her way to the large mill and joined the long line waiting to be fed. Once she'd eaten, she bought a small bag of oats and some flour with the little money she had, before calling briefly to her sister.

Kathleen commiserated with her when Mary broke the news to her about Honora Barry not being able to give her any more work.

'I don't know how we will manage without the money,' she said tearfully.

'Things will get better,' promised Kathleen, telling her the good news that Michael, her fifteen-year-old son, had found employment as a servant in Mr O'Brien's house in Clonakilty.

'The boy who worked for him took sick, so Michael will replace him. To tell the truth, I'm happy for him not to be labouring on the roadworks like his poor father,' she admitted.

'At least they both have work.'

'Though they earn divil a bit for it,' Kathleen said bitterly. 'Not enough to keep a family. At least with Michael away there will be one less mouth to feed, for the boys have me scalded looking for food!'

'Con and Tim are the same, but at least you have the soup kitchen close by,' Mary said enviously. 'The icy roads are too bad these days for the children to walk them.'

'Half the town would be dead without it, for near every soul in Bridgetown has a ticket for it.'

Despite the soup, Mary could not help but notice that her three-year-old niece Lizzie's face was as pale as the snow outside and her stomach distended. Realizing it would soon get dark, Mary wrapped herself up warmly, said goodbye to her sister and set off home.

Chapter 36

DAN TOOK A DEEP BREATH AND FILLED HIS LUNGS WITH FRESH AIR before he entered the workhouse where the conditions were increasingly deplorable. Every square foot and yard of floor space was taken up by a mother, child or decrepit old man near to his end of days. Crowded and stinking, there was little space for a body to stretch or move, and certainly there was no comfort here for the ill or weak. Was it any wonder that in this festering environment, typhus fever and dysentery were rampant among the inmates?

Dan's heart sank in the fever hospital when he spotted three-year-old Will Hayes. The little boy was hunched up under a badly soiled blanket with two other children, all sick with dysentery. His skin was hot to touch, his heartbeat rapid and his breathing shallow.

'Come on now, Will, try to take a little water for me,' Dan coaxed.

At the sound of Dan's voice, the small boy slowly opened his blue eyes. He was seriously ill and Dan asked the assistant to bring him a clean blanket and damp cloth so that he could try to cool him down.

'Will, when you are well again, I promise that I will bring you another ball to play with,' he said, stroking his hand.

The boy gripped the doctor's forefinger and Dan could see he was trying to fight this illness, just as he had once fought to come into the world and to survive in this place.

'You are such a brave boy, Will,' he urged him as he sat quietly by his side. 'Stay strong!'

A short while later, with great reluctance, Dan had to leave his young friend as the matron needed him. The nurses and assistants were doing what they could to help the living and dying, but Dan could see that they too were exhausted and worn out.

'We endeavour to do our best for them, Dr Donovan, but we are overwhelmed and do not have enough beds or blankets, or buckets even,' the usually stalwart matron confided in him, close to tears. 'One of my nurses is sick and I fear another will leave.'

Mr Falvey was equally concerned and called Dan into the privacy of his office.

'The situation here is intolerable,' he said. 'We cannot continue like this, trying to manage such numbers. Some of our staff have fallen ill and others are threatening to leave.'

Dan could see that the poor man was grey-faced and near the end of his tether.

'And such is our dire financial situation, Dr Donovan, that by tomorrow the kitchen will not be able to serve even a small bowl of gruel to the inmates, for we do not have enough money to replenish our stores.'

169

Shocked to hear of the perilous and precarious position of the workhouse, Dan called an urgent meeting of the Board of Guardians of the Union, deciding to move the meeting from their usual boardroom in the workhouse to the courthouse – for their own safety.

'We have one thousand, one hundred and sixty-nine inmates. Three hundred and thirty-two of them have fever and are in either the infirmary or the hospital,' Mr Falvey explained nervously as he addressed the board. 'Gentlemen, these numbers are far greater than the Union was built to hold, and I have no other choice but to request that the Board of Guardians give full consideration to closing the Skibbereen Union to all further admittances.'

'In my medical opinion, given the level of illness and contagion,' added Dan, 'I agree with the master. This is the only safe and wise thing for the board to do.'

'I also must inform the board that there is not sufficient food in the workhouse to provide meals,' Mr Falvey continued, his voice breaking. 'We will not be able to serve the inmates with breakfast tomorrow morning. I will be obliged to pay in ready cash for any food that I purchase, for nobody will give us credit.'

No food! There was utter shock around the table at such a disastrous state of affairs.

'Why is that?' demanded chairman Thomas Somerville.

'I assume it is because we already have many creditors among the suppliers in the town.'

'I am a creditor,' signalled Daniel Welply, the local linen and woollen supplier. 'For I am owed three hundred pounds.'

'And will you give further credit?'

He nodded. 'Given the dire situation, I suppose that I am prepared to give you more if it is required.'

'But where are we to find money for meal, or milk or firing, or other necessities that are required?' worried wealthy landowner James Redmond Barry, who, of late, had taken on feeding a hundred people from the soup kitchen run from his own home at Glandore House. 'There must be some sort of funds, surely.'

'James, we have exhausted our funds,' the treasurer admitted. 'We have one hundred and sixty-five pounds only in the bank, while the demands we have to meet are one thousand four hundred and twenty-nine pounds.'

'Given the urgency of the situation, these funds must be used today to make such purchases,' insisted the chairman. 'We cannot have it that people who fled to the Union for protection and shelter go hungry. They deserve at least to be fed.'

'To fund the Union we will have to somehow raise the poor rate and more subscriptions,' admitted Daniel McCarthy. 'No easy task!'

'There is another matter,' added Mr Falvey. 'Seven members of the resident staff have been attacked by inmates this past week. One of the nurses has demanded her discharge, the apothecary signified his intention to tender his resignation yesterday, and Dr Donovan is nearly broken down in his bodily powers by his persevering exertions.'

Dismayed, the guardians expressed their deep concern for the staff members and thanked Dan warmly for his dedication to his patients and the inmates.

'I am only doing my duty as a physician,' Dan acknowledged humbly.

'So, Mr Falvey, you are telling us here today that the Union is dangerously full with the sick and dying, there is no food, no money to purchase food, and many of the workhouse staff are ready to give notice and resign.'

'I am sorry, Mr Chairman, but that is the extent of it,' the master said with a sigh of despair, relieved to sit down finally after bearing such calamitous news.

Following the recommendations of both Dan and Mr Falvey, the Board of Guardians voted to agree to the immediate closure of the Skibbereen Union Workhouse to all further admissions. They also agreed to issue an urgent appeal for increased funding to ensure that they could continue to operate the workhouse. A few of the guardians decided generously there and then to make a personal donation, while others offered to advance a temporary loan to the Union in order to rescue the desperate situation in which they found themselves.

They all knew it wasn't a permanent solution to the crisis they faced, but at least for the present the inmates would be fed and the sick would be cared for as best they could.

Chapter 37

HENRIETTA WATCHED DAN AS HE PICKED DISTRACTEDLY WITH HIS
fork at the mutton they were eating. He never complained of
tiredness, for he was blessed with a vigour and energy few men
possessed. However, of late, she could not help but worry, for
her husband looked careworn, with dark shadows under his
eyes. He was rarely home any more, gone from early morning
to late at night, seemingly at the beck and call of every beggar
and sick person in the district. When he did appear, he usually
excused himself to attend some committee meeting or other.

The children missed their father and his attention, just as
she missed their chats and walks together, or the hours they
used to spend sitting reading a book, sharing a story or dis-
cussing an item in the newspaper, for Dan was not just her
husband but her dearest friend.

Ellen, Fanny and Harriet vied for his attention, waving to
see if he noticed they had had their hair cut. Dan remained
lost in a world of his own as he ate slowly.

'Dada, you must notice something different about me today,' demanded Fanny, coming over to sit on his lap, waggling her pretty head.

Henrietta laughed to herself and gave Dan a warning kick under the table to attend to Fanny's antics.

'Fanny, you have grown taller!' he ventured, which drew cries of 'no' from his daughter. 'Fanny, you have got heavier since yesterday!'

'No,' she protested.

'You learned to speak French!'

She pouted. 'Dada, you know I can't speak French.'

'I know,' he said. 'You have cut and curled your pretty hair just like your beautiful sisters!'

Fanny jumped up and did a few twirls to show off her new hairstyle. Ellen and Harriet joined in, while young Daniel laughed and their older brother Jerrie threw his eyes to heaven at the antics of his sisters.

'Certain little girls had developed a bit of an aversion to my bristle brush,' Henrietta confided, 'so losing a few inches of hair will make it a lot easier.'

'Of course, my dear,' he said, putting down his napkin and standing up from the table. His eyes showed he had little interest in her simple tittle-tattle about the children.

'Dada, play with us!' pleaded Fanny.

'I'm sorry, children, but I have to work,' Dan said, excusing himself and disappearing to the confines of his small study.

It was late and Dan was still working, no doubt writing his diary again. Passing his study door, Henrietta decided to wish him goodnight as she was about to retire. She found her husband sitting at his desk as usual, but he was not working. Instead, he held his head in his hands, deeply upset over something.

Henrietta flew to him.

'Oh, my dear, what is it?' she asked, fearful that he might be unwell. 'What has upset you so?'

Dan let out a shuddering, heavy sigh.

'Today I lost a patient. A small boy only a year younger than our Daniel, a workhouse boy,' he said, trying to control his emotions. 'He died from dysentery.'

Henrietta had never seen her husband so upset. Every day he saw the most awful sights and endured huge distress dealing with the dead and dying. Often he would discover putrid, rotting corpses and foul-smelling bodies, things she knew well he kept and protected her from.

'But Dan, all the sick you attend,' she ventured gently.

'It is ridiculous of me, but the boy, Will, was a fine little fellow. I helped to deliver him, the day the Liberator came. His young mother abandoned him to the Union's care. Yet the boy had such spirit. Every time he caught sight of me doing my rounds, he just wanted to play or talk to me, even if it was only for a few minutes. He was a bright child and I'm sure he would have made his way in the world when he was older. We were his guardians, responsible for his care, such as it was, and we let him down. I let him down.'

His eyes welled with unshed tears as he slumped in misery.

'You looked after that boy, Dan, and cared for him as best you could,' she assured him, running her hands along his shoulder. 'I know that, for I see it every day – the dedicated way you look after all those who need your help.'

'Instead of any hope of a good life, young Will has ended up buried in the workhouse graveyard.'

'It's not your fault.'

Henrietta held her husband as he gave in to the onslaught of emotion, stroking his hair like a child's. She kissed the top of his head and soothed him until all the hurt and pain that had built up in him was released.

'What must you think of me for being so foolish?' he apologized.

'I do not think it foolish to mourn,' Henrietta said gently. 'Especially when there are so many to mourn and grieve for.'

She took his hand and kissed it, knowing that she loved him more deeply than any other human in the world, and that though Dan may not say he needed her, she would always be there for him . . .

Chapter 38

Creagh

MARY EXAMINED JOHN'S FEET GENTLY AND BATHED THEM IN warm water and salt. They were blistered and sore, and his big and second toe on one foot were blackened and swollen from where a heavy stone had fallen on them yesterday. She suspected they may even be broken.

'Stay home,' Mary pleaded with her stubborn husband, who had also had a fierce bad cough these past few days and looked ill. 'You are not able for such work tomorrow.'

'I'll be grand,' John insisted, though he could barely walk.

Watching him join Denis Leary and Tom Flynn the next morning, she felt increasingly fearful for him, for he was walking like an old man, limping along beside them.

'Oh, dear God,' she cried on his return home that evening.

Her husband's face was grey, and he could barely talk without provoking a fit of coughing. His body was hot then cold, and although she had piled the turf high on the fire he was unable to get warm. She watched helplessly as he shivered and sweated. Mary worried that he had caught road fever like so many of the men had.

In the morning he made an attempt to rise for work.

'You are going nowhere, John Sullivan. You are too sick to work!' she screamed at him like a harridan.

For the next few days he barely stirred, and she dared not leave his side.

'Con, take Nora and Tim and search for anything we can eat!'

She could see the fear in her eldest son's eyes as they set off for the woods and fields.

Despite their best efforts, the children returned empty-handed, so Mary added more water to the remnants of the thin gruel in the pot. She ignored the gnawing hunger pains in her own stomach as she fed her children.

For three days John was lost in a heavy sleep. As he lay wrapped in a blanket, barely waking or drinking, her mind filled with the awful possibility that her already-weak husband might not recover.

If they still had the horse and cart she would be able to take him to the dispensary or ask for a ticket for the doctor to visit him. But she did not dare to leave him, for he was gravely ill. His body and the blanket were soaked in sweat, and as the fever progressed he tossed and turned and wandered in his sleep as if in some kind of nightmare. She feared for him, as the sickness had overtaken him and he had not the strength left to fight it.

The children were scared and watched their father furtively. Nora wept openly at the sight of him in such a state.

'Hush, Nora. We just have to wait and see what will happen,' Mary said, hugging her close.

'I don't want Da to die,' her daughter begged.

'Your father is fighting as hard as he can to get better,' she tried to reassure her, 'but he is in God's hands now.'

All the night long, Mary sat with her husband. She did not know whether to be alarmed or pleased when at last he fell into a deep, heavy sleep. He neither stirred nor made a sound until the early hours of the morning when he opened his eyes slightly and winced at the candlelight before returning to sleep.

Hope flickered inside her. She allowed him to slumber but a few hours later, when she called his name softly, she was rewarded by him opening his eyes again and staring at her.

'Oh, John!' she burst out. 'You are awake again.'

She managed to get him to take a little water, and then a spoon or two of watery gruel. By the end of the week his breathing was easier and his colour had improved, though he was still too weak even to sit up.

Exhausted, Mary curled up like a small girl and slept on the ground near him . . .

Chapter 39

FATHER JOHN WAS FEELING BONE WEARY. HE WAS SPENDING MOST of his days ministering to the sick, giving them the last rites, or praying over those who had already died and trying to console their families. His brother James had written to him of similar conditions in his own parish.

He said prayers over the mass graves in Chapel Lane and in Abbeystrewry, where they had been forced to open deep burial pits to cope with the large numbers of men, women and children losing their lives to hunger and fever.

The parish house was besieged, and the minute he stepped on to the street he was pursued by starving people begging for a penny, a prayer or some bread.

'Father Fitzpatrick, how can you fulfil your duties with so many following you?' ventured his concerned neighbour, Tim McCarthy Downing. 'You can hardly walk a few steps with them. Perhaps you should hire a man to accompany you?'

'Do you really think such a person is necessary?'

'I do, Father, for your own protection and to make it easier for you to walk about and perform your parish duties without being accosted constantly.'

Perhaps Tim was right. He should give it consideration, for he knew plenty of men who would be glad of a little paid work.

The priest's heart had lifted at the news that Daniel O'Connell, the ageing Liberator, had journeyed across the Irish Sea to London despite his failing health. The purpose of his travels was to raise his voice in Westminster and the newspapers and journals were full of it. So too were the people as all across the nation they read of O'Connell's last desperate plea to Parliament for help on behalf of the starving Irish citizens.

'I go to Parliament as a food man,' O'Connell had said as he stood up in the House of Commons to beg Parliament to give Ireland a loan of thirty to forty million pounds to buy food.

'Ireland is in your hands. She is in your power. If you do not save her she can't save herself. And I solemnly call on you to recollect that I predict with the sincerest conviction that one-quarter of her population will perish unless you come to her relief.'

Bridey had hugged Father Fitzpatrick tearfully as he read O'Connell's words from the *Southern Star* to her twice over.

'God bless the man for his love of the people. They must surely listen to him. Help will soon come, Father.'

In every cottage and cabin in Ireland's villages, towns and cities, expectations were high. They were certain that large-scale official government assistance would now follow quickly. Such hopes were soon dashed, for the British parliament and its members, despite Daniel O'Connell's entreaties, refused to provide any further assistance to Ireland.

Heartbroken O'Connell, whose health remained poor, was advised by his doctors to travel to warmer climes. Father Fitzpatrick had heard that it was the Liberator's intention to journey to Rome to see the Pope, and plead with him on behalf of his people.

God speed his journey.

Chapter 40

Oldcourt

MARY LIFTED THE SHOVEL AND BROUGHT IT DOWN AS HARD AS she could to break the stones. She did it once more, watching them crack and split as she hit them again and again. Her shoulders, back and arms ached, for she was still not used to such heavy work, but at least she was getting paid for it.

'A little smaller,' advised Ellen Clancy, the woman working alongside her.

Mary continued to pound the stones with the shovel and was relieved to see that a few had finally broken up to resemble those in the growing pile in the basket beside her.

''Tis the divil of a job but we all need the four pennies,' sighed Ellen.

She went on to explain what was expected of Mary and showed her how to lift the baskets of stones and rocks as needed.

The foreman walked over to where they were working. Mary could tell that he was watching her, but she kept her eyes down, glued to the ground, for she wanted no trouble with him.

'He's gone,' whispered Ellen a few minutes later, and relief washed over her.

With John sick, Mary desperately needed this work. She had come to the foreman to collect John's pay but, seeing the other women at work with their backs bent, she had begged him to employ her until John was fit to return. He'd been reluctant at first, but she had won him over by telling him how strong and steady she was and that she would not let him down. Flor and Molly had kindly offered to keep a good eye on her husband and the children in her absence.

The jagged stone was rough and hard and heavy, and soon Mary's hands were scraped and cut. Her muscles strained as she went from basket to basket. She shivered against the cold, but was glad of the warmth of John's heavy wool coat; many of the women around had only shawls and rags as scant protection from the elements.

The gang of women and young boys put to work breaking and sorting the stones for the men to use was only small in number. They would only get half pay, but half pay was better than no pay.

'My husband died four months ago,' Ellen told her as together they lifted a basket from the cart. 'It was the saddest day of my life . . . but I have two little girls to look after and I'll not see them follow their father.'

Mary was filled with sympathy and admiration for the other woman, who was prepared to work so hard for her children, in much the same way as she was doing for her own family.

'John, my husband, took sick with road fever three weeks ago,' she confided to Ellen. 'He nearly died on me. For six days I didn't know whether he would live or die, but thank God he survived it. He's still very weak, so if he can't work then I will . . . I'll break every stone on this road if I have to for the money they pay.'

It was so cold that the women's breath formed clouds of steam. Mary watched Denis Leary and the other men work, lifting boulders and rocks and layers of stone. A few looked near to collapse as they laboured on.

John had objected to her working, saying the relief works were no place for a woman. Mary did not want to go against his wishes, but she was still strong and prepared to work . . .

At the end of that first day Mary was footsore and weary, her muscles ached all over and she did not know how she would have the strength to walk home. But the four pence she had earned would ensure that tomorrow her family would not go hungry.

Chapter 41

Skibbereen

A FREEZING GALE BLEW UP THE RIVER ILEN AND THE LASHING rain pounded on the roofs and windows of the homes of Skibbereen. On such a night, Dan was glad of the comfort and warmth of his own hearth.

He had decided to hand over to Tom Marmion the task of selecting passengers who were suitable to travel on James Swanton's ship. He had so many competing demands on his time that he could no longer dedicate himself to the endeavour, though he still ensured that those chosen were medically fit to sail.

His rest was disturbed by a knock on the door.

He opened it hesitantly to an awful apparition: a poor woman who could barely stand, emaciated beyond belief and soaked to the skin. She was so pale and skeletal that it was as if she had appeared from the grave itself.

'Dr Donovan, you have to help me,' she wept. 'My boy is dead and I have not even a coffin to bury him.'

Shocked by her appearance, Dan racked his brain trying to recognize her, for no doubt she was a patient of the dispensary.

'Mrs . . .'

'It's Mrs Keating. Mary Keating,' she said, taking a shuddering breath. 'My husband died two weeks ago. I had only buried him in Chapel Lane when my little boy was taken from me. I was sick with the fever myself and there was nothing I could do, but now I have to get a coffin for my boy and bury him decently.'

'Where is your son now?' Dan asked.

'I laid him out in the ditch, near my cabin. A coffin is all I want for him,' she begged, trying to control her emotions. 'You are a good man, and I trust that you will help me, because no one else will. Please, Dr Donovan, help me to find a coffin to bury my boy.'

Dan had the pity of his heart for the woman, but he could not invite her inside. His own wife and children were only yards away from her and she clearly had fever.

'Mrs Keating, you should not be on the streets, for you are unwell,' he advised.

'A coffin is all I am asking for,' she repeated, her hollow, near fleshless eyes mad with grief. 'I am fixed in my purpose. I'll not let the dogs in the fields eat him.'

'I'm sorry but I cannot help with your son's coffin,' Dan said regretfully. He desperately wanted the sick woman away from his family and his doorstep. 'My duty is to care for the living. Do you have other children?'

'I have a boy and a girl waiting on me back home,' she admitted.

'Then you must return to them, Mrs Keating, for they are

the ones who need you,' he cajoled, hoping that she would take her leave. He simply could not put his family at risk.

He felt in his pocket and found a shilling, which he gave to her.

'Please take this money. Go and purchase meal and some victuals to nourish you and the children.'

'Thank you, doctor,' she said, her claw-like fingers grabbing at the shiny coin.

He sighed with relief that at last she might go.

'What about my boy, Dr Donovan?' she continued. 'What am I to do? I cannot leave him in the ditch. He was the blood of my heart and I am lost without him.'

Immediately Dan felt guilty. Here was a mother, who was ill herself, standing in the bitter cold before him, showing how desperately she cared for her lost child. What kind of man was he if he ignored her plea for help?

'I will come and visit you later, to see if we can resolve the situation,' he promised as he watched her shuffle away in the darkness.

The rain had eased but it still was near freezing outside by the time Dan and his assistant, apothecary Jerrie Crowley, drove out to Letterlishe and found Mrs Keating. Her cabin was an absolute hovel. The water poured through the rotten thatched roof and on to the muddy floor.

Jerrie had brought his lantern with him and in the darkness they could see the two surviving Keating children lying on the floor like small skeletons, their ribs and other bones protruding under their skin. Outside, in the ditch near the front door, was a small coffin containing the putrid body of a boy of about seven years old, who must have died ten or twelve days ago.

'Where did you manage to get the coffin?' Dan asked Mrs Keating.

'I bought it with the shilling you gave me,' she admitted. 'And I carried it home.'

'Mrs Keating, I gave you that money to buy food for you and your children,' he admonished her gently.

'The children and I do not care about food now,' she replied flatly. 'It is so long since we've had any to eat, we have forgotten the taste of it.'

Jerrie could not hide his upset at such suffering as he looked over at her starving children.

'I want my boy buried decently,' Mary Keating demanded. 'That is the only help I ask of you.'

'Well, that is what we will do then,' Dan promised, as he and Jerrie took up the shovels they had also brought with them.

They carried their lantern to an abandoned patch of ground at the side of her cabin.

'Will some of your neighbours give us a hand with the digging?' he asked.

'The neighbours did not a lift a finger to help us in our time of need,' she pronounced bitterly. 'Not even a sup of water would they bring to us.'

The ground was wet and heavy as they began their sombre task. Dan found it hard to believe that not one of the neighbours made any offer to help while they continued to dig out the sodden earth, making a large hole rather than a deep grave in which to bury the boy.

They worked in the bitter cold and near darkness until both he and Jerrie were exhausted, sweating and unable to dig any more. Prayers were said as they solemnly lowered the coffin into the ground. The boy's mother seemed satisfied as they began to shovel the soil back into the makeshift grave to fill it in.

Back inside, Dan examined the boy and girl.

'Mrs Keating, both you and the children are sick,' he told her. 'I can make a special arrangement to admit you all to the Union's fever ward tomorrow morning. I promise you will be cared for there.'

'I am grateful to you, doctor, and to you, Mr Crowley, for what you have done here tonight, but I'll not go to the Union and have my children taken from me,' she said, shaking her head stubbornly. 'We are better staying here, in our place.'

As he and Jerrie drove the icy road home to town, they both were filled with concern for Mrs Keating and her children.

'I suppose you cannot blame her reluctance, Dan. We all know how bad things are in the workhouse,' Jerrie sighed.

It was nearly eleven o'clock when Dan reached home. The house was asleep except for Henrietta.

'Dan, you are freezing cold,' admonished his wife. 'You will get a chill after being out so late on such a night.'

She pulled up the blankets and piled them around him, before settling her own warm and drowsy body against his. She rubbed her legs and feet up and down his to warm him up.

'I am a fortunate man,' he said as she touched her warm hand to his icy face, 'to have you, my dearest, to come home to.'

Chapter 42

DAN STUDIED THE TORN FLESH . . . AND EXPOSED BONE . . . BITE marks were clearly visible on the corpse. One arm had been torn from its socket and chewed. Part of the torso had been gouged out and the dogs had done their worst in trying to feed off the man's putrefying body.

Dan sat on his haunches, holding to his nose the lavender-scented handkerchief Henrietta insisted he carry. It was evident that Mr Leahey's body had been savaged by the starving canines. He had seen the damage a few rats inflicted on the dead, but this was different. He detailed the injuries carefully in his notepad, for he had not seen the like of this before. Judging by the various-sized bite marks all over the body, five or six dogs had been involved. The only saving grace was that poor Mr Leahey had been long dead from fever when the pack of starving mongrels had found him in his cabin.

From the reports Dan had received, Mr Leahey's wife and children had kept his body in the cabin for days. They had no way of burying him, but the stench of his decaying corpse finally drove the family out and they had fled.

Mr Leahey's elderly mother had heard growling and barking inside the cabin. On opening the door she came upon the hungry dogs, chewing and gnawing the flesh from her son's bones. She and some neighbours had managed to beat and drive away the animals but, to Dan's mind, the dogs entering the Leaheys' cabin in the first place was his primary concern.

Dogs were known to dig up corpses buried in shallow graves or to prey on bodies left awaiting burial, but for the animals to enter a dwelling to feast on human flesh wasn't something he had come upon before.

Most of the dogs were crazed, abandoned by owners who had died, fled or could no longer feed them. The starving creatures roamed the fields, roads and lanes of the district. It alarmed Dan to see that they were becoming bolder, packing together unafraid, and likely to attack those who were weak.

The matter was serious and Dan intended to write an urgent report. He would recommend that, for the safety of the public during this crisis, all dogs in Carbery be culled. He found it deeply offensive that those with position and money still fed and kept their pet dogs and hunting hounds while the children of the poor starved.

On his return to the dispensary, he felt someone grab and tug at his coattails. Turning around, he discovered Mrs Keating, who was carrying her young daughter in her arms. Dan immediately went to help her but was shocked to discover that the small girl was already dead.

'She died yesterday,' Mrs Keating explained, caressing her

daughter's thin face. 'As no Christian will come near me, I carried her into town myself to lay her alongside her father in the graveyard in Chapel Lane.'

Dan tried not to betray his emotion as he imagined the terrible journey the poor woman must have made along the roads. He ushered her to the dispensary immediately, where he took the girl from her gently and promised the woman that he would look after the burial of her child.

'I am grateful to you, doctor, but it is my poor boy in the grave that you and your friend made the other night that I am worried over,' she explained. 'My neighbours' pigs are scratching and digging at the ground. I fear they will uproot the grave and his coffin if they get a chance!'

'I'm sorry, Mrs Keating, but we did not know there were pigs roaming close by.'

'Doctor, won't you send someone to bury him properly?' she begged. 'Away from the pigs and other animals.'

After seeing what the dogs had done to Mr Leahey, Dan found himself agreeing to help Mrs Keating again. He sent two men to drive out to Letterlishe, exhume the boy's flimsy coffin and have it transported to Skibbereen where it would be buried in consecrated ground. He also agreed to provide a coffin for the little girl's burial.

A few hours later the men returned empty-handed.

'I'm sorry, doctor, but there is no moving that putrefying corpse,' Dinny Burke told him stubbornly. ''Tis in a terrible state and best left buried where it is. Paddy and I will not touch it!'

Mary Keating, however, was made of sterner stuff. She returned home and somehow found the strength and resolve to lift her son's coffin from the earth by herself. The following day she carried it heroically all the way into town, so that her son could be buried properly, with his father and sister.

A week later, Mary Keating accosted Dan once more. Her gaunt face remained pale and worn, her eyes red-rimmed.

'Doctor, I need another coffin to bury my youngest boy. He is the very last of my family,' she pleaded, broken-hearted.

Dan was torn. He had given her the money for two coffins now and she was expecting him to pay for a third. Although he was a doctor and held a good position, he was certainly not a wealthy man!

'In the name of the great God,' she implored him, 'don't let my fine boy, who would be my help and support if he lived, be thrown into the grave like a dog.'

Dan looked at this ghost of a woman, who seemed near death herself. How could he possibly refuse her plea?

Mrs Keating took the money and disappeared to purchase another small coffin. He caught sight of her from the dispensary window as she set off for home with it placed on her head. She was far too weak to be carrying such a load and he ran down the street after her.

'Mrs Keating, you are too sick to go home.' He tried to persuade her to let him help. 'I will endeavour to arrange a bed for you today in the fever ward. Please, I beg you, stay here in town.'

She shook her head firmly, refusing his offer. As he watched her walk away, Dan was overcome with a strange sense of foreboding.

*

A few days later, Dan heard of Mrs Keating's death. The poor woman had collapsed and was found dead at the door of her cabin, the empty coffin beside her. The neighbours were too terrified of contagion even to come near her.

Dan arranged immediately for both her youngest son's body and hers to be transported to Skibbereen for a proper burial in Chapel Lane with her husband and other child. At least she might sleep in death with those she had loved so much in life.

Her passing affected Dan so deeply that he vowed in time to erect a headstone over her grave.

Mrs Keating's reaction to her children's deaths, and Mr O'Shea's to his son's, demonstrated to Dan that people were fixated on the dead and their need for a coffin. In his opinion, the need for prompt burials before putrefaction set in was the most pressing concern. Proper arrangements needed to be made for a cart and a man – or two – to collect the dead both in the town and the district and bring them for immediate burial in Abbeystrewry to stop the spread of disease.

As a doctor, Dan's focus needed to remain on the living. There was little he could do for the growing numbers of dead, except ensure that their corpses were collected and safely interred, but something had to be done to persuade the people to take action swiftly.

Chapter 43

FATHER JOHN FITZPATRICK WAS BUSY WRITING HIS SUNDAY SERMON when Bridey showed in Dan Donovan. The housekeeper knew well that he did not like to be disturbed when preparing for the following day's service.

'John, I need to talk to you urgently,' Dan said, sitting down across from him. 'As you and I are the ones in this town who give care to the dying and the dead.'

'That is the way, with any physician or priest,' Father Fitzpatrick sighed, putting away his pen.

'It is the dead that are my great concern,' the doctor said with worry, wringing his hands.

It was evident that the priest's friend was upset over some matter.

'The starving and poor are spending every last penny they have on the dead,' Dan continued, exasperated. 'They are set on purchasing coffins in which to bury their loved ones despite not having a scrap of food in the house to feed their children, or a warm coat, a shawl or shoes to wear! They come to me, or to the dispensary, begging for money for one. Even worse, they'll keep a putrefying body in their home with the rest of their family rather than admit they cannot afford to bury them in a coffin.'

'I fully agree with you, Dan. They accost me in the street too, or come here to the presbytery, looking for me to arrange the price of one. Poor people, they have no care for their own misery and misfortune, even though some of them are so weak with hunger they can barely walk.'

His stomach turned as Dan told him of a man whose corpse had been attacked by dogs and a poor woman who spent the shillings given to her by the doctor on coffins for her children instead of food! He himself had witnessed the dead bodies of children and parents lying beside the living when there was no money to purchase a coffin.

'The authorities do not seem one bit concerned on the issue,' Dan railed angrily. 'But the situation is now urgent. I intend on putting in place arrangements to have a public cart to transport bodies away from the town and district as swiftly as possible for safe burial in Abbeystrewry. I have also heard of a new type of coffin being made. It has a hinged base that can be used for such occasions and then be reused again and again. It is something to be considered.'

Father John felt a deep despair at the prospect of such necessities. However, he knew Dan Donovan to be a man of great integrity, who would only ever act in the best interests of the community.

'Something must be done to stop this repugnance the people have to bury the dead without proper coffins,' the doctor continued. 'I have told my patients again and again: it is the living we must care for and nourish, not the dead. They do not listen to me, Father. I implore you, speak out about this. You are the only one to whom they will listen.'

'I'm not sure they will listen to me, Dan, but I promise that I will try to convince them.'

Father Fitzpatrick looked down from the pulpit at the good people of Skibbereen. Many of the congregation who sat quietly and respectfully in the pews at Sunday mass, awaiting his sermon, were in rags and tatters, half-starved. These days, he found it difficult to speak to them and console them; to promise them that though they may suffer greatly in this life on earth, they would find their reward in the next life when they entered the heavenly kingdom.

How could he utter such inane words to a man who had just buried his three children in the pit in Abbeystrewry, or to an old woman left to die at the side of the road!

He knew all too well their hardship. Day after day, he visited cottages and cabins where entire families were sick with fever. Often they lay together on nothing but straw, clad only in rags with not even a blanket to cover them, as he gave them extreme unction.

But they were a simple people, who put their trust in the church. Many who continued to attend mass had lost children, husbands or wives and neighbours to the hunger and fever, yet somehow, despite their distress, they retained their faith and belief in God.

Of late, his own belief was being challenged, and his own faith tested every day as he asked himself, where was God's hand in all this? The hand of the merciful God about whom he preached?

'My dear people,' he began, addressing them from the pulpit.

All raised their eyes to him, and the coughing and nose-blowing ceased.

'We are all possessed of a soul,' he continued. 'Even the tiniest baby in arms. For the glory and majesty of the human soul is the most important part of our creation as divined by God himself. Our soul makes us human; the people we are. We all strive to live the best life we can. Some will enjoy a great age while others will have a life shortened by disease and hunger; others may not even get to enjoy a childhood. But it makes no difference, I tell you, for when the time comes to leave this earth, no matter the circumstances of our death, our soul flies heavenward, returning back to God from whence we came.'

He could see and sense that he had their full attention, from the town's well-to-do citizens to the poor dwellers of Bridgetown and the homeless wanderers who took refuge in the church during mass.

'As the soul flies, we leave our frail and often scarred human body. We must leave the world of human flesh behind. The rituals of burials and funerals must be observed as we place and inter our dead in the ground, but it has come to my attention that many here are deeply worried about this, during this terrible time of rampant hunger and disease among us. Many parishioners believe that they must somehow provide a wooden coffin for the burial of the departed, for this is what is expected by our church.

'Unfortunately, with the times we are in, I know well the difficulties faced by many, and there are few coffin-makers. So

I say to you today that the purchase of a coffin for a loved one when you, or your wife or children, are in desperate need of nourishment or shelter is not what the Lord expects.

'Remember, my good people, that the Bible tells us that Jesus himself was taken down from the cross and wrapped in a simple material – a shroud – and laid in a cave as his tomb. There was no coffin, no great funeral, no multitudes, for his was just a simple burial.

'So we can see from the Bible that the dead have no use or care for such earthly forms. I tell you that our Christian duty is to the living. It is paramount that we follow the faith we profess and obey the commandments and, despite all the difficulties we face, continue to love our fellow man,' he concluded, blessing himself.

Father John caught sight of approving nods from some of the relief committee members and their families in the front pews. However, it was to the rear and sides of the large stone cathedral that his missive was directed.

After mass and communion the congregation flocked around him, asking him to clarify what they had heard.

'Neither God nor man expects you to pauper or starve yourself for the sake of a wooden box,' he assured them.

The gratitude, and even tears of relief in some of their eyes, was evident. He prayed that they would accept his words.

Later, as he set about locking up the doors of the magnificent church that stood high over North Street, built to serve the large and growing population of the once prosperous Skibbereen, Father Fitzpatrick reflected on the beggars and destitute, the hungry and the poor of the town. He was tempted to fling open the heavy doors of St Patrick's Cathedral and admit all those who needed comfort and shelter. It is what Jesus Christ would have done. Father John's ideals were in conflict with the bishop's, however, who certainly would not approve of this house of God being used as some kind of shelter for the hungry.

A few members of the congregation still knelt in the pews, their heads bent, praying for help in their time of need.

'The church is closing,' he reminded them gently.

Once they had left, he himself knelt before the cross in the solitude and quiet of the church. He prayed for God to give him the strength and courage to continue to do his work.

Chapter 44

Oldcourt

ON THE STONE ROAD, MARY'S SKIN TOUGHENED WITH THE BACK-breaking work. Her feet were swollen and sore, often numb with the cold and the damp. Her hands were cut, her nails broken, and two fingers were hot with chilblains. But she kept her head down every day as she was set to breaking up stones to make them smaller and more usable. She ignored the stiffness in her arms and shoulders, and the weakness that came over her at times. She forced herself to keep working.

The men were like beasts of burden, made to lift and move the heavy baskets. Sometimes the stones fell, injuring some poor fellow, while other men such as Denis Leary were set to dig the heavy, near frozen earth to create the channels and surfaces where the stones would be laid.

She witnessed one poor man break his arm and be sent on his way with only four days' wages, and only two days ago, a grey-haired old woman, Mary Pat O'Donovan, had fainted on the ground beside her.

'Be on your way, grandmother,' the foreman had told her sarcastically. 'You are no use to us.'

'Not a word,' Ellen had warned Mary under her breath, 'or we will all be in trouble with him.'

Mary, petrified of losing her job, said little as she worked. She missed being with her children as she shivered in the frost and the freezing wind and rain where she felt chilled to the marrow. The one consolation was that she could at least buy some food, though it angered her that the price of corn and meal had risen substantially, making it even worse for them all.

The only good news the family had had was that John had received a short letter from Pat, who was now living and working on a building site in New York. His sea journey had been long and arduous but her brother-in-law was well and living in a fine house. By all accounts he was enjoying his new life in America.

John read his few words over and over again. They were both glad to hear that Pat was well and had escaped from the hard life they were still enduring. She imagined his life in New York, far from the stone roads, the hungry faces and the weeping land.

When she returned home most evenings, Mary barely had the energy to set the pot over the fire. After serving a hot meal to her family, she would curl up and try to warm herself, relaxing her aching muscles as she let sleep overtake her.

On Monday, Mary and the other women were surprised as there was no sign of Ellen.

'She has the road fever, God help us!' one of her neighbours told them. 'They say she is bad with it.'

As Mary hit the stones, splitting them and mixing them together for the men to use, she cursed the officials that had designated such work for the poor and starving.

On Friday, news of Ellen's death reached the women. It upset everyone deeply and they all said a few prayers in remembrance of her.

As she was paid her wages, Mary considered the pennies in her hand. Her head filled with thoughts of how Ellen's children, now orphans, would survive without their mother.

'Mary, you cannot keep on,' warned John when she told him about Ellen. 'I fear you will collapse and get sick, and then what will happen to the children?'

She knew in her heart that he was speaking the truth. The heavy work and hunger were draining the life from her, but there was nothing else for it. She had to work or else they would surely starve.

'I am well again and ready for the work!' her husband insisted, but anyone could see that his eyes were still sunken in his head and he was not the man he used to be. She knew he was still weak and his muscles were gone. There wasn't a chance that he was yet strong enough to swing a heavy shovel or pickaxe.

They argued hotly over it, but Mary refused to give in. As long as she had the strength to work, she would break all the stones in the world if it meant her family would survive the hunger.

'John, I will only do it until you are better,' she conceded. Her back and shoulders ached constantly, but she wrapped herself up in his heavy coat and set off for the works.

Chapter 45

Skibbereen
February 1847

DAN WAS FROZEN TO THE BONE. THERE HAD BEEN A FEW MORE snow flurries during the day and he had got damp doing his rounds. Returning home, he was glad of the warmth of the fire and the plate of comforting beef stew with dumplings. Henrietta, with her hair softly curled and pinned up, looked more beautiful than ever as she served him some tea.

'Dada, we have a big surprise for you!' announced Fanny once he had eaten.

Young Daniel grinned. 'We made it all ourselves.'

Henrietta smiled but would give him no clue as to what they were up to.

To tell the truth, Dan was exhausted. After an awful day he would have liked nothing better than to stretch and relax in the armchair undisturbed, but he could see from his young son's eyes that he was bursting with excitement.

'Very well, what is it?' he asked, curious.

'You have to come upstairs to see it,' coaxed Ellen, pulling him by the hand. 'We have been working on it all day.'

'For days,' Daniel added.

'It was a secret,' whispered Harriet as Dan followed them upstairs as they trooped to the nursery.

Henrietta said nothing as she bounced Margaret up and down on her hip.

'You and Mama are to sit in those two chairs where you can watch the show.'

He laughed. 'What is it?'

'You are invited to the amazing, daring and delightful Donovan Puppet Show,' declared Ellen, pulling back a sheet to reveal a large, home-made puppet theatre.

'Henry and Jerrie made most of it,' said Ellen, beaming at her older brothers.

'And we all made the puppets and painted them,' added Harriet proudly. 'The show will start in two minutes, Father, so do please sit down.'

'They have been working on it these past few days,' whispered Henrietta.

Her eyes shone as the young puppeteers disappeared behind the tall, red-and-yellow striped box. The curtains were pulled back to reveal the painted cardboard figures of Cinderella and her two ugly sisters. Ellen did the voice of Cinderella, and Fanny and Harriet used thin sticks to move the ugly sisters.

It was a wondrous show and even young Daniel managed to operate and move a few figures . . . A dog, a cat, and a jiggling glass slipper.

Entranced, Dan watched and listened to the children having fun as the snow fell outside. He, Henrietta and Margaret gave a huge round of applause as Cinderella and her prince took a final bow.

A few minutes later, Dan was roped in with Jerrie to help tell a variation of the story. This time the dog took to barking at the ugly sisters, and was the one who found Cinderella's lost slipper. It was a long time since Dan had laughed quite so much or had such fun, and he chased the children to bed with the promise of a story.

'Only a happy one, Dada,' reminded Fanny as he tucked her into bed.

'Once upon a time . . .' Dan began.

Chapter 46

'MR MAHONY, WELCOME,' SAID DAN AS HE GREETED JAMES Mahony, the illustrator and journalist from the *Illustrated London News*, at the Becher Arms. 'I trust you had a good journey despite this terrible cold weather.'

'Yes, it was fine, though I saw crowds of hungry walking the icy roads as we passed in the carriage from Cork. At Clonakilty, where we had breakfast, they flocked around us, looking for money and food. One poor woman was carrying the corpse of a fine child in her arms—'

The artist's voice broke off.

'She was begging alms of us passengers to purchase a coffin to bury her dear little baby,' he managed. 'It was an awful sight. One that I will never forget.'

'Unfortunately, you will see many such tragedies in this town, and worse,' warned Dan.

'Dr Donovan, I have avidly read the diary you publish in the *Southern Reporter*, which my own paper then publishes.

Your words have reached many,' he explained, his brown eyes serious. 'Each of your reports is both moving and informative. They are why my editor suggested this visit, so that our readers are made aware of the terrible suffering faced by so many.'

Dan nodded. 'Words in a newspaper can do so much.'

Nicholas Cummins's letter published in *The Times* before Christmas had resulted not only in a huge wave of donations but also in the setting up of the British Relief Association, which had already raised substantial funds to aid Ireland. Dan's published diary had been reprinted not only by some English newspapers but in some American ones too, his words helping to raise much-needed donations and subscriptions for relief from many quarters.

'It is why I allowed them to be published,' the doctor continued. 'Too many people have ignored the plight of the hungry and needy in these terrible times.'

'Then perhaps I can do some good also,' James Mahony offered modestly, 'by my reporting and illustrating the truth of the matter.'

Dan worried that the artist might not be able to cope with the terrible deprivation and human misery he would witness.

'My assistant Mr Crowley and I are more than happy to have you accompany us on our visits to the sick and needy, Mr Mahony. But I have to warn you, it is exceptionally distressing work, even for a medical man.'

'Dr Donovan, I have seen much in Cork City. The hungry and homeless roam the streets and the Cork workhouse is crowded out, but here, judging from your reports, the situation appears much worse.'

Dan had taken an immediate liking to the artist. He had

watched him earnestly carrying his leather bag containing his paper and pens, and had decided that he trusted him. He might have slender hands and the long fingers of an artist, but it was clear that this Cork man was determined to do his best for his fellow man in his own fashion.

'Have you been to other towns yet and seen the results of hunger and starvation there?' the doctor asked.

'No,' Mahony admitted. 'This is my first time undertaking such work. My forte is to paint in watercolour – French and Italian, and sometimes Irish landscapes. I endeavour to capture the beauty of such places.'

'I fear there will be nothing like that for you here,' snorted Jerrie Crowley, who had joined them. 'Believe me, there is nothing beautiful left to see in this poor town of ours.'

'I am fully aware of that, Mr Crowley, and will endeavour to record accurately all that I see.'

'Well then, let us begin with a visit to Bridgetown,' Dan said, 'where there is enormous suffering and many of those weakened by starvation have succumbed to fever.'

'It is a poor area, with nigh on a few hundred cabins and cottages – if you can call them that,' added Jerrie Crowley, turning up the collar of his heavy coat to try to keep out the biting wind as they walked along.

'So many of the people here have no coats or shawls, or clothes,' Mahony remarked as they passed a group of paupers and beggars, and women and children who sat along the street, shivering. 'How do they not perish in this freezing weather?'

'Unfortunately, many do,' Dan admitted. 'In desperation, many sold or pawned every piece of clothing or blanket they possessed months ago to try to feed themselves.'

As they entered the narrow lanes of Bridgetown, Dan could not help but notice the artist wrinkle his nose at the fetid odours of urine and excrement that seemed to envelop the place, where human dunghills abounded.

'Be careful where you walk,' he warned.

'Is it always like this?'

Jerrie grinned. 'It can be worse on a hot summer's day, but you just get used to it.'

The artist stopped and immediately began to sketch. He drew the curving line of low cabins and hovels with their rotting straw roofs and the cluster of barely dressed children and women who moved among the lanes.

'Our first visit is to the Murphys,' Dan said as he led them into the darkness of a low cabin where the sound of moaning filled the air.

In the dim light it was difficult to see, but the family lay on the floor, as near to the dying embers of the fire as they could get. An old woman with streeling white hair lay on the straw in a filthy shift.

'Doctor, my son Paddy died a day – no, maybe two or three days – ago,' she announced. 'The daughter-in-law, Brigid, went not long after him. God be good to them, but I'm weak myself and left with the two young boys here.'

A bout of coughing consumed her as she pointed at the children lying on the rough earth.

'And not even a soul to bring us a bit of food or sup of water.'

Dan caught the look of utter shock and disbelief on Mahony's face as he realized that, with the exception of the old woman, the rest of the family were dead. Their eyes were staring and their bodies were already beginning to decay.

The artist pushed past Dan and rushed outside, gasping for fresh air.

Dan followed him.

'Sit down,' he ordered. 'Put your head between your knees. The faint will pass. Just try to breathe slow and easy.'

He reached for the small bottle of smelling salts he kept in his inside pocket. He opened it and passed it back and forth in front of the man's ghastly pale and clammy face.

'Any better?'

After a few minutes, Mahony nodded.

'Yes. It's just the smell. The cabin and the children. I've never seen such horror. That woman, how did she not know they were dead?'

'She's old with no one to help her . . .' Dan tried to explain.

Dan and Jerrie made their way back inside the cabin to make clear to Mrs Murphy that they would arrange for the bodies of her family to be collected by the death cart in a few hours' time. There was little they could do to comfort her, but Dan promised to return the following day to visit her.

The next stops on Dan's rounds were the Connollys' and the Carews' cabins. Both families had children sick with dysentery. The ominous signs of bloody flux from terrible diarrhoea were spattered all over the mud floor.

'Keep back, Mr Mahony, it is dysentery,' Dan explained. 'There is little I can do about it except tell them to try to keep the children away from the rest of the family. If they don't, they will likely all get it.'

In the Cotters' cabin they were greeted by a skeletal young woman with two small children.

'Have you a biteen of food for us?' she pleaded. 'For the hunger is fierce bad on us.'

'I'm sorry, Mrs Cotter, but we are here on our medical duties.'

Dan examined the middle boy, who was about five years old. The child's belly protruded and his little legs were like gnarled sticks. He was quiet and listless, and his huge eyes simply stared up at Dan.

'Have you been to the soup kitchen today?' he urged the young mother. 'You must go and try to get some nourishment for you and the children.'

'Denis is too weak to walk there, and I do not have the strength to carry him and Peggy together,' she admitted tearfully.

The artist was visibly upset as he began to draw a simple sketch of the cottage and child.

'I will arrange that soup is delivered to you and your family today, and for as long as it is needed,' Dan promised.

With so many too sick or weak to walk to the soup kitchen, Dan and the relief committee had arranged for a number of men to deliver soup to his patients and those in desperate need.

'I will also arrange for fresh straw bedding to be brought here.'

'Thank you, doctor,' Mrs Cotter said, her eyes filled with gratitude.

Over the course of the next few hours, the trio visited cabin after cabin. They saw typhus, dysentery and starvation everywhere. The snowy lanes were quiet, with no sight of a dog nor a cat nor even a bird. The silence was broken only by the scurry of rats darting down the tracks and among the rotting roof thatch of the miserable huts and hovels.

'Rats are the only things thriving in this poor place,' pronounced Jerrie. 'There is not a cat in the place to hunt them.'

One crazed man, Peadar Dempsey, refused to let them take the body of his dead wife.

'She's hungry and tired, but I tell you she's just asleep, Dr Dan.'

James Mahony said little, his skin still pale and his countenance serious as he drew and sketched. He filled his drawing pad with images of the dead and the living; the starving men, women and children of Bridgetown.

After their time in Bridgetown Dan brought Mahony to Old Chapel Lane. There they made their way to a tumbledown house with a window and door missing, which was crowded with destitute people trying to shelter from the cold. Some were already sick with typhus, and two or three were dead, including a big strong country fellow he bent down to examine. The man's body was already cold.

'Doctor, how could he be dead when he was only down here near me a few hours ago?' demanded the man next to him.

Dan sighed.

'I suspect he had typhus. Stay outside, Mr Mahony,' he begged. 'Do not come inside this place, for there is rampant fever here, and I advise you not to engage with those standing around you at the door, for they may also be sick.'

The artist moved down the street quickly, capturing with his pen the house and lane and those waiting admittance. Dan joined him shortly after and showed him the nearby watch hut that overlooked the graveyard in Chapel Lane. A matter of days ago, he and Jerrie had found a family hiding there, amid the decaying bodies.

'They would have died here, among the skeletons and diseased corpses of the graveyard, except for the actions of my friend here,' he said, praising Jerrie Crowley.

'I don't mind telling you that it was a shock to find the living, hidden among the putrefaction of this crowded graveyard, with not even a drop of water to sustain them,' the doctor's man told their companion.

'What happened to them?'

'Fortunately, Mr Mahony, the six of them were removed from this abode of the dead to the fever hospital, where they are improving. I will write it up in my diary,' Dan affirmed.

'Then certainly I must sketch this hut,' Mahony said, trying to find a good angle from which to draw the structure without miring himself in the sodden, putrid ground around him.

With a few swift swipes and scribbles of his pen, James Mahony captured the watch hut from which the family had been rescued.

'Tomorrow I must attend my duties at the Union workhouse,' Dan explained. 'But Mr Everett is a good man. He will collect you in the morning and take you to Ballydehob and Schull.'

'Thank you for your great kindness today, Dr Donovan,' Mr Mahony said as he took his leave of them. 'I hope to see you when I return to Skibbereen to take the mail coach.'

Dan watched the artist walk down the street, hoping that somehow his sketches and drawings would help convey the terrible situation the starving people of West Cork were enduring.

Chapter 47

ON HIS RETURN TO SKIBBEREEN, MR MAHONY CALLED IN TO THE crowded dispensary. Dan was happy to see him again and accompanied him to the Becher Arms where the coach stop was. The coach wasn't due for a short while, so they went inside to take a cup of tea.

'Tell me, Mr Mahony, how did you fare on the rest of your visit?' Dan asked.

'The people in Ballydehob and Schull are in a terrible state too. I cannot understand how the authorities are allowing such extreme suffering to occur. These past few days I have seen women, children and babies all starving before my very eyes.'

Dan could detect the huge emotion and strain in the man's voice.

'I'm sure that you will do your best to reflect this grave situation in which we find ourselves, Mr Mahony.'

'In Ballydehob, Reverend Triphook told me that anyone

who can gather a few pounds is leaving the town to escape the fever and the distress.'

'Aye, Mr Mahony, you cannot blame them!'

'And in Schull, I saw hundreds of women, desperate to buy meal which had been delivered by sloop to the town. Apparently, there are tons of Indian meal on board, but it is being guarded by a government steam ship. I saw only miserable quantities being doled out to those waiting and it was being charged at exorbitant prices.'

'They are saving food for a rainy day,' Dan said, exasperated, 'when it is clear that the full force of the storm is already upon us.'

'I was also introduced to the rector there, Dr Robert Traill. I found him to be a most charitable man. Every day, he and his good wife feed a few hundred people with a warm nourishing soup, from their own door at the rectory in Schull. Such are the numbers that they now employ a number of men to help them make and distribute it. The townspeople are fortunate to have such a dedicated vicar among them.'

'Robert is indeed a good man,' Dan agreed, 'and well respected by all of us.'

'It's strange, Dr Donovan, but in normal circumstances, Skibbereen and these towns and villages are places I would visit to paint or sketch for their great beauty, their inspiring landscapes and views with the sea and river, and the coastline and islands nestling in the shadow of Mount Gabriel. Alas, my work now is of a very different nature.'

'Mr Mahony, your work is of great importance to the people of this town and West Cork,' Dan reminded him.

'As are your reports in the newspaper,' he admitted. 'I

217

perhaps doubted their accuracy somewhat, or suspected they may be highly coloured and exaggerated, but from my visit here I have seen at first hand the terrible truth of the extreme suffering of the people. Neither pen nor pencil could ever portray the misery and horror to be witnessed at this moment in Skibbereen.'

Dan nodded gravely as he sipped his tea.

'If anything, Dr Donovan, you have tried to make the reports less graphic and more palatable for the readers by hiding the hideous reality that you and Mr Crowley have to contend with day after day.'

'That is true,' Dan admitted calmly. 'I have found that the human mind can only deal with so much distress and horror.'

'I have observed that there is little sympathy shown between the living and the dead,' Mahony continued. 'Men driving carts filled with corpses show little respect for them, and foremen and managers on the work schemes show no care for the men they oversee. Men who may have walked miles stand in the mud and cold to break stones and build roads, with not even a scrap of food in their belly. It is a cruelty beyond any belief.'

Their conversation was interrupted by a shout that the coach to Cork would be ready to leave in a few minutes. The artist nodded and stood up to leave.

'I'd better take my seat.'

'Mr Mahony, we are very appreciative of your visit, as distressing as it has been for you. Thank you for coming to Skibbereen.'

'Dr Donovan, I have filled my sketch pads and am as well informed of the situation as I can be. I promise you that I will endeavour with fidelity to portray what I have witnessed in order to make the suffering and afflictions of this famine-stricken people known to the charitable public and readers of the paper.'

'Sir, God bless you and your work.'

Dan caught Mahony by the shoulder and gripped his hand firmly as they bade each other farewell.

A crowd of beggars swarmed around the horses and coach as the artist took his place aboard.

'The hunger is on us,' they called and shouted, over and over, as the remaining passengers climbed inside and sat back in their seats. 'The hunger is on us!'

The driver ignored them as he checked his fares were safely ensconced. He grabbed the reins swiftly and urged on the horses to pass the crowd and leave the hungry town behind them.

Chapter 48

FATHER FITZPATRICK'S HEART HAD GROWN HEAVY. NEARLY HALF
the town had fallen victim to the fever that was raging across
the population. The wealthy and powerful had been afflicted
just as badly as the beggars in the street.

With his own eyes he had witnessed vermin, dogs and even
pigs lay claim to abandoned and poorly buried bodies. On
Windmill Lane a pair of dogs had tried to pull apart the body
of a small baby but for the quick intervention of two soldiers
who killed them.

Anger and rage grew in him that the British authorities,
who did so little to sustain the living as the country starved,
still permitted food, grain and livestock to be exported to English cities, and made absolutely no provision for the inevitable –
the interment of the dead.

It was the town officials who declared that all dogs be culled,
though it brought cries of outrage and protest from many who

were reluctant to relinquish their animals, even if it was for the common good. Shame on all of them!

Never had he imagined such a terrible end for the innocent people of Skibbereen.

Charles Trevelyan, who controlled the Treasury, considered the failure of the potato crop and the ensuing hunger divine retribution from the Lord on the ever-growing Irish Catholic population for their indolence and laziness. That a man in such a crucial position should entertain such unchristian thoughts grieved and upset the priest deeply.

He sat down to write to Frederic Lucas, editor of the English Catholic journal *Tablet*, which had published some of his letters, to thank him and his readers for their generosity towards the town's starving and sick. He'd been overwhelmed by the post office orders and donations sent to him by congregations, charitable ladies and good men from Aberdeen to East London, and Cardiff to Cornwall. The British people, unlike the government, had shown themselves to be both charitable and most generous. Mr Lucas had kindly opened a bank account in London for such purpose.

Father Fitzpatrick had also appealed for much-needed clothing by asking readers of the journal to send him items care of Thomas Galwey at the Skibbereen coach office in Cork, and this had already borne results.

A British Relief Association had been founded, raising huge sums of money, which the charity intended to be used to give grants of food aid, and Queen Victoria had issued her Queen's Letter, an appeal for money to relieve distress in Ireland, to which many had contributed, including the Queen herself, who had donated one thousand pounds.

The priest's eyes grew heavy and he was suddenly conscious of Bridey trying to rouse him.

'Father, you must away to your bed or you will not be fit for tomorrow,' she warned.

He stood up stiffly. His back and right knee ached.

'You need your rest, Father,' she persisted.

'I am finished here,' he assured her, signing and folding the letter. 'And will be glad to get some sleep.'

Lying in the darkness, his mind was crowded and tormented by the memory of those to whom he had attended during the day. He said a quiet prayer for them all, before rolling on to his side and giving in to the utter exhaustion that he felt.

Chapter 49

'DAN, IS IT TRUE THAT POOR JOHN CLERKE IS VERY ILL?' HENRIETTA asked, for he and the bank manager were close friends.

'I fear his condition is grave,' her husband admitted, his voice breaking. 'The Provincial Bank sent a replacement manager to take over the running of it, but apparently he has already fled the town for fear of contagion. The new official they sent is apparently no better as he too is threatening to leave!'

'You can't blame them, Dan. Anyone with an ounce of good sense would pack up and go,' she said pointedly.

'Unfortunately that is precisely what the matron, the apothecary and some of the staff in the workhouse have done,' he told her, clearly worried. 'And a number of staff there have also fallen ill.'

'Oh, Dan, what will you do?' she asked, shocked at such news.

'We will have to manage with a limited staff.' Her husband sighed, a heavy tiredness in his eyes. 'We must treat the sick, feed the hungry and bury the dead. Fortunately, Mr Mahony's graphic illustrations of the tragedy of our terrible situation have resulted in massive donations to help Ireland and our people. Hundreds of thousands of pounds by all accounts, not just from the readers of his paper but from all around the world.'

'Oh, thank heaven,' she said, relieved.

'Such contributions are badly needed and we have now arranged to have soup brought to the sick in the town and delivered by cart to Kilcoe, Ballydehob, Rath and outlying areas to stop more people flooding into town. We are feeding near eight thousand people, Henrietta, and delivering fresh straw for bedding throughout Bridgetown and the lanes to try to cope with the filth and sickness. Unfortunately, there are even fewer people now to assist us with such work.'

'Dan, you are working too hard. You must rest,' she pleaded with him, 'or you will fall ill yourself.'

'I have a strong constitution, my dear,' he reminded her gently, 'and my duty is to attend to my patients.'

As she made her way to the market that morning, Henrietta was lost in thought. She stopped in her tracks when she bumped into Reverend Townsend, who doffed his black hat to her.

'Good day, Reverend,' she greeted him politely.

He paused, appearing upset by her words.

'I'm afraid that as far as my household is concerned, Mrs Donovan, this is not a very good day. For we have suffered a great loss.'

'Oh, no. Is Mrs Townsend unwell?'

'She is quite well,' he assured her, 'but she is distressed by events. Our two servants were both stricken with fever these past few days. Despite our best efforts, both died during the night.'

Henrietta felt herself grow weak as she thought of the new pretty little maid who had played with her children only a few weeks ago.

'I must call to her,' she blurted out, knowing how deeply affected her friend would be by such loss. 'Is she at home?'

'Yes.' He nodded gravely. 'I need to attend to the arrangements for them. Please convey our gratitude to your husband, for he was most kind and attentive to them during their travails.'

Henrietta watched as he walked away, and decided to call to Glebe House immediately.

Through the long drawing-room window she could see Elizabeth sitting sewing, head bent in concentration. She rang the bell twice and her friend came to answer the door herself. Her eyes were red-rimmed from crying and she looked utterly grief-stricken.

'I met your husband and he told me about what happened to your servants,' Henrietta ventured. 'I wanted to come and offer my condolences on their deaths.'

'I still cannot believe it!' Elizabeth's voice broke with emotion. 'The two of them taken from us like that in a matter of days. Young women with their lives ahead of them, taken by fever. How can such a thing happen?'

'I am so sorry. I know how good you were to them.'

'Kate had worked for us since she was sixteen years of age.

She had such a kind heart and helped out with serving in the soup kitchen only last week. And as for young Jane, she was like a little bit of sunshine that came into our lives. They were part of our small family and will for ever be greatly missed,' she sobbed.

Henrietta took hold of her arm gently and led her back into the drawing room, where Elizabeth lowered herself into the velvet armchair.

'Do you need anything?' Henrietta offered. 'Can I help in some way?'

Elizabeth Townsend shook her head and slowly took up her sewing again.

Henrietta realized that the linen she was stitching neatly and carefully was a white shroud.

'This one is for Jane,' Elizabeth explained.

Another shroud lay spread out on a nearby chair.

'Would you like me to make you a cup of tea?' Henrietta offered.

'Thank you, but I just need to finish my sewing so these will be ready for the funeral of my two girls.'

'I am so sorry for your loss,' Henrietta repeated, words escaping her.

Tears ran slowly down Elizabeth's pale face. 'They were like our family. I don't know how people can bear such sadness – children, sons and daughters, husbands and wives, parents all stricken by fever.'

'These are terrible times,' Henrietta consoled her friend.

'Nobody is safe from this disease and torment, no one!' warned Elizabeth.

*

Distressed, Henrietta hurried home, her head bent low as she avoided meeting or talking to anyone. Skibbereen had become a blighted town and she dearly wished that Dan would give consideration to fleeing as others had done. However, she knew well that, despite her entreaties, her dutiful and steadfast husband would never desert the town and people he loved so much.

Chapter 50

'YOU HAVE VISITORS, FATHER,' INTERRUPTED BRIDEY, AS FATHER Fitzpatrick ate his breakfast and read the newspaper. 'They are gentry,' she reassured him, showing in two well-dressed young gentlemen who were students at Oxford.

'Father Fitzpatrick, we apologize for disturbing you so early in the morning,' explained Frederick Blackwood, as he also introduced his travelling companion, George Boyle. 'Both Reverend Townsend and Dr Donovan told us we should speak to you before we leave Skibbereen later today. We have a great interest in Ireland and are keen to record the effects of this terrible calamity on this good land.'

Father Fitzpatrick sighed, for only a few days ago a wealthy philanthropist – an editor from an American newspaper, Mr Elihu Burrit, who was devoted to helping mankind – had called on him with similar intentions. He had agreed to take Mr Burrit around and had taken him to the soup kitchen and to the hovels and cabins where he ministered to the dying.

Shocked by such scenes, Mr Burrit said he had no language to describe the suffering of the people consigned to this battle-field of life. With disease raging, the priest had worried for the health of the American visitor but admired the man's courage and zeal to help the poor and vulnerable.

He smiled at his two young visitors for he could see they displayed a similar zeal!

'We arrived only yesterday,' Mr Blackwood went on, 'but Reverend Townsend has been most generous with his time. He has shown us around the cottages, the town graveyard, and we have met some of his parishioners. Dr Donovan has also told us of the terrible state of affairs and of the people.'

'Then you will have witnessed terrible things,' replied Father Fitzpatrick, feeling pity for the privileged twenty-year-olds and their innocence in coming to visit a place like Skibbereen.

The pair intended to write an account of their journey to inform family and friends of the distress and suffering in Skib-bereen and took notes as he endeavoured to answer all their questions.

'It is far worse than we ever could have imagined,' admitted Mr Boyle, trying to control his emotions.

'We visited filthy hovels around the town where people lie dying with no food or furniture.' Mr Blackwood's voice broke as he folded his notes away. 'How could we ever believe the terrible conditions that exist here if we had not travelled and seen them with our own eyes?'

'Now, excuse me, please, gentlemen, for I am afraid that I must finish,' Father John said, shaking their hands. 'I am expected soon at St Patrick's. Perhaps we shall meet and talk again later.'

George Boyle informed him that they were planning to leave on the next coach to Dublin.

'Then I wish you both a good journey and safe return to Oxford.' The priest smiled, sensing their reluctance to stay in the midst of so much disease any longer.

By chance, only a few hours later Father Fitzpatrick met the young men again, outside the Becher Arms.

'The coach to Dublin was full,' explained Mr Boyle, 'but we have managed to hire a jaunting car with an extra horse to transport us to Cork.'

'We have ordered some bread from the bakery to be distributed among the people here before we leave, Father,' added Frederick Blackwood as they said goodbye again.

Father Fitzpatrick was heading home when he noticed a huge crowd surging along North Street towards the Becher Arms. What could it be? The noise was deafening. A hundred or more screaming women and children gestured wildly, begging and shouting up to a hotel window above them. Freshly baked loaves of bread were being thrown down from it, cascading into the grasping hands of the crowd below.

Word had spread of the young men's deed and more people joined the fray, gathering outside the hotel as the bread rained down on them like manna from heaven.

Father John grew alarmed as women and small children screamed, fought and scrabbled fiercely over the scraps of bread and loaves that had fallen to the ground. Those who were successful held on tightly to their bounty. His young English friends were well-intentioned, but as the flow of bread from above began to dry up, the cries of the huge crowd intensified.

'Bread! More bread!' they demanded angrily. 'Feed us! More bread for the hungry!'

He watched with dismay as the two students emerged from the hotel in fear. Struggling with their baggage, they had to fight their way through the crush of starving people to get to their waiting jaunting car. The two horses, terrified by the noise of the mob, reared and thrashed as some of the crowd began to run alongside the car, pleading and begging the gentlemen for more.

As the crowd realized their benefactors were well on their way, they dispersed with their precious spoils and the priest returned to his business.

A few weeks later he received a published copy of their journey from Oxford to Skibbereen, with the young Frederick Blackwood promising him that all the proceeds from their work would be donated to Skibbereen.

Chapter 51

THAT MORNING, FANNY WAS STRANGELY QUIET AT BREAKFAST. Despite Henrietta's entreaties, she refused to take even a spoonful of porridge.

'I'm not hungry, Mama,' she declared.

By mid-morning Fanny was burning hot and running a fever. Henrietta tried not to give in to the mounting sense of alarm she felt as she tried to cool her daughter with a flannel cloth soaked in water.

'Sally, you must mind the others while I stay with Fanny,' she told her maid.

Children always get fevers, she tried to reassure herself as she wished that Dan was at home rather than being away at the workhouse or seeing one of his patients.

During the course of the day Fanny slept fitfully and Henrietta was up and down attending to her.

'Mama, my head hurts,' she cried quietly.

As she helped her back into bed, she noticed a reddish rash developing on her child's stomach, which she had itched.

About half an hour later, Sally called to her. Young Daniel was now sick too.

'He has vomited his lunch, ma'am, and says he has a bad headache.'

'Young man, you are going back to bed too,' Henrietta ordered, plumping his pillow as she settled him and brushed back his fair hair.

She made her way into the bedroom next door to check on Fanny, whose condition had deteriorated rapidly. The poor child was shivering, her teeth chattering with rigors. She would barely open her eyes when Henrietta tried to rouse her.

'Sally! Sally!' she shouted in alarm. 'You must go to the dispensary immediately and fetch Dr Dan. Tell him that the children are sick and he must return home.'

Nearly two hours passed before Dan returned. By that point Fanny was in a deep sleep, her skin burning with fever, while young Daniel tossed and turned in his small bed.

Dan examined each child in turn, talking gently to them as Henrietta looked on.

'It is typhus,' he announced.

'Oh, Dan, don't say such a thing!'

'They both have the symptoms,' he admitted dejectedly. 'Half the town is sick with it.'

'Then you must make them better,' she demanded in fear, her hysteria rising.

233

'My dear, the fever will run its course. Unfortunately there is little else I can do except ensure the children are kept comfortable and drink some water.'

'What about all the people who have it? What do you say to them?'

'Many who have the fever are severely malnourished and weak, but our children are strong, young and healthy,' he explained quietly.

'You are a doctor and you will make them better,' she insisted. 'I will not have anything happen to our children, Dan. Do you hear me?'

Henrietta broke down when she saw the powerlessness in her husband's eyes and the pain he felt that the disease was now within their own home.

Harriet too soon fell sick with fever. The Donovan family were now in the grip of typhus, as were so many other families in the town. As death lingered at her own door, courting her beloved children, Henrietta was filled with a mother's fear like that of every poor mother in the town.

Dan too was consumed with worry, but he still had to attend to his professional duties. Henrietta knew that her husband blamed himself for their children being ill. She thanked heaven that Henry, Jerrie, Ellen and twenty-month-old Maggie displayed no signs of the fever yet and insisted that Sally tend to them.

Fanny's small body was now covered with a dark spotty rash and her fair hair clung damply to her head in curls. Her fever refused to break and her breath came raspingly in her small chest, like a butterfly trying to escape from a net.

'She is much worse,' Dan sighed as he took her wrist and felt her pulse.

Henrietta had no words for him, for her heart was heavy with anger. How she wished she had packed up the children and fled this place when she was able to. She had condemned them to this. Why had she not acted to protect them!

Chapter 52

DAN HELD FANNY IN HIS ARMS AS SHE SLEPT. SHE WAS STRUGGLING to breathe, her small life slipping away. His heart was heavy as he looked at his sick daughter, for he knew only too well the path of the disease at this stage, and how little could be done to aid the afflicted.

He slipped her back into the bed gently and dampened her bare skin with a flannel he'd soaked in water, washing her face, brow, neck and chest, and wetting her cracked, dry lips.

'Dada is here with you, Fanny. You must try to get better.'

He wanted her to hear his voice, to cling to it, and to fight to hold on to life.

'Mama and I, and all your brothers and sisters want to see you back up playing and running around, singing your funny little songs for us.'

Fanny exhaled, and fell deeper and deeper into sleep. Dan stretched out in the chair beside the bed and watched over her. She was normally so lively and full of chat. Named after his mother, Frances, his daughter had inherited much of her grandmother's spirit. To see her lie so quietly like this was alarming.

As the week ended, young Daniel seemed a little better.

'Good boy,' Dan praised his son, who, with a little coaxing, took a few spoonfuls of broth. Harriet remained weak and slept a lot, but he was hopeful that she too would recover. Unfortunately Fanny's condition showed little improvement and her breathing was still laboured. His wife was so tired that she felt giddy.

'Henrietta, you must sleep,' he insisted.

'How can I sleep, Dan, when I fear the worst will happen to one of them if I am not there?' she protested.

'I will stay with Fanny, and will wake you if need be.'

All through the night Dan sat with his young daughter as she moaned softly in her sleep. Her skin was clammy to touch and all the colour was gone from her face. Looking at her pretty face and pert little nose, he was overcome with emotion. He held her small fingers to let her know he was there and that she was not alone.

As he watched the sun come up, he breathed a sigh of relief that his little daughter had somehow survived the night and seemed to be sleeping easier.

Hearing Henrietta stir, he went to tell her the news, only to find her slumped by her bedside, saying that the room was spinning all around her.

'Oh, my dear,' he said, rushing to her side and putting her back into bed.

'I must stay with the children,' she protested, trying to get up, but a fresh wave of exhaustion overcame her and she fell back against the pillows.

'Henrietta, you are most unwell. You need to remain here in bed.'

His wife eventually closed her eyes, too weak and sick to move. Her throat and head hurt, she told him, as she was stricken with a sudden bout of coughing.

Dan removed her dressing gown and the warm blanket from the bed, for she was too weak even to move a muscle as she gave in to the waves of fatigue that overpowered her.

Chapter 53

FATHER FITZPATRICK WENT TO CHECK THE ALTAR AND ENSURE that the chalice, chasuble and heavy leather-bound Bible were stored away safely for the night.

He said mass every day and these days he presided over funerals mostly. Often they took the form of a simple blessing and prayers over a shrouded corpse, for most of the deceased were penniless. Earlier that morning he had officiated at the funeral of William Crowley, a young man of means, who had been struck down with famine fever and now lay buried in Abbeystrewry with so many others from the town.

He was about to go into the sacristy when he became aware of a man kneeling in a pew to the side of the altar, his head held in his hands, lost deep in prayer. The man's tall black hat sat beside him on the bench. It was Dan Donovan. The priest hesitated but decided not to disturb him and moved on to the room behind the altar.

The people came to the church every day, heads bent in

prayer, begging the Lord to help them in this time of need. Father Fitzpatrick ensured that the church door was opened early before mass so at least his congregation could come inside to shelter from the harsh elements and could sit quietly or doze in the pews. He had been warned not to leave the church open all day and night for it would soon become home to the poor and needy, and those who walked the roads.

The bishop had reminded him that the church was a sacred place, the house of God meant for prayer and contemplation and the sacraments. However, Father Fitzpatrick suspected that if Jesus Christ still walked the earth, every Christian church in the country would have flung open their doors to the hungry and sick during this time of calamity.

When Father Fitzpatrick returned from ensuring that his vestments were clean and in good condition for Sunday mass, he was surprised to find Dan still kneeling down, his shoulders hunched, his countenance miserable. Filled with concern for his friend, he went over to him.

'Dan, are you all right?'

The doctor looked up with reddened eyes.

'Father John, it's Henrietta and the children. They are sick, so sick with fever.'

'I'm sorry to hear that.'

'I blame myself, Father, for bringing sickness and contagion to our door. No matter what time of day or night I return home, the sick are there awaiting me. I tell them to go to the dispensary, but they all know well where my home is. We have had to harden our hearts to those who come inside our door, but now illness besets my family. I have been so busy with my medical duties that I did not pay enough attention to my own family and wife. What kind of man am I?'

'Dan, I know you to be a good person, who does his best for his fellow man. The town is filled with fever – not just in the poor lanes and cabins, but in the big houses too. Death, unfortunately, does not discriminate the way we do.'

Dan sighed heavily. 'I know you are right, Father John.'

'Will we say a prayer or two together, for Henrietta and the children?' the priest offered.

Dan nodded, his face filled with misery and despair as they began.

> *Pater noster, qui es in caelis,*
> *sanctificetur nomen tuum.*
> *Adveniat regnum tuum.*
> *Fiat voluntas tua,*
> *sicut in caelo, et in terra . . .*

When they had finished, the priest urged his friend to return home.

'The Lord will understand, Dan. Your place is not here in the church with me, but at home with your family, where you are needed. I promise that I will keep them all in my prayers.'

241

Chapter 54

THE MORNING SUN STRETCHED ACROSS THE BED AND ITS SILK counterpane. As Henrietta began to wake, she felt its warming rays on her face. It was as if she had been in a deep sleep for days, but the reality was that she had been ill with fever and had little memory of it, only Dan tending to her, washing her and changing her like a child, and encouraging her to get well again.

She opened her eyes slowly as she became used to the light. She took in their bedroom, and the heavy oak wardrobe and chest of drawers. Dan, his long thin face serious, sat in a chair, watching her, his writing pad on his lap.

'My dearest, how are you feeling?' he asked with concern.

'Strange,' she replied, her mouth and lips parched.

He filled a glass from the water carafe on the small table. He helped to prop her up in the bed and held the vessel to her lips.

'It is good to see you sitting up and able to speak to me,' he said, overcome with relief.

She was filled with a profound alarm.

'The children?' she asked, dreading his response.

'They are well,' he reassured her. 'All of them, I promise you, are well.'

Hours later she woke again, conscious of someone watching her.

Harriet sat in the chair next to her, sipping from a cup of milk.

'Oh, Harriet, you are well again,' she said with relief, and reached for her daughter's hand. 'I was so fearful. So fearful.'

'Dada said I must drink some milk to help get my strength back.'

Harriet gave her mother a smile and licked at the creamy whisker of milk on her top lip like a little kitten.

'Well, your dada is right, and tomorrow I will take a little milk too. Where are Fanny and Daniel?'

'Daniel is downstairs, playing with Henry and Jerrie, and Ellen is next door reading a story to Fanny. She still has to stay in bed,' she said seriously, 'but Mama, I am much better.'

'I can see that, darling girl.'

Later that evening, Henrietta went and sat beside Fanny's bed. Her daughter's face was pinched and gaunt, but her eyes lit up when she saw her mother.

Dan appeared in the doorway and smiled.

'You are the best medicine for her.'

Chapter 55

DAN'S BREATH FORMED ICY CLOUDS IN THE COLD AIR AS HE DROVE out to Lough Hyne. He was thankful for his heavy grey coat and Henrietta's gift of a knitted scarf and gloves to keep him warm, as it was near freezing outside. He was on his way to see Daniel McCarthy's wife after his fellow committee member had stopped him at the end of Monday's meeting and asked him to pay her a visit.

McCarthy's voice had been filled with concern. 'I don't like asking you to come out so far with this bad weather, but she is tired all the time, and her legs and feet these past days are badly swollen.'

Dan knew the worry of having a sick wife and had agreed immediately to see Mary McCarthy.

He turned his horse off the main road and took a small winding track down through the green forest that led down towards Lough Hyne. The ancient saltwater lake was a place of stunning beauty. Shaped like a bowl and surrounded by tall trees and steep rocks, its crystal-clear waters contained fish like you'd never seen before. It was a wondrous place.

The track began to slope suddenly, and grew slippery with ice. Dan soothed his mare as she began to lose her footing on the steep descent. He stopped for a minute, got down from the trap and began to lead the horse instead.

The McCarthys' large house with its magnificent view of the lough came into view, but he also became aware of a group of men working down at the edge of the water. Surely they were not doing works in this appalling weather?

As the ground levelled off, he climbed back into the trap and continued towards the house. He watched in disbelief as men in rags stood partially immersed in the freezing water, lifting heavy stones, shivering and shaking with the wet and cold. They were building some kind of sea wall in the rapids at the edge of the lough.

'What is going on here?' he demanded, slowing the horse and coming to a halt.

'We are part of the public works scheme,' replied the foreman, a tall fellow in a warm, heavily-lined coat. 'The men are building a wall here.'

'The men cannot work in such conditions,' Dan said, getting down. 'You can see how poorly clad they are. I am the Union physician and I am telling you that these men will meet their end if they continue to stand in the water like that. Tell them to come out. This is no work for such men in this weather.'

'If they want to get paid their eight pennies they will work,' the foreman replied stubbornly.

The men could hear the argument but kept their heads low, not wanting to cause a disturbance.

'I order you to take these men from the water immediately,' Dan countered firmly. 'I will check on them on my way home.'

The uselessness of the situation assailed him, as did the absolute folly of the public works. He had protested about them so much already and this despicable display of lunacy would no doubt cost lives.

He turned into the avenue leading to the McCarthys' home. The maid showed him to the drawing room where McCarthy greeted him and offered him a warm drink.

'Did you see the men working down at the lough?' the doctor demanded of his host.

'Aye, they've been working there these past two months on a public works scheme to improve the lough.'

'Are you telling me that these men have been working that long in this terrible snow and the cold?'

'Yes, I protested to the county supervisor, Mr Treacy, and Major Parker,' McCarthy said angrily, 'but to no avail. Wrixon Becher is the landlord here and owns most of the land around the lough. Even this house of mine is part of Lord Carbery's estate, so there is little I can do. Believe me, Dan, it upsets my wife and me to see them treated so.'

'How is your good lady?'

'To be honest, I am worried for her.'

'Let me see her.'

'She is upstairs. I'll ask Peggy to tell her that you are here.'

'I will see her upstairs if I may.'

'Of course.'

Peggy, the maid, led him up to the enormous bedroom, which was lavishly furnished and had a breathtaking view of Lough Hyne.

Mary McCarthy sat at the window in a loose gown.

'Dr Dan, thank you so much for coming all this way to see me. I feel foolish dragging you out here, but my husband insisted.'

Dan could see immediately that Mary's hands were swollen, as were her feet. She had a slightly puffy look about her, which some women develop in late pregnancy. But Mrs McCarthy was not that far along.

'Will you sit on the bed and let me examine you?' he asked politely. 'Is there any sign of cough or fever?'

'Of course. And no, my husband insists that I stay away from town lest I catch something.'

'He is probably right, Mrs McCarthy. You have a lovely comfortable home here, where I believe you should rest.'

'Rest?'

'Your child is not due for another few months, but I think you should do little until it is time for your confinement, which may be a bit sooner than we expected. The baby is growing fast.'

She sighed. 'I feel like I am very big and heavy.'

'I want you to get as much bed rest as you can, here at home. No gallivanting into town or carriage rides,' he said sternly.

'Yes,' she mumbled. 'I will stay home.'

'Good,' he said, satisfied.

He did not want to say anything more at this stage, but he was concerned by her size. He worried that either there was something amiss with the baby or that there was the possibility that she could be carrying twins.

'I will visit you again in two or three weeks.'

'Thank you for coming, Dan. I know how busy you are with

other, far more important things in town,' she said, her blue eyes filled with gratitude.

Back downstairs, over tea, Dr Donovan explained the situation to her worried husband and told him to ensure his wife had bed rest. He was to send for him immediately should there be any sudden change in her condition.

Peggy offered Dan a plate of scones. He was not hungry but asked if she minded if he took one for later.

'Take two,' encouraged McCarthy. 'You won't get the like of them in the workhouse.'

It began to sleet as Dan climbed into the trap and guided the horse slowly back down the avenue towards the lough, where the men were still working in the water. It was unbearable to watch.

One poor fellow looked blue with the cold. Every vein on his skeletal frame stood out. His teeth were chattering and his entire body was overcome with shivers and shakes.

'I told you to stop this work,' Dan bellowed, approaching the foreman. 'I will complain about the inhumane treatment of these men when I get to Skibbereen. Mark my words.'

The foreman shrugged, uncaring.

'These public works schemes are all due to shut down soon,' Dan warned the bully of a man, 'and your role here will be well remembered in the district.'

The fellow grew visibly uncomfortable at Dan's threat.

'Get that man out of the water,' Dan continued. 'I am taking him with me, for he is too unwell to walk home. But first you must pay him for the work he has done.'

Muttering and complaining as the other workers looked on, the foreman reluctantly tossed the man a few pennies.

Dan helped his patient into the trap. He handed him the rough towel he kept for the horse and made him dry himself off with it then wrap the rug around his shivering body.

The climb back towards the main road, away from the lake, was desperately steep and the horse struggled. Dan walked beside her, calmly urging her along the slippery surface. Heaven knew how the weak men managed to make such a trek after working all day down at the lough.

The old man lived alone only a mile away. He neither spoke nor stirred the whole way home. There was not a scrap of clothing left in the small dirty cabin and so Dan left him with the warm rug from the trap, though he knew Henrietta would scold him over it. He also took out the scones and placed them near him.

'Thank you, doctor,' the man said weakly, his eyes welling with tears.

'In a while, when you are warmed through and feel better, eat those, little by little,' Dan ordered gently. 'You must not return to that work. I will call to see you again in a day or two.'

Chapter 56

Oldcourt

SINCE ELLEN CLANCY'S DEATH, MARY KEPT HERSELF TO HERSELF as she worked on the road, and thought only of what she could buy with her hard-earned pennies. She pitied the old widow women who worked alongside her, as they grew weaker and frailer by the day.

One of the men working nearby had collapsed. Denis Leary and a few of the other fellows tried to give him some water and a little bread to revive him, but their efforts came to nothing. The foreman ordered three of the men to lift the man's body carefully on to one of the carts and to cover him with a bit of tarpaulin. He instructed two others to take him into town to the dispensary.

Ten days later the foreman called the workers together to inform them that the public relief works scheme was ending. Come Monday there would be no more work for them.

Mary's heart sank at his words. The implications for her and her family were too terrible to contemplate.

'We are willing to work,' big Tom Corrigan shouted angrily. He was a six-foot-five giant of a man. Although he was lean, he could still swing a pickaxe higher and harder than anyone. 'You cannot just dismiss us when we all have hungry mouths to feed. We have killed ourselves working for you.'

'We need the work,' Denis joined in. 'We have families to feed.'

'Who has decided it?' called another voice from the crowd.

'The British government has issued orders that all public relief schemes across Ireland are to end and I must follow such orders,' the foreman informed them dispassionately.

'Please, sir, let us work,' cried one of the women. 'Our children will starve.'

'I'm sorry to impart such news,' the foreman said, looking embarrassed at the tattered and exhausted motley group of workers before him, 'but this is no decision of mine. I too must follow orders.'

'We are willing to work,' a few shouted. 'Give us work!'

'There is not the money to pay for further works,' the payment clerk interrupted loudly, daring them to challenge him. 'You will receive the wages due to you tomorrow but that is all, for officially this scheme is ended.'

Angry, dissenting voices murmured their disapproval and upset.

'Get back to work,' threatened the foreman, 'if you do not want to be docked a few hours' pay.'

*

As she walked home across the fields, Mary's upset at such bad news gave way to a strange sense of relief that neither she nor John would have to undertake such terrible work on the roads. Far too many lives had already been lost over those paltry few brass coins. Surely there must be some other means and a better way for their family to survive.

Chapter 57

Creagh

WITH THE RELIEF WORKS CLOSED, MARY WORRIED FOR HER FAMILY, for they now had little to eat. Two or three times a week they walked with the children to the small soup kitchen set up only a mile and a half away at the home of Reverend Caulfield, the church rector, and his wife. It made a huge difference to the Sullivans, for the children were far too weak and no longer able for the eight-mile round trip to Skibbereen to take the soup. Flor brought Molly in the rickety cart pulled by Smokey the donkey, as both her legs and feet had become strangely swollen and she could not walk far.

'Little Annie can sit with me,' Molly volunteered. 'Poor Smokey is old like myself and not able for much of a load these days.'

Some days they were fed and others they had to quell their disappointment, when too many families came and the soup ran out.

John took the boys out hunting for any wild thing they might find or catch that could go in their pot. On one occasion he had killed a fat wood pigeon, using a stone in a sling he had fashioned, and she had plucked and cleaned the bird as she would have done one of their old hens.

Each day, they foraged and hunted in the fields. Nearly every bush and hedge was picked clean, and there wasn't a rabbit or hare to be found, or a bird's nest to rob. They collected snails, which she boiled up with some herbs and salt water. Her stomach turned as she swallowed them, but they said nothing to the children who sniffed at them before eating them. All except Annie, who kept her mouth closed stubbornly in refusal.

They dug up roots, which she boiled and mashed, and picked mushrooms and puffballs in the shady woods and young nettles.

'But I want taties to eat,' Annie whined.

'Well, there is not a tatie to be had in the county, so you will have to make do with something else,' she told her firmly. 'Your grandfather Corney used to always say that nature's bounty is there for the like of us.'

Con and Tim had found a hedgehog hidden under a pile of leaves. John cut its throat and covered it in clay before they roasted it over the fire. It was fatty but the meat tasted a bit like rabbit.

In desperation, they also fished in the river for little pinkeens, speckled trout and carp, even though the old heron had long since disappeared. They had little luck. At low tide they searched the rocks and pools for baby crabs, cockles and mussels, limpets and periwinkles, and gathered dulse, kelp and carrageen moss.

Famished, Mary even resorted to digging up earthworms. She watched them wiggle as she washed and cut them, and put them in her pot. She prayed that they were safe to eat.

But still the Sullivans grew hungry . . .

Chapter 58

'AWAY! AWAY!' MARY SHOUTED.

The mangy dog kept watching her as she tried to shoo it away with her broom. She could see it, sense it. A scrawny thing that insisted on hanging around. No doubt the mongrel was hungry, but there was little she could do about it. Every scrapeen of food they had was for them, not some cur of a dog that had appeared out of nowhere.

But it kept showing up. As time went on, Mary hadn't even the strength to chase it away.

The family were growing weaker and weaker by the day. The watery gruel she heated up to feed the children simply passed through them, only filling their small stomachs momentarily.

She kept a careful eye on the dog, making sure it did not come too near the house or the children. She feared it was just biding its time.

*

The following day she spotted the animal further down the field, chewing on something. A bone. She had no idea where it had found it or from where it had dug it up. It turned and growled at her. The pit of her stomach turned in fear.

'Go! Go! Off with ye!' she screamed, but it continued to gnaw at its filthy bone.

There wasn't another creature to be seen – not even a fox, or a rabbit or a hare – and yet this dog was still here . . .

There was nothing to put in the pot. Water, a bare handful of Indian meal, salt, and a few herbs and nettles to cook over the fire. What kind of a meal was that?

Then she saw it. The dog had come nearer to the house than ever before, as bold and brazen as you like.

Suddenly fearful, Mary grabbed the broom to chase it away, but as she did so the animal raised its snout. Growling, it bared its teeth, ready to attack and bite her. As she swung the broom, the beast jumped up and snarled, trying to grab at it with its teeth. She made contact with its head as hard as she could. Again and again, she struck the dog until it was still. Its tongue hung from its mouth in a small pool of blood, its eyes glazed over.

She had killed it. Triumph filled her and a feeling of inexplicable joy took over her.

Close up, it looked to be about two or three years old. Its head and paws were big but its body ill-fed. Still, it was a good size. Mary studied the animal further, wondering where she would bury it or how she would get rid of it before the children and John returned home. She went to lift it and was surprised at how heavy it still was. The weight of a lamb or a piglet . . . And then it came to her . . . She knew what to do.

Mary dragged the animal's lifeless body to the back of the cottage where John often worked, and laid it on a stone slab. She took a sharp knife and quickly began to skin it, removing its short coat deftly. She then opened it up and pulled out its entrails before cutting off its head, for she could not bear to see its sad eyes. She butchered it as she used to prepare their lambs, removing its paws instead of hooves and its long narrow tail.

Meat still sat on its bones. Not a huge amount, but enough. She set about quartering it and then divided it into fleshy segments that she could manage.

The smell of meat cooking filled the air as she stirred the boiling water and added a few herbs to the pot.

The children sat around the turf fire, watching and waiting, and John returned with a bucket of water from the well.

'What is it?' he whispered, coming over to investigate.

'A kid goat I found caught in the thorns out back, half dead,' she lied.

'Whose goat is it?' asked Tim, curious.

'I don't know, but it was lucky for us that I found him before someone else came along.'

Nora said nothing and sat staring into the fire.

The meat was strong . . . and tough. It was much like mutton but they ate it slowly, spoonful by spoonful. Mary dared give only a little mouthful to Annie.

'Only a small bit tonight,' she warned the children. 'For fear the taste of meat in your belly after so long will make you sick.'

'It will not make me sick.' Tim grinned, wanting some more.

'You may have more tomorrow,' she promised him.

As she ate, she tried to push thoughts of the animal out of her head, knowing that the meat of the poor creature would somehow help them to survive.

She cooked up more of the dog meat the next day and roasted one of its legs slowly over the fire.

'Eating dog will do us no harm,' John assured her once she had shared her secret with him. 'A sailor once told me that in some far-off countries in the Orient they eat them all the time.'

'God preserve us!'

'We will do what we have to. Anything to keep us from starving,' he said matter-of-factly. 'If I had seen that dog, Mary, I tell you, I'd have killed him myself.'

She had never expected to become so hard, so strong and determined. She may have a woman's light touch with her needlework, but deep inside Mary knew that if the situation demanded it, she would fight like a wolf to protect those she loved.

Chapter 59

THE LAST OF THE DOG MEAT WAS GONE AND THE CHILDREN GREW
weaker, whining and complaining of pains in their bellies
much of the time. Mary couldn't bear it, so, with an eagle eye,
she searched their cottage for anything left to pawn or sell to
buy meal.

She bundled up the warm patchwork counterpane she had
made for their marriage bed, which left them with only a grey
blanket. She gathered up her only good dress, the pin-tucked
dresses she had made for Nora and Annie, and John's tweed
waistcoat, and folded them up neatly to take into town.

'Near everything we have is gone to that man!' John shouted
angrily as he watched her. 'Hegarty and his like are robbing
the people blind with the hunger and making money.'

Skibbereen was busy, with beggars, hands outstretched looking for food or money. She pushed past them all and joined the
short line outside Hegarty's pawnbrokers. As the young couple

ahead of her moved forward and put down their heavy load on the floor in front of the shop counter, Mary kept her eyes low.

'The chair and footstool were made by a craftsman and are in perfect condition,' the young man began.

Mary could tell Hegarty was intrigued, but he feigned disinterest.

'I have a warehouse of furniture. What am I to do with them?'

'We have to sell them, for we are taking passage to America.'

'Sir, we are not looking for a fortune, but we are here to sell them today,' the young woman insisted.

The proprietor shrugged. 'Perhaps you could try somewhere else?'

'I am selling my bridal dress too. It is made of fine lace and embroidery, and is precious to me,' she continued, the desperation in her voice growing.

Mary remembered how bad she had felt when she brought her own wedding dress to the shop last year.

Hegarty fingered the young woman's garment and carefully examined its pearl buttons and delicate stitching. His wife and daughter were known for their fashion and Mary could see at once that he was tempted by the gown.

'For a young couple going to the New World, I will be generous. What do you say if I give you two guineas for the furniture alongside the dress?'

'It is not enough,' blurted the husband. 'They are worth far more.'

'I will take the dress with me,' the woman added defiantly. 'Sell it when I get there.'

The pawnbroker sighed, exasperated. 'Three pounds and not a farthing more.'

The couple stood still, taking stock of the offer. Mary could see that the young wife was ready to argue with Hegarty, but her husband's fingers caught her wrist, warning her to say no more.

'Thank you, sir. We will accept your offer,' he muttered.

Before Mary could step forward, an old woman with a bundle pushed ahead of her. The woman's grey hair fell lank around her shoulders and her dress was soiled and muddy. Mary caught the stale odour of the woman's body as she reached to untie her parcel of scraps of material.

'It's just rags,' the pawnbroker retorted. 'Rags are no good to me.'

'A few pennies are all I want, sir,' the woman argued loudly. ''Tis all I've left to sell.'

Mr Hegarty cut short her pleas and ordered her from his premises.

'I can't have beggars like her in here. This is a place of business,' he said brusquely, beckoning Mary to come forward.

'Mr Hegarty, I have a few more items that I wish to sell,' Mary said, placing them in front of him. 'I made the counterpane and dresses myself. It is good work, for I am a seamstress.'

As the pawnbroker thumbed the coloured patchwork cover, she could sense his greedy brain working and assessing what price the items might fetch. They finally settled on only four shillings and Mary hid her disappointment as she bid him good day. It was little enough to buy what she needed.

As was her habit, Mary paused outside Honora Barry's dressmaking shop. Honora was inside and so Mary knocked on the glass, filled with a wild hope that her former employer might have some mending work for her. Miss Barry let her in and enquired politely how she and her family were faring.

'Things have been very hard,' Mary admitted. 'John took ill and could not work, so I had to work breaking stones on the road these past weeks.'

'My poor dear child,' she sympathized. 'Look at your hands and fingers!'

'Just a few bruises and scratches,' Mary said defensively. 'I can still sew.'

Their conversation was interrupted by the arrival of a customer at the door to collect an item. Honora disappeared into the back of the shop for a minute and returned with a white garment, which she rolled up carefully and wrapped in paper as the tearful older woman paid her.

'Thank you, Miss Barry, for your kindness to us in our time of trouble,' the woman said, dabbing her eyes with a handkerchief.

'I'm sorry for your loss,' the dressmaker said, walking her to the door.

'Mrs Callaghan's daughter died two days ago,' she explained to Mary once her customer had left.

She gestured to a roll of creamy white material on the far side of the room.

'All people want me to make these days are shrouds to bury their dead in. For God help us, there are no coffins. This is what keeps me busy. Have you ever made one of them, Mary?'

'No.' She shook her head. 'Never.'

'I didn't ever think that I'd see the day I'd be taking on such work either,' the dressmaker admitted ruefully, 'but it is what is necessary. I promise that they are easy enough to make. That is, if you are interested in helping me?'

Eager for work, Mary agreed without hesitation.

'They are a simple pattern,' she explained, 'and people will pay promptly for them.'

Mary studied the shroud that the dressmaker had been stitching when she came in.

'I can teach you how to make one,' Honora offered, leading her to the workroom.

The dressmaker showed her quickly how to cut out the pattern, wasting as little material as possible, and how to shape it and sew the simple seams.

'No one is going to examine it stitch by stitch,' Honora reminded her, 'but people do expect good work for their dear departed . . . despite the circumstances of their burial.'

It was certainly not the type of work Mary had expected to be offered, but work was work. She promised to return next week with the five shrouds they had agreed upon.

'Do you have a good supply of thread and needles?' the dressmaker asked as she carefully measured out and parcelled up the lengths of material that Mary would need.

Mary blushed. How could she admit that she had come here looking for work and yet had barely a spool of thread at home! The other woman lowered her eyes discreetly and generously added a packet of needles and a few spools of thread to one of the packages.

'If you want, I could let you have an advance of six pennies now and the rest when you are finished,' she offered.

Mary was overcome with gratitude for the kindness of her old employer, who was proving herself a true friend.

'But you must promise to have the shrouds back to me by Tuesday,' she urged. 'And they must be spotlessly clean, with no smudges of turf or dirt on them.'

Mary agreed without question and watched as Honora took some coins from the small drawer and counted them into her hand. It was little enough but it would buy a small bag of oats to take home with her.

'Take this too, for it doesn't agree with me,' insisted the kindly woman, wrapping up a half loaf of rye bread for her.

Mary carried the parcels through the town, deciding to stop at Kathleen's as she hadn't seen her sister for weeks. Sarah and Lizzie were both sick, and her sister looked more tired and thinner than she had ever seen her before.

'We are lucky we can take the soup every day,' she sighed, 'but it runs through me.'

Mary looked around the cottage. The straw underfoot was dirty and foul and in need of changing. The whole place could have done with being swept out and washed down.

'I haven't the energy for cleaning it,' admitted Kathleen, as if reading her sister's mind.

Mary told her about getting work making the shrouds.

'God between us and all harm, but I suppose someone has to do it!'

'I'm happy to have work,' she said defensively.

'If only my Joseph could find some kind of job now the roadworks have closed down,' Kathleen complained, 'we wouldn't always be in the terrible state that we are in.'

Walking home, Mary couldn't wait to tell John the good news of her new job, even if it was as a shroud-maker to the dead.

Chapter 60

Skibbereen

DAN STOOD IN THE GROUNDS OF ABBEYSTREWRY GRAVEYARD. IT was a beautiful spot, situated on the Ballydehob side of town on a sloping hill with some shady trees, and overlooked the broad expanse of the river. However, the peace and beauty of the burial place was now destroyed by the large, deep trench that had been dug in the graveyard to receive the large numbers of bodies of those who had died overnight or during the day. With such large numbers of decaying corpses being brought to the graveyard, immediate interment was imperative.

Many of those poor souls who had died in the workhouse during the night and in the early morning would be buried here in the deep pit – the mass grave that had been dug to contain them. It was his duty to ensure that the bodies were disposed of as quickly and safely as possible, and to ensure that once one section of the pit was full, it would be covered with lime and filled in with earth as a new pit was dug and prepared to receive more bodies. There was no time for gravestones or crosses to mark the last resting place of so many.

He watched as the cart arrived and the men made ready the hinged coffin they used to place the remains of the deceased, one at a time, into the burial pit. Dinny Burke and his helper approached the grave and released the coffin base, so that the body of a skeletal middle-aged woman fell on to the decaying corpses below.

No prayers or blessings were uttered for the deceased. Father John and his curate tried to attend some days but often, like himself, they were too busy administering to the sick to come and say a few words of prayer over those who had left this world.

The men returned to refill the coffin and repeated their actions.

The stench from the pit was overpowering. The gravediggers most certainly needed to close this section once these new bodies had filled it. Dan stared down at the young men and women who should have had their lives ahead of them, the innocent children and babies who deserved better than this undignified end in a crowded, unmarked grave. How much longer could this appalling situation continue without some proper form of rescue for the people? Dan sometimes felt like a moth batting against a lantern as he tried to attract attention and aid for his patients and the hungry.

As he walked over to the gravediggers to tell them they must close this pit and begin a new one, a woman arrived at the site. Dressed in nothing but rags, she staggered over to him, her legs bloated with oedema. She was almost too weak to walk but she demanded to know where they were interring her husband, who had been on the cart.

267

'Where is my Paddy?' she wailed. 'I'll be in the grave with him before too long.'

The man's body was gone from the cart and had been deposited already. For a moment, Dan thought the poor, crazed woman was going to jump into the pit herself to join him.

'Your husband is at peace,' he said, taking her arm gently, 'but you are most unwell and need to be cared for.'

Tears ran down the woman's dirt-creased face.

'Your husband would not want you left here like this. I am a doctor in the Skibbereen Union where I promise you will be cared for.'

'I'll not go to the workhouse,' she spat stubbornly. 'I'll stay here close to him.'

'The men will lock the graveyard soon,' he cautioned. 'So it's far better that you come with me to the Union where you will have, at the least, some nourishment and a place to lie down.'

The woman swayed on her feet, near to collapse. She was starved but when he observed her he could detect no sign of fever. With the help of Dinny, Dan managed to get her to his carriage where she lay down, exhausted. She closed her eyes and said nothing more as Dan drove towards the workhouse and down the avenue leading up to it, passing all those waiting outside in the desperate hope of admission.

'Dr Donovan, you know better than anyone else that we are full,' the newly appointed matron protested sternly as Dan pleaded for the woman to be admitted to the women's section.

'I could not leave this poor woman lying near her husband's grave, waiting to be thrown into it,' he petitioned her.

The matron's cheeks flushed and she acceded reluctantly to his request.

He was all too aware that Skibbereen Union Workhouse was overcrowded, but he was very hopeful of acquiring a warehouse down by the quay that could be used soon as an auxiliary workhouse to accommodate more women during this crisis.

As he turned the carriage for home, Dan felt himself grow weak. He found himself having to stop for a few minutes to get his breath back. He checked his pulse and temperature, aware of the worsening of the headache he had felt since earlier that morning. He had stayed at the dispensary for three hours, but in the end had to refuse to see patients, and made the excuse that he was urgently needed somewhere else.

By the time he arrived at the house on New Street he felt wretched and wanted nothing more than to crawl into bed. His body was already feverish as he made his way upstairs, undressed and lay down on the cool sheets.

As Henrietta followed him, she was unable to hide her concern.

'What is it, Dan?'

'You must fetch Patrick Dore,' he told her. 'Tell him I have the fever . . .'

Chapter 61

HENRIETTA COULD NOT BEAR TO SEE DAN SICK. WATCHING HIM arrive home in a state of near collapse, she had been overwhelmed by fear and panic but composed herself. She knew that her husband would not wish for her to be in such a state. She had asked Sally calmly to go to North Street to fetch his friend and colleague Patrick Dore.

Thoughts crowded her mind as she considered the many diseased hovels her husband attended, as well as the workhouse and graveyards, but she reminded herself that in the years since they had first met, Dan Donovan had never been sick a day or complained even of being unwell or in pain. He was a strong man and, as he said himself often enough, had the constitution of a horse.

She dispatched the children to play in the back garden and warned them to be quiet as their father was not feeling well.

Meanwhile, Dr Patrick Dore arrived promptly and went

upstairs to examine Dan. His face was serious when he told her that Dan had contracted typhus fever, was very poorly and would need good care and nursing.

'I have already had typhus,' Henrietta informed him as she promised to follow all his instructions with regard to Dan's medical care.

'I will call to see him tomorrow,' the doctor promised, 'but if there is any change for the worse during the night, please send for me.'

Henrietta slept in the chair at Dan's bedside as his fever raged. A reddish macular rash covered his body and his head was splitting with the pain, causing him to thrash around and moan. She did everything in her power to cool him down with cold compresses and keep him comfortable.

The following day he would not even open his eyes and lay curled in their bed like a small child.

When he made his promised visit, Dr Dore reassured her that even though Dan appeared seriously ill, it was the normal progression of the disease.

'I may consider bleeding him in the next day or two, if it is needed,' he told her. 'But, knowing Dan, I am hopeful that he has the strength to fight this disease.'

Patrick Dore was a fine physician and he and the town's other doctors, Cornelius O'Driscoll and Thomas Tisdall, all assisted by seeing patients at the dispensary, while Patrick temporarily took over Dan's workhouse duties.

Father John was the only visitor Henrietta permitted to see Dan, and both of them prayed for his recovery. The priest told her that their friend Tim McCarthy Downing was, like Dan, very ill. Poor Mary Hegarty from the hotel was bereft as her daughter had died a few days ago. So too had Major Parker.

The next week and a half passed in a blur, and the children remained wide-eyed and fearful for their father's health. The older boys and Ellen hovered at the bedroom door, terrified whenever Dr Dore called to see their father.

'What will happen if Father dies?' Jerrie asked with worry.

'I will not have you talk like this,' Henrietta said, hugging him. 'Your father is a man of good health and his body will fight this illness.'

Her reassurances were as much for her own benefit as for her son's and she prayed with all her might for Dan to recover.

One evening, when Henrietta had dozed off in the bedside chair, Dan stirred and sat up. To her amazement, almost in a whisper, he asked her for a sip of water before slumping back on to the pillows and falling into an exhausted sleep again. The following afternoon he asked for fresh sheets on the bed and the morning after that, to her relief, Dan took not only more water but also three small spoons of milky porridge.

Each day, Henrietta watched as her husband, little by little, regained his strength. Ellen would come in to sit and read a story to him that she had written, while young Daniel and Harriet showed him drawings they had made for him: Dan in his tall hat and long coat in a sunny garden, and a family portrait of Dan and Henrietta surrounded by all seven of their children.

'What wonderful artists you are!' he encouraged them. 'I

will treasure them always.' Henrietta's heart soared to see Dan gladdened by the short visits of his children.

In no time Dan began to demand that he be allowed to dress and return to work.

'You have been very sick, Dan,' Henrietta pleaded with him. 'Dr Dore says that you must have a period of convalescence.'

'Henrietta, I have had more than enough of lying down and convalescing,' he complained, exasperated. 'It is high time for me to return to work and tend to my patients.'

Two days later she watched as her husband, in his usual long frock coat and black hat, set off for the dispensary, medical bag in hand and a zealous glint in his eyes.

Chapter 62

EVERY WEEK MARY WALKED TO TOWN WITH HER WORK STRAPPED to her back.

'Let me come with you,' Con begged and pleaded with her, but she refused. Truth to tell, she did not want her son to see the hollow-faced hungry and sick who besieged the town.

The dressmaker inspected each shroud as if it were a pretty dress or fine coat for a customer, meticulously checking the seams and stitching. Happy with Mary's work, she went to the drawer in the back room and, taking out some money, counted the coins for her.

'Would you be able to make another eight shrouds for me for next week?' she asked.

Mary nodded, delighted to have more work.

'Then I will measure out the yards of linen for you.'

'If it is all right with you, Miss Barry, I will return in a while and collect it on my way home?'

'Aye, it's better not to be traipsing it around,' agreed the dressmaker. 'I'll have it ready for you.'

Mary made her way to the soup kitchen, took the broth and was grateful, for it sustained her after her long walk. Then she went to see her sister.

Bridgetown had become a place of sickness and reeked with the smell of human ordure. Brazen rats scurried along the filthy muddy lanes, under the eaves of the thatched roofs and across the filthy floors as there was not a dog nor cat left to hunt them.

'The Murphys and Molloys should have kept their cats,' complained Kathleen, 'for now we are plagued night and day by those stinking, filthy vermin. I heard that one or two have trapped and boiled them, but they can make you fierce sick. That is one thing I would never do.'

Mary's stomach heaved at the thought of it.

The cottage was even dirtier than on her previous visit. The straw had not been replaced and the children were unwashed. Her once pretty sister's face was haggard and grey, her body run to bones, just like her own. Four-year-old Lizzie was weak and listless, her small stomach swollen like a ball. She lay on her sister's lap as pale as a ghost.

'She will not take even a spoon of water and gruel for me,' fretted Kathleen.

Mary gave her sister two of her precious pennies to buy cow's milk for Lizzie in the hope that that would help.

'I shouldn't take it off you, but the milk might give her new strength,' thanked Kathleen. 'We have nothing since the works closed. Every day Joe disappears down to the river for hours, sitting on the bank fishing.'

'Maybe he'll have luck,' Mary encouraged.

'Joe's no fisherman and the river has been near fished out,' her sister said bitterly.

'Are you all right, Kathleen?' Mary asked, suddenly concerned for her.

'I'm tired, Mary. More tired than I have ever been in my life,' she admitted quietly. 'I don't know what will become of us.'

Mary had never seen her sister like this. Kathleen had always been the headstrong, carefree older sister who had gone against her parents' wishes to marry handsome Joseph Casey. She usually shrugged and laughed off all her cares and woes, but now she seemed defeated, done in by her circumstances.

'I'm glad that Mother and Father did not live to see these terrible times,' Kathleen continued despairingly, 'and what has befallen us and our children. And poor James and Denis, and their families at home in Goleen. 'Tis meant to be fierce bad there. I thank God that I have you, my sister.'

'We have each other,' Mary reassured her as she hugged Kathleen goodbye, promising to see her again the following week.

Mary felt like crying as she handed over the meagre pennies she earned to buy some oats, flour and tea in Healy's. The prices had all gone up. As she turned for home, she called in to Honora's shop to collect the material.

'I have already sold two of the shrouds so I have added more material for you to make an extra two for me if you can,' Honora declared.

Mary accepted, but was torn between delight at the fact she would earn more pennies and guilt that so many shrouds were needed.

Her load of material was extra heavy as Mary walked the road to Creagh, and every time she heard a cart, or a pony and trap near her, she looked up hopefully. But no luck. People passed her by and then it began to rain. She wrapped her shawl around her precious bundle of linen and provisions, trying to ignore the pain in her back, shoulders and arms, and kept going.

She was about two miles from home when she spotted Con sheltering under a tree, waiting for her.

'Da sent me to help you.' He grinned and took the wrapped oats and flour from her arms.

With her load lightened, she was glad of her eldest boy's company.

'I worry for your aunt and her family living in Bridgetown,' she confided in him as they walked home, telling him how terrible things were for the people in the town.

She cooked a large pot of meal that evening. When they had finished eating, she sent John over the fields to Flor and Molly's with a bowl of it along with a screw of tea. The old couple barely stirred from their cottage these days. The Sullivans had little enough to share, but she and John did their best to visit the pair, for they were family.

Chapter 63

Creagh

SILENCE . . . EVERYTHING WAS STILL AND HUSHED, FOR THERE was not a bird in the sky or even a field mouse to be seen. Nests, burrows and lairs had all been pulled apart and searched, robbed in desperation. No spring bird song, mating calls or flurries disturbed this strange empty peace.

The fields about the Sullivans' cottage were quiet too, lying fallow and unplanted. The children said and did little, for the hunger had weakened them so much. They did not have the energy for playing and chasing about the place. It grieved Mary to see them so.

The neighbours kept to themselves, all fearful of sickness and disease. Even Nell Flynn had stopped begging from her, for she knew that Mary had nothing to give her.

Brigid and her family struggled and whenever the women met, they hugged, for there were no words to describe the great sympathy they had for one another, nervously asking, 'Are the children well?'

Truth to tell, all Mary cared for was John and Con, Nora, Tim and Annie. Her husband and family were the world to her. She called in to see Flor and Molly regularly, and it saddened her greatly to watch as her two elderly relatives grew weaker by the day. Their flesh had already melted from their bones and Molly's skin hung loosely from her poor skeletal frame.

'I am too tired for it all,' admitted Flor. 'Molly and I are not able for going to the soup kitchen or to hunt for food any more. We are content to rest easy here.'

Every few days, she and John brought them a little gruel, some oatcakes or a cup of nettle broth. What little they had, they tried to share.

'I don't know how much longer they can manage,' John said, worried. 'We cannot starve ourselves for them.'

'We may be family but they don't expect it of us,' she reassured him.

When she brought them a few spoonfuls of warm, watered-down meal the following morning, she broached the subject of the workhouse.

'Mary, girl, the workhouse is not for us,' Flor said, shaking his head.

'Flor and I would be in different parts,' Molly protested. 'We have never been parted since the day we married and will stay together for the rest of our days.'

Mary understood. They were proud people, only expressing the same love that she and John shared.

Less than a week later, John called up to them with some turnip, but Flor told him not to cross the door or come inside.

279

'Molly's sick,' he reported to Mary when he arrived home, 'so I left the bowl of food at the door and fetched them some water.'

Over the next few days, Mary and John continued to call up to the cottage, bringing any food they could manage to spare and re-filling the large water jug that was left at the door. Flor had also fallen sick and they could hear him coughing as he begged them to stay away for fear of spreading the fever.

Mary placed the small pot of meal at the door, knocking to let them know that she was outside.

Flor called out from inside to thank her, but his voice had grown weak.

'Mary, promise me that you will bury us together.'

Alarmed, she gave him her word but asked him to let her in to assist them.

'Molly is asleep,' he said quietly.

Mary sobbed as she walked home, deeply upset by the suffering and hardship the old people endured, locked away in their cottage with not a child nor grandchild to help or comfort them.

The following day, on her return, the food and water jug lay untouched, and there was not even a whisper of smoke from the chimney. She called their names again and again, and knocked and rapped on their door, but Flor and Molly were silent.

She rushed home to John.

*

The couple had died as they lived, asleep together in their pallet bed. Peaceful, eyes closed, tucked in together.

Mary blessed herself.

'What will we do?'

'I'll bury them in the same graveyard as my father,' John said resolutely, 'where the Sullivans are buried. It's the least they deserve.'

There was not a penny for a coffin but John knew his duty. He harnessed their old donkey to the turf cart and, having wrapped his uncle and aunt gently in their blankets, placed them in it.

'I will ride to Creagh with them and find the gravedigger there,' he sighed. 'You stay here with the children.'

The neighbours came out and stood at their doors, blessing themselves as the cart passed. The children were all upset at the loss of their old grand-uncle Flor and kind grand-aunt Molly, who used to make them scones and cook up the best pot of rabbit stew they had ever eaten. Molly, with her endless patience, sitting with a glint in her eye by the fireside, telling them stories of the *sidhe*, and their old uncle Flor, who could not only play the tin whistle but was also blessed with a fine singing voice, often singing as he worked or walked in the fields.

It was late when John got home.

'It's done and they are buried together,' he told her.

'In a pit?' she asked, worried.

'No, thank heaven. The gravedigger laid them together in a shallow grave. The poor donkey was barely up to it, but he got them to Creagh at least.'

They watched the clouds scud across the yellow moon.

'They always loved each other dearly,' John said after a while.

'I know,' she said, reaching for him. 'Like I love you.'

He kissed her softly and she kissed him back, for life and love were more precious than all the gold in the world, once she and John had each other.

Chapter 64

MARY AND JOHN WERE WOKEN IN THE MIDDLE OF THE NIGHT BY the loud braying of Smokey the donkey. The poor animal sounded very distressed. Alarmed, John jumped out of bed immediately.

'What is wrong with the creature?' Mary fretted, also getting up as her husband pulled on his trousers and jacket.

'He's old and half lame but he seemed fine when I left him. Unless a pack of dogs has found him,' he said, rushing out of the cottage in the darkness.

Con and Nora had both been disturbed by the commotion and were stirring. Mary soothed them gently and told them to stay in bed.

'I'm running out to see if your father needs help,' she explained.

She didn't want him to confront a pack of hungry dogs on his own and so, pulling on her shawl, grabbed a blackthorn stick from by the door before running blindly across the field.

The noise from the old donkey had stopped but, in the silence, Mary could hear shouting.

Wary, she kept a firm grip on her stick. The darkness was beginning to lift and ahead of her she could make out John with three other figures. Relief washed over her that there was no sign of any dogs.

As she neared the group, she recognized Nell and Tom Flynn, and their older boy, Paddy. What were they doing out here at this hour? John was shouting at them angrily, and there was some kind of argument going on.

Then she saw it. The donkey lay dead on the ground, blood seeping from where its neck had been sliced open by Tom, who still held the bloodied axe in his hand.

'Why did you kill him?' she cried, rushing over. 'He was Flor and Molly's animal.'

'They are both in their grave and have no need of him now,' Nell said boldly, 'while others do!'

'Flor Sullivan was my uncle and that animal was his property, Nell,' John said through clenched teeth. 'You and your family had no right to lay a hand on him!'

'There's good eating in a donkey,' snivelled Nell.

'How do you think we felt, watching that yoke wandering the fields and us starving with hunger pains in our stomach?' Tom defended himself. 'I have to think of my wife and the boys.'

'Flor and Molly loved that animal,' Mary countered. 'He used it to take his cart to the bog and the cove. You know well that he let most of us borrow it when we needed to. If he had wanted to kill it for food, he would have done so.'

'He was a fool, then,' Nell muttered sarcastically. 'He should have done it and saved himself and Molly!'

Mary was tempted to raise her stick and belt her neighbour with it but John, as if reading her mind, stayed her arm.

'You have done something you had no right to do,' he said coldly. 'Stealing an animal is a crime.'

Mary saw a dart of fear flash between Nell and her husband.

'They meant no harm to you, Mr Sullivan,' Paddy piped up, shamefaced. 'They thought that old Smokey was there for the taking.'

'Sure, what difference does an old donkey make to anyone?'

'The difference was that he was ours.'

'The beast is dead,' argued Tom. 'There is no bringing him back. We'll skin him and butcher him and share him with you. There is not a lot of meat on him, but enough for two families.'

Mary's stomach turned at the mere thought of it as she remembered Uncle Flor giving the children rides on the back of the gentle animal.

John considered Tom's proposition. He was torn between anger and fury at his neighbours for what they had done, and a grudging acceptance of the situation.

'Mary, you go home and I will return later,' he decided. 'Not a word of this to the children.'

Mary nodded, relieved to escape Nell's smug glances.

John returned as the sun rose, and explained to the children that the old donkey had died.

Mary cooked the meat slowly in the pot. It was lean but

stringy, and had a sweetish taste when mixed with wild garlic and the last few wizened turnips. She would make soups and stews from it and use a little grain to eke out every bit of it. However she might regret the beast's death, she knew that it would give them renewed strength and nourishment.

The following day she and John went to check on Flor's cottage. To their dismay they found that there was nothing left in it. Even the old couple's bolster and pallet bed, few pots, cups, jug and Flor's tin whistle had disappeared. Mary noticed that Molly's shawl, which she kept on a hook on the back of the door, had vanished too. Her heart broke as she realized how much she would miss her relative.

'The turf pile, and Flor's spade and few tools are all robbed,' John declared in fury as they looked around them. 'This is the Flynns' business. Nell and Tom have been here. They have always been thieves, with no regard for their neighbours.'

'How could they do such a thing when poor Flor and Molly are barely cold in the grave?' Mary cried in despair.

'I am going over there to tell Tom Flynn what I—'

'Shush,' she said, grabbing hold of him. 'We want no more fighting with the likes of them. They are not worth it.'

'I'll not let them away with it,' he said, enraged, as he pulled away from her.

'No, John, you must promise me not to go near them,' she begged, standing in front of him. 'Flor is at peace now. He wouldn't want you to get in a fight with Tom.'

'He never trusted him.'

'No one trusts them any more. The hunger has changed them, made them worse.'

'They were always like that.'

Somehow, she managed to persuade him to return home with her, and he agreed reluctantly not to set foot near Tom, or his wife or children.

Nell fell sick with the fever first, then their youngest boy got it and then Paddy. There was no donkey and cart to take them to the workhouse fever shed, just Tom Flynn and his middle son to push them in a small handcart on the long road to town.

Chapter 65

Skibbereen
April 1847

'THE POOR MAN,' HENRIETTA HAD SIGHED WHEN DAN TOLD HER that his friend Reverend Robert Traill of Schull had contracted typhus. Mindful of the terrible effects of the illness, she had prayed for his recovery.

Two days later, as they sat in the drawing room, Dan broke the news gently.

'I'm afraid, my dear, that Reverend Traill has unfortunately died.'

'It's so desperately unfair, Dan,' she said, unable to hide her anger. 'He was such a devoted minister, and he and his wife, Anne, worked tirelessly, feeding hundreds of people in Schull every day. Now, because of his good works and charity, he has been taken.'

'Fair doesn't come into it, my dear! Robert Traill was a dedicated church man with a fine mind, who deserved a better end.'

288

'I must write to Anne to express my sympathy,' Henrietta said, thinking of the poor widow and her children, now left to cope alone.

'I see here that the government has finally opened a soup kitchen,' Henrietta observed as she read aloud from the newspaper article describing the official opening of the government's first large soup kitchen in Dublin, at the esplanade near Phoenix Park, beside Dublin's Royal Barracks. 'At last, they and the Lord Lieutenant are doing something to address the situation.'

'About time too,' Dan said caustically.

'It was a grand affair, by all accounts, with his Royal Highness Prince George of Cambridge, Lord Bessborough, the Lord Lieutenant and the Lord Mayor of Dublin all in attendance for the gala launch. It was quite a social occasion for Dublin's fashionable young women and gentry. Apparently, Dublin society paid five shillings each to watch the paupers feed, and there is also to be a Government Fever Ball later this month.'

'My dear, opening a soup kitchen for the poor is certainly not what I consider a social occasion, and how rude to treat the hungry as if they were animals from Dublin Zoo!'

Henrietta smiled wryly and carried on, for she could see he was curious.

'A renowned French chef from London's Reform Club, a Mr Alexis Soyer, has developed the nutritious soup recipe himself, and it says that he can make up to one hundred gallons of soup for less than a pound. The soup kitchen has a three-hundred-gallon soup boiler and an oven that can bake one hundredweight of bread at a time.'

'That is bigger than our boilers!' remarked Dan rather enviously. 'But I know well that to make that quantity of soup for less than a pound is near impossible.'

'And more soup kitchens are set to open throughout the country,' Henrietta continued as she passed him the newspaper.

'The more the better,' he agreed, re-reading the article avidly and scratching out notes in the small leather notebook he always carried.

Dan pored over Soyer's recipe assiduously.

'If this is made in the quantities Mr Soyer suggests, it would have little nutritional value,' he insisted, and was delighted when, not long after, an article in *The Lancet* concurred with his findings, declaring Soyer's soup 'quackery'.

Dan's sentiments were further vindicated when Sir Henry Marsh, the Queen's own physician, came out and declared that the soup would pass through the human system too quickly to assuage hunger and nourish the body.

Chapter 66

A STRANGE STILLNESS HAD DESCENDED ON THE TOWN OF SKIB-
bereen. The sick and starved sat listlessly on the ground and in
doorways, the streets otherwise quiet.

Honora Barry barely spoke to Mary when she delivered her
work. The dressmaker looked ill, with a sickly yellow pallor to
her skin.

'I should have moved away, Mary, while I could,' she pronounced as she paid her. 'Death stalks this town, and no lock
or key can stop him from entering every door.'

Mary felt a fear rise in her.

'Don't dawdle here,' Miss Barry warned, as she gave her the
lengths of calico and linen she needed. 'Away home to your family.'

Mary had intended to take the soup but, seeing so many in
such a bad state, decided to ignore her hunger pains. Instead,
she made her purchases quickly and decided to call briefly to
her sister before returning home.

*

Her nose wrinkled at the putrid odours that dominated the lanes of Bridgetown. As she neared Kathleen's cottage, she was surprised to see little Sarah and Jude, both sitting on the step.

'Is your mammy gone out?'

'She's inside,' Sarah replied quietly, her head down, barely looking at her aunt.

'She's as cold as stone,' sniffed Jude.

Alarmed that Kathleen had fallen ill, Mary pushed in the door. The room was gloomy and she wondered how Kathleen could be so foolish as to let the turf fire go out. In the poor light, she could make out the form of her sister, lying curled up on the settle bed.

'Kathleen, are you sick?' she asked, trying to keep the fear from her voice.

Kathleen said nothing. Perhaps she was asleep or too ill to talk.

A noise reached Mary's ears and she saw some movement under her sister's filthy blanket.

'Kathleen.'

She bent forward to rouse her, but was greeted with a flash of squirming and screeching. With horror, she saw the eyes and hunched backs and tails of three – no, four – rats that ran over her sister's body, their sharp teeth busy gnawing at her flesh.

'Get off!' she screamed in the near darkness. 'Get out of it!'

Grabbing the nearby broom, she frantically beat the teeming rats away from her sister.

'Get off her!' she cried over and over, belting and chasing them as they scurried and jumped all around her.

'Kitty!' she yelled, agonized. 'For God's sake, Kitty, wake up!'

But Kathleen did not stir or move.

'Wake up!' she sobbed again, stretching out her hand to touch her sister, whose skin was ice cold.

She levelled one last whack at a furtive rat that had burrowed under her sister's skirt. As she gently turned Kathleen over, she discovered little Lizzie, curled up and hidden protectively in her mother's arms. Both dead . . . Both gone from the world.

Shock overcame her as she took in the damaged face and left eye of her beautiful sister, and the myriad bites that covered her neck, torso and left arm.

Bile cascaded from her mouth as she retched on to the earth floor again and again, despite her empty stomach. The only mercy was that Kathleen had been dead when the rats had attacked her.

Wiping her mouth with her handkerchief, she stood, shocked and shaking, as she considered what to do. As she battled to regain her composure, she pushed out the door to the waiting children.

'Is Mammy really sick, Auntie Mary?'

She nodded, not trusting herself to speak for a minute.

'Your mammy is gone to heaven,' she said eventually, hunkering down beside them, 'along with little Lizzie.'

'They've been sick these past few days.' Sarah sobbed quietly. 'Mam told us yesterday that we were to stay outside so we wouldn't get sick too.'

'Your mammy loves you both very much and always wanted the best for you,' she explained. 'She is at peace now.'

The children looked miserable, dirty and half-starved. And now they were motherless.

'Where is your da?'

'He never came home these past five days,' whispered Sarah.

'Mam was fierce worried for him. She searched the town and kept asking for him, but no one has seen him.'

'Maybe Da went looking for work,' argued Jude defensively.

'I must go to the dispensary straight away,' Mary said gently, 'and tell them about your mam and sister's deaths.'

Sarah's scrawny body was racked with crying and Mary took her niece protectively in her arms.

'Hush, pet . . . Hush,' she soothed, realizing that the children were in no state to be left alone. 'We'll go together.'

Mary went as fast as she could to the dispensary, where a kind man dutifully took down Kathleen and Lizzie's names and their address, and details of how they had been sick with fever.

'The cart will collect them in an hour or two,' he told her. 'There are a few stops to be made in Bridgetown before they go to Abbeystrewry for burial.'

'It is better you two stay outside,' she told her niece and nephew on their return to the cottage, for she did not want them to see their mother the way she was.

'That's what Mammy told us to do,' acknowledged Jude, wiping his tears with his raggedy sleeve as he sat back down on the stone step.

Mary swept the room noisily to rid it of any bold vermin that might have returned in her absence, before taking some linen from her pack. Carefully, she wrapped a length of it around Kathleen and Lizzie's bodies, before taking her needle and thread to stitch the shroud, so that they would be buried together.

Finding a little turf, she blew the ashes in the grate and relit

294

the fire. She set the pot to boil before bringing the children inside. She would make a little gruel for them with some of her oats.

'What will happen to us, Auntie Mary?' asked Sarah nervously.

'Will we have to go back to the workhouse again?'

'Jude, what do you mean?' Mary countered.

'Mammy took us there on Sunday to look for my da,' Sarah explained. 'She told them that she and Lizzie were both sick, but they said that the workhouse was full.'

'Mam got angry with them, told them that our da helped build the workhouse, and said they must have space for us,' Jude continued.

'They could see Mam was sick,' Sarah finished bitterly, 'but they told her to go home.'

'There will be no workhouse,' promised Mary.

She made up her mind there and then that somehow she would take on minding her niece and young nephew. It was what Kathleen would have wanted – for her children to be raised with their own.

It was midday by the time the death cart came to collect the bodies. Two men with cloths wrapped around their noses and mouths lifted Kathleen and Lizzie with little gentleness on to the mounting pile. A few neighbours looked on from their doorways and Mary told them that she was taking the children with her, in case Joe reappeared, looking for them.

Along with a few other Bridgetown residents, Mary and the children followed the cart slowly across the river to the nearby graveyard where the large pit lay open to receive the dead. It was hard to believe that it was where her beloved sister would be laid to rest – a crowded grave with other poor souls from the town. Kathleen, with her green eyes that would crinkle with laughter, her red-gold hair and a smile that could charm the hardest heart, buried like a pauper.

They watched from a little way back as the men unloaded the bodies, one at a time, into the hinged coffin, which was carried to the pit and lowered before being lifted up to be used again. She made the children close their eyes, for she did not want them to witness such a terrible thing.

'Your mam and Lizzie's souls have gone straight to heaven,' Mary assured Sarah and Jude once the men had left.

Her niece broke down in sobs while Jude stood silent and red-eyed, staring at his mother and young sister's last resting place. There had been no priest to say a few words so she wrapped her arms around both children and said a few prayers herself.

The breeze blew in from the water and across the Ilen as she did so, and the reeds whispered a lonely song.

The trio walked back to Creagh almost in silence, all lost in their own thoughts. Mary had no idea how John would take the news that there would be two more hungry mouths to feed, but she would not see Jude and Sarah put in the workhouse. As far as she was concerned, they were in her care now until their father returned.

Chapter 67

Creagh

BY THE TIME SHE AND THE CHILDREN ARRIVED HOME, MARY WAS heartsore and weary. Never had she been so glad to see their cottage, as she led an exhausted Sarah and Jude inside.

Her own children were full of questions at the arrival of their two cousins, but a stern look from her ensured they said little. John, as if reading her mind, assured Kathleen's children that they were family and welcome to stay with them.

Straight away she busied herself tending to their immediate needs. She made the two siblings strip out of their filthy rags and washed their dirty bodies all over with warm water. Despite their protests, she tended to their hair with the lice comb before putting Sarah into a clean shift, while Jude had to make do with a patched pair of Con's britches and a shirt.

'Let's get you both something to eat and then you need to sleep, for you are all done in and need to rest.'

They managed a few oatcakes but their eyes were heavy with sleep. Con had fixed some fresh straw and a blanket on

297

the side of the room where his sisters normally slept and the exhausted children lay down together, safe and warm.

'They have suffered terribly,' Mary explained to her family, 'and are in need of kindness. They have lost their mother and sister, and their father is nowhere to be found. What little we have we will share with them.'

'Poor things,' said Nora. 'Sarah can share with me.'

Once the rest of the children were asleep, Mary told John of the terrible circumstances in which she had found her sister and her youngest child. His eyes filled with anger.

'Poor Kathleen,' he said, shocked. 'What a terrible way for her to die!'

'I know that taking in the children means we now have two more mouths to feed,' she admitted despairingly, 'but I could not bear to see them end in the workhouse.'

'We will manage,' he vowed, taking her hand in his. 'Like we always have.'

Mary worried for the young Casey children. Sarah often sobbed herself to sleep, while Jude said little of his family and roamed the nearby fields on his own. She did her best to eke out the little food that they had, but Con complained constantly that he was hungrier than ever, as did little Annie.

John had worries of his own, for there was talk of evictions across the district. George Hogan was said to be giving the tenants of Sir William Wrixon Becher orders to leave their holdings.

'There is a new law that has come in,' he told her one day. 'I am going to go over to meet Michael Hayes and a few of the men to find out what it means, but I fear it is not good for the likes of us.'

In the still of the night Mary sat quietly, sewing the linen shrouds and watching the low flames flicker in the grate, wishing that these bad times would soon come to an end.

Chapter 68

Skibbereen
May 1847

'IS IT TRUE, FATHER?' BRIDEY ASKED, RUSHING INTO THE ROOM. 'Is it true that he is dead?'

Father John nodded solemnly, deeply saddened by the news of Daniel O'Connell's death. He found it hard to believe that Ireland's mighty champion would no longer rise up to defend his people. The great Liberator, who had won Catholic emancipation, fought for repeal of the Act of Union and, only a few short months ago, pleaded to Parliament on behalf of his starving people, had died in Genoa, far from his native land. It was the worst of news.

'They say that he was going to see the Pope, Father?'

'It would appear that he intended to travel from Genoa to the Vatican to appeal to Pope Pius for assistance.'

'Oh, God be good to him!' Bridey broke down. 'To think that he stayed here under this roof and I cooked him his breakfast.'

Although he was well used to death, Father John, like

Bridey, felt overcome by a great sense of loss as he thought of the man himself, sitting by his fire and chatting with him less than four years ago.

The great Daniel O'Connell was, at last, reunited in death with his wife, Mary, and much-loved young grandson. It was a sad day for Ireland and her people, for all hope was destroyed. Who would champion their cause now?

Father John resolved that he would arrange to say a special mass in the morning for the remarkable leader.

'The best of men taken from us.' Bridey continued to sob. 'For without him we are lost!'

The reaction to the devastating news was the same everywhere. In every street, lane and cottage in Skibbereen, the people were shocked to hear of the Liberator's death.

The following morning the townspeople crowded into St Patrick's Cathedral and prayed fervently for Daniel O'Connell. They mourned the loss of Ireland's great leader, giving thanks for his long life and his deep love of his country and its people.

'We'll not see his like again,' murmured Tim McCarthy Downing as they gazed across the river and up towards Curragh Hill where the great man had spoken to them all.

A week later, Father John heard that O'Connell's last wish had been for his soul to go to God, his body to be returned to his beloved Ireland for burial, but that his heart be removed and sent in an urn to the Pope in Rome.

He smiled, thinking of O'Connell's huge funeral, one last great massive Monster Meeting to be held in Dublin to welcome their great hero home to his native land.

Chapter 69

SINCE KATHLEEN'S DEATH, MARY HAD SPENT MUCH OF HER TIME caring for her sister's broken-hearted children.

'You two are my kin,' she assured young Sarah and Jude. 'You are my blood, and I promise you that John and I will take care of you. You have a home here with us.'

John had gone to town in search of Joe Casey twice. He had made enquiries everywhere, but no one had seen sight nor sound of Kathleen's husband. Her brother-in-law seemed to have vanished, unaware of the death of his wife and child.

'Perhaps he's gone away to Dublin or Liverpool for work?' John suggested to Mary.

'Joe would have told Kathleen if he had found work. He would know how happy that would have made her.'

Mary had written a simple letter to Kathleen's eldest boy, Michael, who was still employed in the big house in Clonakilty, telling him of his poor mother and Lizzie's deaths. She assured him that she was caring for his sister and brother.

Her own children found it strange at first to have their two cousins now living with them, but had pity for them and did their best to be kind.

Mary had finished making the shrouds for Honora Barry, but worried that the dressmaker would be annoyed with her. She should have returned them nearly two weeks ago and had used some of the material for Kathleen and Lizzie. Truth to tell, she had not been able to face visiting town since finding her sister dead, but she could no longer put off returning her work, for she needed the payment badly.

She rang the shop bell but there was no sign of the dressmaker. She peered through the window and rapped loudly at the door, calling her name. When there was still no answer, Mary decided she would try the back door, and was just about to knock on it when a maid came out of the next-door building with a bucket of ashes for the bin.

'If you are looking for Miss Barry she's not there,' she said matter-of-factly. 'Took sick a few days back. All on her own, she was, when they found her and took her to the fever sheds. Poor woman, she died there the next day.'

Mary stood rooted to the ground, shocked by the news of Honora Barry's death and the loss not just of her employer but of her friend, who had been both generous and supportive to her since she had first started working for her.

'Oh, I'm sorry to hear that,' Mary said, dismayed. 'She was a good woman, and always kind to me.'

'Sad, no husband or child or relation to mourn her by all accounts!'

The maid turned her back on Mary and disappeared inside.

A strange instinct made Mary check beneath the loose stone near the back step where the dressmaker used to keep a key. She couldn't believe that it was still there. Taking it, she let herself in to the empty shop.

She walked through the workroom that housed the cutting table and sewing table where she used to work. The wooden shelves that once were laden with bales of satin, silk, velvet, lace and sprigged cotton were now bare. Two or three unfinished garments hung forlornly and forgotten from the work rail.

Miss Barry had been telling her the truth about her business drying up. She thought back to how busy the shop used to be, with plenty of customers. The needle and thread, and measuring tape and scissors were on the go constantly. Poor woman, Mary thought, to have to watch her business all but disappear. She must have struggled to stay open these past awful two years.

Mary put down her packet on one of the tables and wondered what she was meant to do with the shrouds now. It was likely there was no money to pay her for her work.

Curious, she walked around the empty shop and went upstairs to Honora's living quarters. She had never crossed the door of her employer's abode. Its kitchen was small and the dining and drawing room was a simple affair with few luxuries, only a couple of tasselled, pink and green satin cushions on her chairs and a small table with a vase of faded flowers. It certainly was not what she had imagined for the stylish dressmaker. As she continued to look around, she could not help but wonder if some of her employer's finer items had already been sold or pawned.

Opening the bedroom door, Mary was assailed immediately

by the smell of sickness and stale air. She reached to unlatch the window in the simple but pretty room. A large bed lay tousled and bare, with only a blanket, some dirty sheets and a rolled-up bolster on it. Folded away neatly on a chair was a beautiful French lace counterpane and two delicately embroidered pillowslips. A few fine dresses, along with a satin wrap, a cloak and a velvet-lined coat hung in the mahogany wardrobe.

As Mary sat on a carved chair in front of a mirror, she thought of Honora. Despite how little she really possessed, the older woman had always shown great kindness towards her. She had not only given her work but also had insisted on several occasions that Mary take some bread, eggs or salted fish back home to share with her family.

A small, nearly empty glass bottle of perfume sat on the neat dressing table. Unthinking, she opened it and the scent reminded her immediately of Miss Barry. She sprinkled a little around the room before replacing the stopper.

A sense of guilt engulfed her. She felt she had let Honora Barry down, just as she had Kathleen. If only she had returned the shrouds when she was meant to, she would have seen her employer was sick. Perhaps she could have fetched the doctor, or helped her in some fashion.

Back downstairs, Mary remembered the money drawer in the back room of the shop from which Miss Barry had paid her once or twice. Bent down, she reached around and found the narrow drawer. Her hand closed in on a few brass and silver coins.

She counted out her wage fairly, unsure of what to do with the rest of the money. Should she just leave it there, where likely the next person to enter the shop – be they beggar or thief – would come upon it? Then her fingers touched some paper, a rent book and an envelope with a sheet of paper, which contained a note in Honora's hand. 'For Mrs Mary Sullivan', it read, and detailed the money due to her.

Tears pricked Mary's eyes as she realized that she had not been forgotten. Across the back of the paper was an additional note, scribbled in larger, looped writing: 'In the event of my demise, I bequeath to my employee, Mrs Mary Sullivan of Creagh, all of my remaining personal possessions to dispose of as she wishes.'

Mary read it and re-read it, over and over again. This good woman in her hour of sickness had made a special point of remembering her.

She took a while to compose herself, considering what she should do. The note made it clear that Honora had left her few possessions to her, but what if a distant relative of the dressmaker appeared, or her landlord made a demand for rent? She wished that she could go home to consult with John, but worried that on her return to the shop she would find the place boarded up and empty, which is what happened to so many vacant buildings in the town to prevent trespassers and beggars from entering the premises.

Honora knew well the desperation of Mary's circumstances and her family, and so Mary decided she would follow the wishes of her employer. Returning to the bedroom, she gathered up the heavy lace counterpane carefully along with the embroidered linen pillowslips. She was torn about selling the dressmaker's personal things but it was what the good woman had wanted, her last wishes. She also took the satin cushions and bundled them all together. She would go to Maguire's pawnbroker, who took furniture and household goods only, to see what they would fetch.

There were only two people ahead of her. Most people in town had sold off their valuables and possessions a long time ago.

Julia Maguire raised her head suspiciously at the likes of Mary having such fine items to sell. She fingered the French lace, admiring its beauty.

'My employer, Miss Barry the dressmaker, sent me with them,' Mary lied, hoping that the news of Honora's death was not yet known through the town.

The other woman smiled. 'I have done business with her previously, but today can only offer her two pounds for the lace and a guinea for all the cushions and bed linen.'

Mary hesitated, for she knew well that they were both worth a lot more. She was, however, in no position to argue the case and accepted the payment.

On her return to the dressmaking shop, Mary searched the shelves and living quarters for any remaining items to sell. The little furniture was likely the landlord's so she dared not touch that. Her heart lifted when she found a teapot and some cutlery, which might fetch a pretty price. There were also a few items of clothing of Honora's which might sell too.

As she continued her search, she found a packet of needles of all sizes and Honora's large fabric scissors, along with a tray of spools of coloured thread and a pincushion. Tears welled in her eyes as she remembered the sight of the dressmaker busy at work, her head bent and concentration on her face. She would keep these items in memory of Honora.

This time she took her collection of items to Hegarty's. Denis Hegarty ran his fingers over the stylish satin dresses, warm woollen coat and fine leather boots.

Mary held her breath and prayed that he would not question her about them, but with two women and well-dressed gentlemen behind her, all pushing and demanding attention, he concluded their business quickly and gave her two pounds for everything.

She returned to the shop one last time to lock it up. Silence hung around her as she replaced the key under the stone and took the shrouds with her.

She called to the dispensary and explained the situation. She asked if they knew anyone who would be willing to buy them from her. The apothecary himself told her immediately that he would happily take all five of them, and paid her generously sixpence for each one. She couldn't quite believe her luck.

Using that money, she purchased a few items of food before setting off home.

On the long walk to Creagh, Mary's heart sat heavy in her chest at the death of her friend. The realization that there would be no more work for her hit her hard. However, the knowledge that she had a few pounds in her purse provided her with a sense of comfort, for which she would always be grateful.

Mary was determined that Honora's gift to her be set aside for a special purpose, used only to protect and save her family.

Chapter 70

Creagh

JOHN HAD SAT AND LISTENED QUIETLY AS MARY TOLD HIM ABOUT the death of the dressmaker and her unexpected generosity. Upset and nervous, Mary showed him the money she had raised from pawning the woman's few possessions.

'Am I a desperate thief for taking Honora's things and selling them?' she fretted. 'Perhaps I should have left everything as it was.'

John studied the few short words.

'Miss Barry wrote you this note,' he said. 'Obviously the poor woman was all alone and afraid of dying. You were the one who visited her more than most. She helped you as best she could, by giving you some work when she had it.'

'I feel so guilty that I did not get the chance to say goodbye to her or pray over her.'

'She is at peace now,' he soothed, 'but I think it is clear that as she neared her end, she intended for you to get your wages and follow her wishes.'

'I will never forget her for it,' Mary said softly, finally giving in to tears at the loss of her friend.

As spring turned to summer and the days grew warmer, the Sullivans' fields lay bare. Like all their neighbours, they had no money for seed potatoes and were still afraid to plant them. Mary had sown half a field of turnips and cabbages because at least they were crops upon which they could rely.

All around them her family saw small farms and holdings empty as starving families were forced either to abandon their holdings or give up their land. The landlord's agents were ruthless and turned out men, women and children on to the roads.

'If they come near us we will use Honora's money to pay the rent,' Mary offered.

'I fear it is too late,' John said. 'The landlords and their gombeen men want to rid the land of people like us. They want to clear small tenants off their holdings and turn the fields to tillage and pasture.'

Fear crawled in Mary's stomach. What would happen if they were put off their land? They had six children to think of now.

'Four families were evicted off their holding up near the Old Hill Road four days ago,' John said, his face serious. 'I am going to the Learys' to meet Denis and a few of the other men to talk about it. There's a rumour that anyone with more than a quarter-acre will get no relief or assistance of any kind unless they give up their holding.'

The sun was dipping in the red sky when he returned home that evening. Anger and dismay were written across his face as he beckoned her to come outside.

'What is it, John?' she urged.

'It's all true. This new quarter-acre law affects tenants like us. Anyone with more than a quarter-acre must give up their holding if they want to get a bowl of soup or a bed in the workhouse. Imagine, a man must renounce the field he has worked for thirty or forty years in order to get any type of assistance – a bite to eat for his child or a bed for his sick wife to lie in. What kind of law is that?'

'It's cruel!'

'Cruelty doesn't come into it!' he spat bitterly. 'All across the Mizen they are tumbling the cottages, pulling down the thatch and kicking out the doors so people cannot find any shelter there. They're forcing people to move from their home place. All they want is to clear the place of small tenants.'

'Where are people going?' she ventured.

'It's some choice,' he said scornfully. 'The road with nothing, or the workhouse. I've heard that the Union's guardians are making each landlord pay a contribution to the keep of their tenants there. Some are offering to assist with paying their passage to Québec and New York. I'll not give up this place easily.'

Mary could sense her husband's rage and sadness at the prospect that they might be forced to leave Creagh.

'John Sullivan, I tell you, if we are put out of here, this family will not set foot in the workhouse,' she told him firmly. 'Flor and Molly wouldn't go because they would have been separated, and I'll not be separated from you and the children.'

'Then we'll take passage to North America, like Pat did.'

'Leave Cork? Leave Ireland?'

'Aye, what else can a man do if he is left with no roof over his head and no land to work but travel the ocean in search of a new life away from this misery? Pat was the wise man who left when he could.'

Mary tossed and turned all night as John's words ran through her head, over and over. How could they ever leave this, their home place?

Chapter 71

July 1847

'MAMMY!' SCREAMED NORA AND TIM, RUNNING ACROSS THE FIELDS as fast as their legs would carry them. 'Mammy, the men are coming! The 'viction men are coming!'

Mary could see the upset and fear in their eyes.

'They were up at Learys' cottage,' Nora panted, coming to a stop.

'We saw them batter their door and pull down the thatch roof,' added Sarah.

Mary tried to control the trembling that overcame her body.

'Run and get your father,' she told them. 'As quick as you can. He's up in the woods with the boys.'

It would be only a few minutes before the landlord's eviction gang reached their cottage, and she was sick to her heart at the thought of what to say or do.

Frantic, she began to put things in order. She folded up into a sacking bag whatever food they had left, along with spoons and a knife or two, and a pot with tin mugs and bowls. She hid them in the corner.

Over the past few days, she and John had discussed over and over again how this might come to pass. Despite his misgivings, she had hoped naively that they would not face such disaster.

Quick as a flash she saw them come – ten, maybe twelve of them, in a group, surrounding the cottage and trampling over her young cabbages. Some she recognized: James Murphy, Denis Carmody and his younger brother, Sean, who had the reputation of being a powerful fighter; the others burly strangers bearing sticks and cudgels. George Hogan was at their head.

'Sullivan,' they shouted. 'Sullivan!'

Mary pulled her shawl around her and stood at the door to face them.

'I'm Mary Sullivan,' she said coldly. 'My husband is not here at present but is due back.'

'We have orders to follow, Mrs Sullivan, from your landlord and his agent,' George Hogan boomed, his long and narrow face serious as he gazed around him, taking in the well-cared-for cottage and her vegetable patch. 'Any tenants behind in their rent must leave their dwellings and the holdings that they have occupied.'

Just as he finished speaking, John arrived with the children behind him. Relief flooded over her as he came and stood protectively beside her.

'What is your business here, Mr Hogan?' John asked.

'I have orders to clear these holdings today, Mr Sullivan. My employer has been patient for far too long with unpaid rent monies, but now seeks the return of his property.'

314

'You know well that not a man in this district could pay his rent with the hunger,' he stated firmly. 'I promise you that when the crops return and the land is fertile again, Sir William will have his full rent. But we can only offer you a part payment this day. The Sullivans have always been good tenants here. You know that well, Mr Hogan.'

The overseer barely acknowledged John's words.

'Give me a chance to pay the rent,' John continued. 'It may take a while but every penny and shilling will be returned to you.'

Mary could see a frown crease the man's brow.

'I'm sorry, Mr Sullivan. The decision has been made that this area is to be cleared and tenants moved off Sir William's estate and properties.'

'We will not give up this place,' John said loudly, his temper rising. 'You cannot put us off these fields and land, for we have earned them with our labour. You have no right to do such a thing.'

'You are wrong, Mr Sullivan. A legal eviction order has been issued for this property and holding.'

'There is no justice when a scrap of legal paper declares this land can be held for eternity by a man who cares not a whit for it or those that work it!' John said contemptuously.

'My advice is for you and your family to go quietly and cause no trouble here. Pack up any of your belongings and leave this place.'

'Leave our home, our land?'

'The land agent, Mr Marmion, is a fair man and arrangements have been agreed with the Union workhouse for payments to be made for tenants agreeing to enter there.'

'You would put my wife and children and me in the work-house?' John shouted, unable to control his anger any longer. 'We who have done nothing wrong but try to feed our children? With not even a penny of help or as much as a bag of grain from our landlord, I may remind you.'

Mary could see Mr Hogan growing uncomfortable and one or two of the men looked shamefaced, but he continued with the job he had been sent to do.

'Otherwise, for all tenants giving up their holding, there is an offer of paid passage on ships to North America.'

'Leave our home, our land *and* our country? What choice is that?'

Mary swallowed hard, trying to control her impulse to scream and kick at the men.

'Do not cause trouble, Mr Sullivan,' George Hogan warned again.

'What kind of man do you think I am, Hogan? I will not give up our holding.'

With that, John grabbed his wife's arm and beckoned for the children to follow as he stepped back inside the cottage. He closed the door behind them firmly and put on the iron bolt.

'Don't be a fool, man!' Mary could hear the exasperation in Hogan's voice on the other side of the door. 'Step outside.'

John, Con and Tim blocked the window quickly with the wooden pallet and pushed the settle bed against the doorway. The girls stood by, terrified. John and the boys braced themselves, ready to hinder the group of men for as long as they were able.

'We Sullivans will not go from here easy and give up what is ours without a fight,' he told the children as the men began to push and rush against the door, pummelling the wood. 'Do you understand?'

The words had barely left his lips when the wood began to splinter and crack, gaping as sticks and heavy shoulders pushed at it.

'Hold firm!' he urged as Mary and the boys used all their strength to resist the attack, trying to push the settle bed back against the men while Nora, Sarah and Annie stood at the window.

Despite their best efforts, the settle bed was shoved backwards and, with a mighty bang, the cottage door gave way. At the same time, over their heads, men began to strip the thatch from the roof.

Poor Annie began to scream, petrified.

'Shush, shush,' said Nora, taking her little sister in her arms.

Dear God, they were going to pull and tumble the place down around them.

John and the boys pushed hard against what remained of the door, trying to hold back the men, but they were no match for the might of the group. Mary braced herself as five of the men entered the cottage. Part of the roof was already open to the sky as she and the three girls managed to flee outside. John pushed against Sean Carmody, telling him to leave the place for this was no fight of his, and earned a few punches in the stomach and ribs for his trouble.

'Leave my father alone,' Con shouted at them angrily, his eyes blazing.

Hogan entered the cottage and gave a signal to the men to stop.

Annie whimpered like a little puppy as John and the three

boys appeared slowly, standing in front of the battered wall and door.

'Former tenants of Sir William Wrixon Becher if not entering the Union,' Hogan announced, 'may avail themselves of fully paid passage to Liverpool or North America. Tickets for those wishing to travel will be issued at the shipping office in either Baltimore, for those who wish to make the long journey, or Queenstown in the coming days and weeks.'

John said nothing and stared blankly out over the fields.

'My employer has generously agreed an amount with the shipping agents, who have a complete list of our tenants,' Hogan continued. 'My advice, Mr Sullivan, is that you and your wife and family avail yourselves of this good offer, for we will not tolerate tenants remaining on this property or attempting to stay on these lands. You and your children cannot remain here. Is that clear?'

Mary's breath caught in her throat, but she would not give Hogan and his men the satisfaction of seeing her break down and cry.

'Is that clear?' the overseer repeated.

'Yes,' John said, meeting his gaze directly. 'This injustice, this act of putting my family from land that we Sullivans have tended all our lives, will be remembered, Mr Hogan. I promise never will it be forgotten.'

Mary could see an angry purple blush blaze against the overseer's cheek.

Behind him, a few of the younger men had pulled every last bit of thatch from the cottage roof and broken the roof supports. They had knocked the chimney so that their home now lay ruined, open to the sky and elements.

'You must leave this place today,' Hogan ordered. 'Are you agreed?'

'There is nothing left for us here,' John replied bitterly. 'You have made sure of that.'

'Is it to be the Union or the road to Cork, or wherever? It is not my concern where you go once you leave this place.'

'Passage,' interrupted John. 'We will take assisted passage for my family to sail to North America.'

'A sensible decision,' pronounced Mr Hogan, relieved that his business was done. 'Passage will be arranged for you and your good wife and children to sail from Baltimore. I believe that I have a list of all your names.'

They watched as he mounted his horse and turned to ride away, the rest of the men following in his wake.

Mary felt like a wet rag as they disappeared. Sarah and Jude looked at her, wide-eyed and scared.

'You are coming to America with us,' she reassured them both. 'You know that we are your family now.'

She ran her eyes over the broken and battered cottage. Her marital home, her children's home; Sullivans' Cottage, where John had spent his boyhood. Soon they would be gone from it and rain and wind, weeds and wildlife would claim it. She was heartbroken at the thought of the children never playing in the surrounding fields again.

Slowly, she went around and gathered up the few things they had. The precious vegetable patch had been trampled, her young cabbages and turnips all but destroyed underfoot. She did her best to salvage what she could, for they still had to eat.

319

A tearful Brigid and Denis came to say goodbye to them with their children.

'There's nothing left for us here,' proclaimed Denis. 'We are going to my brother's place in Tipperary. He's an old bachelor and we are hoping he would not see us on the roads.'

'God bless you all,' Mary said, embracing her friend for the last time.

'We'd best be leaving too, and get on the road to Baltimore,' John said quietly. 'We cannot stay here.'

Without a word, Con went up to his father and hugged him, burying his head in his chest. Eight-year-old Tim stood in front of the cottage with his feet apart, taking it all in.

'I want to remember every stone and every bit of straw and every blade of grass in this place,' he said solemnly. 'I want to make a picture of it so I will never ever forget it.'

John went and took a few small bits of stone that had come off the fireplace and doorway and handed him one.

'Tim, you will always have this place and the memory of it,' he told him. 'We all will. No one can take that from us.'

Mary reached for John and held him close. She noticed him wince with pain but he assured her that he was fine.

'We'd best get on the road,' he said gently, pushing back a lock of hair that had fallen across her face. 'My darling girl, 'tis time for us to go . . .'

At the end of the road, hand in hand, they turned and looked back, knowing full well that they would never see this place again.

Part Three

Part Three

Chapter 72

Baltimore, County Cork

THE HUNGER HAD STALKED AND STARVED THE LAND. THE ONLY sound to be heard was the forlorn cry of a lonely corncrake as the Sullivans packed up and made ready to leave.

They took only a few possessions with them: two pots, a knife, spoons and bowls and mugs, and the tin bucket, all items needed for their journey. Mary took her precious scissors and dressmaking tools with her while John carried his shovel and fork in the hope that he might sell them, for he had no use for them now.

With heavy hearts they said a final goodbye to their home place, with its unplanted potato patches and empty cottages with not even a curl of turf smoke in the sky. Scraggy thorn trees, leafy ferns and bushes of gorse and bramble lined the stony road, broken by the shimmer of blue as the broad, curving river Ilen flowed out to meet the wide sea.

As the family walked down the curving hill towards the village of Baltimore, they passed the school, a tavern and Dún na Séad, the once grand castle of the O'Driscolls.

'Is that the ship?' Con shouted excitedly, running ahead. They took in the large vessel moored down below in the harbour with its tall mast and rigging, sailors busy scrubbing the deck and checking the thick ropes. 'Can we go and see it?'

'Later,' John promised. 'First, we need to find the shipping office.'

The office was part of a chandler's, overlooking the harbour. A few men stood outside, smoking their pipes. A gaunt-looking man with his wife and three boys was ahead of them in line. They were tenants like themselves, booking passage for a ship that was sailing in three days' time. The wife looked ill and coughed constantly.

Once they were finished, the shipping clerk beckoned the Sullivans forward. John duly gave his full name and the address of their holding, and told him their circumstances and desire to book passage to America for the family.

'It will be to New York if you sail this week. Otherwise you will have to wait until we have one sailing in twelve or fourteen days.'

'As we have left our holding, we have no need to wait.'

The man looked down at the pages of names and record numbers from the Becher estate, running his stubby finger along the list.

'Sullivan, Dan . . . John . . .'

'That's it. John Sullivan, sir.'

'Aye, here it is. John Sullivan and wife, Mary, and four children, I see it noted here.'

'There are six children in our family that will be travelling,' John informed him calmly.

'Six? I have only four listed here,' the clerk looked up, puzzled. 'There is a Cornelius, Nora, Tim and Annie Sullivan. This is what is entered on the estate record. Have you had more children?'

'We have two other children who are our family now. They were orphaned and had to come to live with us,' he explained. 'Their names are Jude and Sarah Casey.'

'That may be, Mr Sullivan, but they are not listed as tenants of the estate. As such, they do not qualify for the estate's assisted passage payment to North America.'

'They are my wife's family and will travel with us,' John told the man firmly. 'We will not leave them behind.'

'I have my orders to follow, sir. I can issue boarding tickets for the *Lady Jane* for you, your wife and four children as former tenants, but I have no authority to issue passes for others travelling with you, be they family members or not.'

'There must be some way we can bring the children,' he pleaded, trying to gain the man's sympathy. 'We cannot leave them behind.'

'Free passage does not apply to extra family members or friends,' the clerk responded tetchily. 'Otherwise we would have half the people of the parish wanting to bring relations on board with them. If they want to travel with you, then you must purchase tickets for them.'

'How much is the passage for New York?'

'Seven pounds per passenger is the normal fare.'

'Seven pounds,' John repeated, incredulous. There was no possibility they would be able to pay such a vast sum of money.

Mary felt giddy. After all that had happened that day, she could not believe they were facing such a dilemma.

'Are you telling me that it costs seven pounds to bring a young orphan child across the Atlantic?'

Sarah had begun to sniffle loudly, drawing everyone's attention.

'Seven pounds is the adult fare but for children it is less. Given they are travelling as part of a family situation . . .' The clerk began to tot up figures on a piece of paper with his pencil. 'They can both travel for two pounds and five shillings, if you wish to pay passage for them.'

John's eyes met Mary's. She had given him all the money she had earned, every penny of it, along with what she had got from Honora Barry. He carefully counted out the coins. Jude and Sarah's names were added to theirs on the steerage passenger list, and all of them were issued with official boarding tickets.

The clerk gave them details of their ship, the *Lady Jane*, and its departure time. He also told them what rations of food and water would be provided for passengers.

'We advise people to purchase extra oatcakes and food supplies for the long journey, and a chamber pot or bucket for their personal needs. We offer all of these items in our small provision store here.'

John was tense and worried by the time they stepped outside, and the children were silent and watchful.

'We have all got our tickets,' Mary said, trying to cheer the situation, 'and will set sail in two days' time. Until then, we need to find somewhere sheltered and dry to sleep.'

Baltimore harbour looked out over the water and Sherkin Island in the distance. The sea was a mixture of blue and green, shimmering in the sunshine as the waves rushed against the harbour. Further out, beyond the wide curving bay, lay the blue ocean. There was a fine church in the village, and a scattering of houses and fishermen's cottages dotted along the shore, but few vessels, as many fishermen had sold them in order to feed their families.

It was a place of trade, where boats and ships carrying timber, grain and flax loaded and unloaded their goods to be transported between Cork and Liverpool and Cardiff, and upriver to Skibbereen.

The Sullivans went to look at the large ship that would carry them to the New World. Its mast reached up skywards like a tree, supporting the great folds of heavy white sails, its boom and rigging. Only a few sailors were working on the large wooden deck as the waves lapped gently against the ship's timbers.

'Soon we'll be sailing across the wide Atlantic Ocean in that ship,' declared Con proudly. 'Just look at her sails!'

'I hate big ships,' said Annie stubbornly, 'and I'll not go on one!'

'You will too,' encouraged good-hearted Nora, promising to look after her younger sister.

A curious seal bobbed its head up and down, diving in the foam nearby and making the children laugh with its antics.

Down by the cove they found a sheltered spot. John lit a fire and Mary cooked up the ends of the food they had brought with them. They were all tired and exhausted.

Lying in the darkness under the moonlight that night, Mary could hear the waves lap against the shore and felt strangely comforted by the familiar childhood sound.

*

By mid-morning the harbour had come to life rapidly as the sailors began to load the ship and make ready for the long sea voyage. The crew were busy with their preparations, climbing along the rigging, and creeping up the stays and out the yard arm as the heavy sails were readied and raised.

'They say that the *Lady Jane* is not regulated or as well-equipped as the bigger ships that leave from Cork and Queenstown,' John said with worry in his voice.

'This is the ship we have paid passage on,' Mary assured him. 'And for the children's sake, we must try to make the best of it and put our trust in the Lord.'

John finally managed to sell his shovel and fork to a man from Clear Island.

'He got the bargain,' he said ruefully.

Following the advice of the shipping clerk, they purchased two cheap rolled-up ticking mattresses for the hard, slatted wooden bunks, and oatcakes and oats for their journey. Most of their money was gone and they had not even left Cork!

The children played for hours down at the shore, paddling and splashing in the water, and it did Mary's heart good to hear them laughing.

That night Mary slept fretfully, dreaming of towering waves and crashing seas. She tried not to give in to the terrible fear that engulfed her. What would happen if the ship was wrecked or foundered crossing the vast Atlantic Ocean?

'Mam, look! Our ship is nearly ready to sail,' announced Con with delight early on Thursday morning. 'We'll be sailing soon, before the tide turns.'

Mary, John and the children hastened to join the line of

passengers waiting to board, many of whom were tenants from their district.

The ruddy-faced captain's mate, Mr Dwyer, examined their tickets and called out names on a passenger roll. Each traveller in turn was checked over to ensure they were well enough to travel before they were directed below deck to the steerage part of the ship.

'There is one bunk per three or four people,' Mr Dwyer informed the passengers, which drew groans of protest. 'Everyone must share.'

Stepping across the gangplank, Con and Jude jumped up and down in excitement at the adventure that lay ahead of them. Mary was glad to be escaping the hunger and sickness. Although she was filled with trepidation about the sea journey, relief coursed through her veins that she, John and all the children, including Kathleen's two, had somehow survived and were bound for a new life far from this torn land.

As they made their way down into the murky hold, it took her eyes a few seconds to adjust to the lack of light. As soon as she could make out her surroundings, she rushed to place their belongings on two bunks. There was no separation of men and women so, acting quickly, Mary decided that she would share with Sarah, Annie and Nora while John and the boys would sleep together in the bunk above them.

She felt the narrow rough slats of the bunks and was mighty glad of their two mattresses as she unrolled them. Though there was such little space to sleep, she was relieved, for at least they were together and not forced to have some stranger lie with them. Already, she could hear people around them fighting and arguing about not wanting to share.

It was horrendously crowded down in steerage, the bunks all on top of each other with only a narrow passage running between them. Some bunks were even worse, with wooden posts between them, and the roof was so low that John, and many of the men and taller boys, tipped their heads against it. There was no privacy or ventilation, and already the air below deck was heavy. The bunks she had chosen for them were near the steps, where there was at least a little more light and fresh air, but Mary worried for the modesty of the women on board, for there was no provision to protect themselves from the prying eyes of the men and boys around them.

'We all better get used to this,' a big man called Denis Murphy declared, looking around at them all. 'We'll be living here on top of each other like pigs for the next six or eight weeks, so they say. There's no point in fighting with each other, for it will do us not a bit of good.'

'Hear, hear,' added two other men.

The ship's bell cut through the chatter, signalling the vessel's departure, and there was a change in mood as everyone pushed and rushed to climb up the steps and back on to deck. The sailors had untied the coiled ropes and hauled in the heavy anchor. The ship was ready to sail as the tide and the wind in her hoisted sails began to lift and move her.

The *Lady Jane* began to tilt and rock, and every man, woman and child was up on deck as she began to move through the waves, leaving the harbour, the wide cove and the headland behind.

Mary felt immense sadness and grief for the land they were leaving but, as the ship began to cut through the waves and

John reached for her hand, she felt a strange rush of hope and excitement that this was a new beginning for them.

They drank in the view of the harbour and shoreline, the cottages, green fields and rolling hills, the woods and gorse and bracken. They savoured their last glimpse of the tall headland as the *Lady Jane* caught the waves. Within minutes, they had left Baltimore far behind, as they headed out past the sandy beaches of Sherkin Island and Clear Island towards the open sea.

A few women sobbed, and a young woman holding a baby started to pray out loud. The other passengers joined in with her. Tim and Annie clung to Mary nervously, scared by the strange rocking of the wooden deck under their feet. She caught sight of tears in her husband's eyes and she knew how much leaving their home place grieved him.

'This is a sad day for all of us, but at least we are going to a country that is no longer shackled by British rule and parliament,' declared Denis Murphy loudly, to nods and murmurs of approval.

Con and Jude bounded up and down as the wind caught their breaths.

'America!' they whooped and hollered at the grand adventure that lay ahead. 'We are going to America!'

Standing in the sea spray as the rolling waves around them rose and swelled, they took in every last vestige of the rugged coastline that they would never see again. Every rock, stone, hue, tree and field, the sheer beauty and wildness of their beloved land, they seared into their memory.

Chapter 73

'THE SICKNESS WILL SOON PASS,' MARY PROMISED THE CHILDREN, trying to comfort them.

No sooner had the voyage begun than they had fallen seasick, like most of the passengers. The rough motion of the ship as it was tossed by the ocean waves left them puking and retching, covered in sour vomit. Their throats burned and they lay curled together in their bunks, clammy and miserable.

'Let me die,' roared an old man, crouched in his bunk like a child.

Their clothes and blankets reeked, for there was not enough fresh water for washing to rid the hold of the pervading stench. Water was strictly rationed, with only one gallon allowed per adult for drinking, cooking and washing, no matter how much the passengers begged for more.

Annie got the seasickness worst. She lay beside her mother like a little ghost, whimpering and distressed. Dark circles grew under her eyes as she became ever more listless, unable even to hold down a few sips of water.

John recovered first, followed by Con and Jude, who found their sea legs quickly, running and playing around the steerage accommodation.

'Mr Dwyer showed us four dolphins swimming by the side of the ship this morning, when we went up on deck to empty the piss bucket,' Con declared with excitement. 'Mam, you should see them. They are the biggest fish, and he said they can talk and signal to each other, and jump and swim faster than any horse. The ocean is full of such creatures!'

The rest of them suffered terribly. It was five days before the awful queasiness and retching began to ease. The captain agreed to let the steerage passengers up on deck to take some air while they tried to clean part of the hold.

As she gazed at the vast blue ocean, spread like a field all around them, Mary made the children take in deep breaths of fresh sea air to try to revive them. The wind and salt and spray stung her skin, and though there was no sight of land, only endless blue sea and sky, life coursed through her, for the past and their home place now seemed so far away.

Mary had never imagined such a voyage, cramped together with barely space to walk around or turn in your sleep. The air below deck was heavy and pungent from foul human ordure as people shared buckets and chamber pots or tried to use the water closet that hung over the side of the ship, perilously close to the waves. Most just chose to do their business in corners and hidden parts of the deck with no regard for their neighbours.

Every day the routine was the same. The ship's mate would

ring the bell to summon the passengers to line up for their food rations.

'There's barely enough to feed us,' complained John as they each were given only a pound of bread, or meal or hard biscuits. Con, Jude and Nora got half portions, while the younger ones received barely a third. Some days, there were no rations at all, and the mate simply ignored their complaints. The bread and rock-hard biscuits often were green and mouldy, and the meal was not much better.

Up on deck was a caboose, with a grate for cooking over the fire. Crowds gathered around it with their pots and pans, and Mary waited patiently for her turn to use it to cook her family's portion of the meal.

'I've no pot of my own,' wailed a young woman from Coronea who was travelling with her husband and a three-year-old. 'What use is a pound of meal if I cannot cook it?'

Mary took pity on her and generously let her use her pot.

Con and Jude befriended the Murphy and Collins boys, who were about their own ages. The seven youngsters, their heads down, jostled and laughed, whispering and plotting together to pass the time. Nora and Sarah grew to become like sisters. They slept curled up beside each other and walked arm in arm around the crowded hold as if they were strolling down an avenue in New York, both of them full of plans for the future. Tim and Annie stayed close to Mary, frightened by the rough men who played cards and drank and cursed each other, day and night.

'They are just bored like us all,' she tried to reassure them.

In the murky gloom of steerage, the days ran together. Sleep was their greatest friend as it helped to pass the desperate hours. However, even that was usually disturbed by the cries of children who had woken, terrified or sick, and who clung to their mothers as Mary lay awake in the cramped bunk, listening.

Then there was the constant snoring and sounds of the other passengers at night. The loud, rough banter of some men who played cards into the early hours of the morning as they smoked their pipes; while others looked to satisfy themselves with a wife or woman under the cover of darkness. Women, on the other hand, desperately sought some privacy to relieve themselves.

John was quieter than Mary had ever seen him since they had first walked out together. She knew that his heart was broken by the loss of their land and home place. He brooded over it and it was doing him no good.

'John, we have to try to be glad that we and the children have a chance of a new life where we are not beholden to any agent or landlord.'

'It is not that easy to leave the place where I was raised, where I farmed, and where our children were born,' he told her despairingly. 'I think of it night and day.'

'You and I will never forget it, I promise, but America is where our new home will be. Let us talk of New York,' she encouraged. 'Do you think Pat will be able to help you to get a job and help us find a place to stay?'

'My brother will likely suit himself, as he always does.'

She pondered on it.

'He is your flesh and blood and cares for you and the children. I'm sure Pat will do his best for us when we arrive.'

One of their fellow passengers, Johnny Meagher, had a tattered map of New York which he had acquired from one of the sailors in place of a half bottle of *poitín*. He and John and the rest of the men pored over it for hours, sharing information they had, and trying to learn the names of the districts and streets where they might find work or rooms to rent. John's eyes lit up when he recognized his brother's address.

'There are factory and labouring jobs aplenty to be found,' John reported to Mary, 'and up north or out west there are thousands and thousands of acres of government land being sold cheaply to any man who has a few dollars and is prepared to clear the land and farm it.'

'Land that would be our own!' she ventured, seeing the hope in his eyes.

'Aye, all legal and proper like, once a man has the money in his pocket to pay for it. 'Tis not like at home at all. In America work is rewarded and we will be no man's servant.'

Relief flooded her heart. She could see that planning for the future finally was helping her husband to banish the terrible despair that had clung to him since they had boarded the ship.

She too had her own ideas for life in America. Once the family and children were settled, she would try to find work as a seamstress. In a city the size of New York, there would surely be a workroom or dressmaker's or garment factory that would employ her or give her piece work. She had no intention of sitting idle.

Chapter 74

Skibbereen

DAN DONOVAN WAS RETURNING FROM OVERSEEING THE OPENING of a fresh pit in Abbeystrewry graveyard. Despite his best medical efforts, the numbers of those falling ill with fever continued to grow, and the fever wards and sheds were now full.

The Union had opened a new auxiliary workhouse for women on Levis Quay, and another, smaller government soup kitchen had been set up on North Street. They were feeding near eight thousand people. Two men with a horse and cart brought soup and biscuits to be distributed to outlying areas such as Kilcoe, Ballydehob and Rath, and also to the sick and weak. The guardians and the relief committee were doing what they could to cope with the enormous numbers now being dispossessed who found themselves in need of assistance. It was disheartening to say the least.

He stopped to gather his thoughts and took in the sight of the riverbank and the beauty of the Ilen as it wound its way towards the curving stone arches of the town's bridge. It was a calm spot away from the misery and deprivation all around him. Scraggy thorn branches bowed low over the river, and a light breeze rippled through the rushes that grew along its edge. The sunlight sparkled on the clear water, where ducks, swans and waterfowl aplenty used to swim and dabble. However, such creatures were long gone.

The river was low that day and Dan's eyes were drawn to something caught among the silt and stones and rushes. He left his horse and walked down to the water's edge to investigate. It soon became apparent to him that what he could see was a body that somehow had fallen into the river and become trapped among the rushes. He surmised that it had been there for a few weeks at least, for nature and the river had done their worst.

He climbed back up the bank, mounted his horse and returned to the graveyard where he ordered the men there to give him a hand in raising the body. Between them, they managed to use their shovels to catch the dead man by his coat and drag him out and up on to the riverbank.

'Putrid,' grumbled Martin, the older gravedigger.

Dan knelt to examine the body, which was clearly emaciated. Most likely the man had drowned either by throwing himself in the river or falling into the fast-flowing water. It was hard to tell, but then he noticed the remnants of a fishing line and two hooks that had wrapped themselves around his torso, which indicated that his fall had probably been accidental. There were no signs of identification on him and the state of the decomposition made recognition impossible.

'What do you want us to do with him, doctor?'

'You can put him in the cart and bury him today.'

There was no need for Dan to do an autopsy on this poor fellow who had been fishing and likely fallen into the river when he lost his footing.

He wondered if the man was from Bridgetown or Windmill Lane. Did he have family there, or was he just another stranger passing through the town? At least whoever the poor man was, he would be buried in Abbeystrewry.

Chapter 75

Atlantic Ocean

THE LADY JANE HAD BEEN AT SEA FOR NEARLY THREE WEEKS, when the Sullivan family noticed people sickening around them, coughing and spitting up and burning with ship fever.

The woman they had seen at the chandler's office, Mrs Cassidy, had died a few days earlier. Her scrawny body had been committed to the ocean by the captain and his men, with a few prayers said by her fellow passengers. Her son, a sickly boy, soon followed his mother to a watery grave, for there was no doctor on board.

One of the Murphy boys, Michael, also had taken bad with the fever. He began to complain that his head was going to burst and then developed pains in his legs and all over his body. Within a day or two, he was covered with spots and awful sores.

'Keep away from him,' Mary scolded Con and her nephew. 'Or else you will get sick too.'

'But we are friends,' her son pleaded.

'Friends doesn't come into it!' she warned, giving him a sharp clip to his head to scare him into obeying her. 'You stay far away from those Murphy boys.'

Fear stalked her that the ship fever would spread to her children and she kept them close to her and John. The boys grew scared when thirteen-year-old Michael Murphy lay quiet and still after drawing his last breath in his bunk. At midnight, his poor mother's wailing at the loss of her once healthy boy woke them all.

'We should never have come on this voyage to hell,' Mrs Murphy lamented as her husband and younger sons tried in vain to comfort her.

Chapter 76

MARY WORRIED FOR ANNIE, WHO WAS FADING AWAY LIKE A LITTLE brown bird. She was watchful for any change in her, coaxing her gently to try to eat or drink a little. Con too had grown quiet since his friend had died. He no longer played with the other boys and at night she could hear him cough in the darkness in the bunk above her.

'Mary! Mary, wake up!' John was standing before her. 'It's Con. He's burning up.'

Mary moved Annie off her. Climbing out of her bunk, she could see that Con was curled up tightly on his side, his head and neck wet with sweat. Jude and Tim lay beside him fast asleep. She woke them gently and told them to go down below with the girls as she tried to rouse Con. He moaned and complained that his stomach and head hurt before lapsing back into sleep.

Mary tried not to give in to the panic she felt. John fetched a damp rag with which to cool him down, despite her son's groans of protest. For the rest of the night, she sat on the corner of the bunk, watching over him as John lay beside him. In the morning, he was no better and pulled the blanket over him as the others got up. His cough had worsened, racking his chest, and he had developed a few sores on his body.

'What are we to do?' she pleaded with John. 'There is no physician on the ship.'

John and Nora took over caring for Annie as Mary minded Con. She spent the hours talking and singing to him, as she had done when he was younger. He was drowsy most of the time, retching bile into the bucket a few times before slumping back on to the bunk. Although his body was burning up, his teeth were chattering, and he shivered with rigors as he groaned and mumbled in his sleep, thrashing around on the mattress. With a damp piece of cloth, she desperately tried to keep his fever down.

Kate Connolly, a kindly woman from Sherkin Island, gave her a special poultice she had made of herbs and seaweed from the island to put on his chest.

'It may do your boy some good,' she offered quietly, but Con pushed it off him roughly.

As time went on, her eldest son's condition worsened. Though she tried to make him drink, he refused, saying he was not thirsty. His breath grew laboured and it sounded as if he had a whole bag of water in his chest.

The other children were scared. They tried to talk to him and encourage him to get better, but Con looked away and closed his eyes. It was as if he could no longer see them.

Mary railed against God for allowing her child to fall ill. She had done everything in her power to protect him from the hunger and fever, and still her boy was sick . . . Sicker than she had ever seen him, struggling for his life.

For two full days he thrashed and moaned as she sat with him and stroked his head.

'We will be in America in a few days, Con,' she promised him. 'You will see your uncle Pat and New York. Everything will be grand there for us.'

She rambled on, trying to get him to fight and cling on to life. John told him of the day he was born and how much he loved him from the first second he held him in his arms. Mary's eyes welled with tears at the memory of it.

But all their words and all their prayers and all their love were not enough. Late into the long night, as the ship moved on the ocean waves, Con simply closed his eyes and, with only a few deep, shuddering breaths, was still . . .

With his arms stretched out peacefully on the mattress beside them, Con's young beating heart finally stopped. Mary sat in silence, holding her own breath, for she too felt that she might die, while John sobbed openly, his head in his hands, broken-hearted.

Chapter 77

MARY WASHED HER SON'S BEAUTIFUL LONG BODY AND COMBED HIS light-brown hair. She had taken her scissors and cut a few locks of it, sewing them quickly into a small pouch she had fashioned from a piece of material from his shirt. She kissed his handsome face for the very last time as the first mate, Mr Dwyer, and two of the sailors came to take him from her to bury him at sea.

'I'll carry my boy,' John insisted hoarsely.

Mr Dwyer told the others to step back as he helped John wrap Con's body loosely in a light sheet and carry him up on to the deck.

The sun nearly blinded Mary as she stepped into the light. The sky and the sea were so blue that they made her feel giddy. Nora, Sarah and the boys all cried as the ship's captain appeared. He began to read slowly two passages from the Bible and they all said the 'Our Father'. Annie stared out at the sea, still as a statue, and said nothing.

There were two bodies to bury at sea that morning. The

other casualty was a thirty-year-old man who was travelling on his own and planning to journey out west and stake a claim for some government land. Three of the men he had befriended on the ship were the only ones there to pray over him.

'Let us pray for the soul of Peadar O'Malley, who has gone to his rest and is now reunited with the Lord,' said the captain, blessing himself.

The sailors lifted the loosely wrapped body on to a wooden plank, which was tilted and then lowered into the sea, consigning the man to the deep water.

Mary began to shake with disbelief as they took Con's body and moved it on to the plank in the same way. John came and stood beside her, gripping her shoulders.

'May God and his grandparents watch over him!' prayed John.

The captain began to recite the 'Our Father' again and everyone present joined in.

'Let us pray for the soul of this young man, Cornelius Sullivan, nearly thirteen years old and taken before his time, who has this day gone to his rest and is now reunited with the Lord,' the captain intoned.

Mary watched as they began to lower and tilt the plank towards the water. Con's body slipped down into the cold, cold sea, floating there for a few minutes before the ocean's waves knocked and pulled him down below into the dark blue depths that would for ever be his grave.

She wanted to fling herself into the churning water after him, but Nora and Annie had taken a grip of her hands. She began to sob and ran to the side, peering down into the depths to see if she could catch any further glimpse of him.

'Mr and Mrs Sullivan, I am sorry for your loss,' the captain said solemnly as he took his leave of them, gesturing for Mr Dwyer to escort them all back down to steerage.

'Please, I want to stay here with him,' Mary begged. 'Just for a little while longer.'

Two sailors suddenly appeared, carrying the ticking mattress and soiled blanket on which her boy had lain. Despite her protests, they tossed them into the waves.

Mary watched the ship lurch and roll, the wind in her sails, as the vessel skimmed and moved through the waves, carrying them further and further away from her first born. Her eyes raked the rippling field of waves, but she could see no trace or sign of Con.

Back below deck, John cared for Annie, for all Mary wanted to do was lie down in the bunk, close her eyes and somehow pretend that Con was still alive. She imagined she would hear him laugh or talk beside her.

For three days, Mary could not eat or drink, though she had no fever. The young woman from Coronea kindly offered to cook meals for their family, while her friend from the island, Kate Connolly, gave her a bitter herb to take at night to dull her terrible pain.

As she lay in the bunk, watching the ship's timbers and feeling the constant rise and fall of the vessel, she knew her heart was broken. She had been fooling herself to think that somehow they could escape fate and the hunger. Like a ghost, it had followed them on to this ship and across the ocean.

'Annie needs you,' said John tentatively. 'I need you.'

She could see the fear in his pleading eyes. She nodded

dumbly as he helped her up. Though her legs felt weak, they walked slowly around the narrow rows of steerage.

'We are sorry for your loss,' people murmured.

'He was a fine boy!'

'Thank you.' She nodded, trying not to cry.

The children stared at her as she fetched the cooking pot.

'What is this I hear, Annie Sullivan, about you not taking a sup of food from your father?'

'I don't like it!' the small child said stubbornly, her face the colour of snow.

'Well, there will be none of that kind of talk. I am going up top to make us some gruel and woe betide anyone who doesn't eat it. We all need to keep our strength up.'

Her nephew was quiet and she feared he too might be getting ship fever.

'Are you sick?' she asked him, feeling his brow.

'No!' Jude blurted out tearfully. 'I'm so sorry, Auntie Mary, but Sarah and I are the ones who brought the sickness to your door. It should have been me that died, not Con!'

'Jude, hush with that talk.' She could not believe that he was blaming himself. 'Con's death was not of your doing. He was as right as rain when we all boarded the ship. It was here that he got the fever, the same fever that took that boy Michael and a few others.'

She could see the relief in the young boy's eyes as she hugged him and kissed the top of his head.

'Now, Jude. You stay well, do you hear?' She smiled. 'I made a promise to your mam that I would look after you.'

Chapter 78

SIX WEEKS OUT, THE LADY JANE GOT CAUGHT IN A TERRIBLE STORM and was tossed like a log in the towering Atlantic waves. The wind roared like a banshee, and thunder and lightning flashed above them. Sea water poured over the deck and in on the passengers, flooding the low steerage hold. For once, Mary pitied the crew.

'Hold on to the bunks!' John ordered the terrified children, using his belt to tie Tim and Annie to the upper one.

All around them people prayed that they would not drown.

As the ship gave a huge creaking lurch, Sarah was flung on to the soaked floor, howling in pain as Mary and John pulled her back up, for her arm was badly hurt. One man smashed the bones in his leg and a woman had her eyes blackened and nose broken as she was thrown against a wooden beam. Everyone was terrified, for they did not know how much more the ship could take. Some resorted to prayers while others sat in silence, watching the water rise, terrified they would drown.

There were tears of relief when the gales and waves finally abated, although there were bruises and cuts aplenty among the passengers. Despite the severity of the storm, Mr Dwyer reassured them that the ship was undamaged and he gave the orders for the water below to be bailed out as the *Lady Jane* sailed on across the tall, churning waves.

Six, seven weeks, all the days ran together. The family's supply of oatcakes was long gone and the food they received was not fit for a dog. However, they had no choice but to eat the meagre rations and the little water that was allowed. Bored, some passengers played cards, listened to the fiddle, or told stories of their townland to pass the hours on the seemingly endless voyage.

Suddenly there was a change at sea and the sailors gave orders to clean up the bunks and the steerage deck. All the filth, the stinking mouldy mattresses, the straw and the blankets were jettisoned to the churning depths of the Atlantic Ocean. The deck was washed with lime and new bedding straw appeared. The over hatch was left open and fresh air finally filled the fetid, squalid darkness.

'We have entered American waters,' declared Johnny Meagher. 'I tell you, soon we will be landed.'

The excitement was contagious as the passengers roused themselves from the terrible inertia and despondency that had hung over them for the past seven long weeks. Faces were scrubbed and children wailed in protest as mothers combed and tried to clean their hair.

'America! We are nearly there,' John told his family proudly.

However, their hopes of landing any time soon were halted as the captain announced that an inspector was due to board the ship shortly.

'Those who are deemed ill or display any symptoms of fever will be removed from this ship immediately to a nearby quarantine facility for medical care. By law, they must remain there until they have recovered sufficiently.'

Consternation spread among the passengers, for many among them were unwell and incredibly weak.

Mary looked at Annie, who resembled a ghost child. She had kept down little food during the journey and deep circles shadowed her eyes. Her lips were parched and flaking, and she sported a dark bruise on her leg where one night the previous week she had hit it on the bunk.

What would they do if she was removed to this quarantine place? They had all heard terrible tales of what happened to the patients of such hospitals where fever, as in the workhouse, spread quickly. They knew stories of families who had endured the long ocean crossing, only to succumb when they landed there.

'Mammy, what is happening?' Annie asked, fearful.

'It is all right, pet. No need to worry,' she reassured her little daughter. 'The captain said our journey is nearly over. Sit up and let me plait your hair.'

Chapter 79

'THERE IS TO BE A MEDICAL INSPECTION OF PASSENGERS AND CREW before we are allowed to sail into New York harbour,' announced Mr Dwyer as the *Lady Jane* dropped anchor near Staten Island. 'Anyone found with fever or contagion will be removed from the ship to Staten Island's Marine Hospital – a quarantine station. It is the law here.'

The passengers grew nervous and uneasy as a smaller ship docked beside them and an official inspector came on board.

'I heard that if a large number of passengers shows any sign of fever, the ship itself could be quarantined for thirty days,' Johnny Meagher had told them grimly.

'Thirty days!'

Mary's heart sank at the thought of having to spend another month in these conditions. Surely people would not be so cruel to them when their journey's end was so tantalizingly close.

She watched silently as two men, unable to hide their disgust at the foul conditions, moved quickly among the passengers while another sat grim-faced at a long rough table. A sailor stood beside him with the ship's manifesto, as he called people forward.

The medical inspector's expression was serious as he examined each person from head to toe. Eyes, nose, ears and throat. Feeling their neck, looking under their arms, and examining their skin carefully, looking for tell-tale typhus pustules and ship fever spots.

Poor Mrs Murphy, Mary thought. The inspector, who had already been informed of Michael's death, examined her, her husband and two younger sons. He pronounced gravely that they all were infected and were to be taken to the hospital. A young wife, who had lain in her bunk, sweating and tossing and turning since last week, was also lifted off the ship, accompanied by her upset husband.

Mary and John stepped forward slowly when their names were called. She worried for all the children, but mostly for Annie who looked wretched. She gave her daughter's cheeks a quick pinch to try to give her some colour.

'I see you already have lost a son,' the medical officer stated matter-of-factly, as he began to examine the children.

'Yes, sir.' John nodded, trying to disguise the concern on his face as the man began to examine Annie.

The poor child was terrified of him, her eyes welling with tears.

'I am well, sir,' said Tim, standing straight and strong when his turn came.

Nora, Jude and Sarah were all nervous and quiet as the inspector made them cough and stick out their tongues.

Then it was Mary's turn. She blushed at the filth and odour

of her skin and clothes as the man ran his fingers over her neck, shoulders and legs, and studied her throat and mouth, examining her as you would an animal at the market. He then called John forward and repeated the exercise all over again.

'Mr and Mrs Sullivan, I have to admit that I have concerns about your youngest child, Annie. She seems very weak.'

'Sir, she's had the seasickness since we left Cork,' Mary tried to explain. 'She has kept little down and has just lain in her bunk the whole journey, only eating like a little mouse.'

'Aye, so that is it,' he said, writing on the list. 'Mrs Sullivan, my advice is that once you land, your child will need good care and nourishment if she is to be well again.'

He gestured for them to move away as another passenger's name was called.

Mary's legs nearly went from under her with relief as she grabbed hold of Annie in her arms and hugged her tightly.

Ten passengers in all were removed to the hospital from the ship, along with a seaman who had been ill and unable to do his duties the past few days. Fortune had smiled on the rest of them and the captain was given permission to continue their journey.

The *Lady Jane* sailed slowly through Upper Bay to the wharfs and piers of New York where the rough Atlantic Ocean met the mouth of the broad Hudson River. A strange mixture of excitement, nervousness and emotion overwhelmed Mary as she, John and the children caught their first glimpse of the country that would be their new home.

'Look, Mam, just look at it!' declared Tim, his eyes shining as they took in the city with its tall structures and streets all crowded together, the roads and warehouses, the horses and carriages. 'It's huge.'

New York. The name tripped off their tongues and John gripped Mary's hand tightly as they approached the wharf where they would anchor.

The buildings, people and horses were getting closer and closer. The children began jumping up and down, giddy with excitement as at last they reached land.

Chapter 80

New York City
October 1847

HOLDING HER BUNDLE, MARY STOPPED TO CATCH HER BREATH AS she stepped up on to the gangplank. Her thoughts were with Con, who, only two months ago, had crossed it back in Cork, filled with hopes and dreams. Their son should be here with them in New York today, instead of lying buried in the depths of the cold ocean.

'Mam, come on,' Nora called, her eyes shining. 'Mam!'

Mary tried to gather herself, seeing the hope and excitement written on the children's faces.

'I'm coming.'

Taking hold of Annie's hand, she smiled as she, John and the children crossed the narrow gangplank and put the first foot on this new land . . . America.

Crowds milled everywhere. As they stood to take it all in, a group of young boys and men, runners from the various boarding houses near to the wharf, accosted them.

'I know of a clean room, missus. With a large bed for you and the children!'

'Welcome to New York, good sir! Come with me to cheap boarding in a well-run Catholic establishment. Only a ten-minute walk for you and your family.'

'Rest your head in the cheapest lodgings in the whole of the city.'

The boys and men clustered around the exhausted passengers, trying to grab their bundles and baskets, to lead them towards their employers' boarding houses.

Johnny Meagher had warned them about such a thing happening, so Mary held on to their small bundle tightly, anxious as her legs and body struggled to adjust to the feeling of standing on dry land again after the constant movement of the ship.

A large, red-faced woman in a fashionable blue dress and bonnet approached her as if they already knew each other.

'It will all be strange to you, my dear, but if you are in need of clean lodgings, I am an honest woman.'

'Madam, we are to find my brother's place and hope to lodge with him,' interrupted John. He held Annie in his arms, fearful she would be hurt in the crush of people and carts around them.

'Well, good luck to you all.' She smiled and took a printed card from her large pocket. 'Here is my address should you be in need of somewhere to lay your heads.'

'Thank you,' Mary said, grabbing the card and putting it into her bag.

The boys had started to run around, glad to stretch their legs and enjoy the warm sunshine and salt-scented breeze. Above them, noisy seagulls whirled and dived as goods and passengers were unloaded from the ships all around them. Carts and horses were quickly packed and laden with goods to be taken to nearby warehouses and businesses.

'Move out of the way!' shouted their impatient drivers.

Mary, jumping aside, had never witnessed such a frenzy of activity. She began to fret about what lay ahead of them in such a large strange city that was so different from their tranquil home place.

'Come, we must make our way to Pat's address,' John insisted. 'Hopefully he will have space for us to rest and stay with him.'

'Your brother is in for a surprise,' she teased as, arm in arm, they set off with the five children in tow.

John had only his brother's letter to guide them but, having gained some knowledge of the streets and layout of the city, he had some idea of the direction they had to take.

The streets were lined with tall wooden buildings and crowded with shops and stores, slaughterhouses, tanneries and breweries. There were all kinds of wares on display, from tin and copper to linen and lace, sides of beef and haunches of bacon.

They passed a long avenue which was home to fancy shops and provision stores. Mary had never seen the like. They were well-stocked with food and bread, clothes, boots and shoes, hats and gloves, furniture and linens to entice the customer inside. Fashionable, well-dressed ladies and gentlemen paraded by, ignoring them. Mary was all too conscious of her family's dishevelled and pitiful state.

'More filthy Irish,' a man in a velvet coat sighed, holding his handkerchief to his nose.

Anger burned inside her and she was tempted to shout back

at him. Did he have any idea what they had endured these past eight awful weeks at sea, these past hungry years? Instead, she concentrated her attention on trying to find Pat's address, which they were told was in the Five Points district.

They took a few wrong turns on the way, and Nora and Sarah grumbled about how tired and hungry they were.

'After all that time on the ship, we are not used to walking. That's all it is,' she tried to reassure them.

'We will eat soon,' John promised. 'Once we find where your uncle lives.'

They had turned off the main roads and larger avenues to an area of crowded, narrow streets. Ones where tall houses were cramped together near yards, stables and busy factories. Rubbish was strewn everywhere – outside the factories and the houses, in the yards and dung heaps – and waste food scraps and unwanted goods were piled high. Pigs rooted and scrambled and searched among them, gobbling up the city's rubbish. As they passed through Mulberry Bend and Cross Street, John asked a burly cart-hand who owned the animals.

'They are the city's pigs,' he responded.

A short walk later, a look of concern crossed John's face as he recognized the name of the street from his brother's letter.

Pat Sullivan was living in Little Water Street, a rundown part of the city from what he could tell, in a shabby wooden house with ramshackle windows, a peeling door and broken steps. It was certainly not the fine dwelling he had boasted of to his brother.

'Is this it?' Mary could not hide her disappointment.

'It seems so. I will enquire for him.'

Mary stood by his side as John rang the bell again and again.

It took an age before a heavy-set woman in an apron came to the door.

'We are looking for my brother, Patrick Sullivan from Ireland. Does he live here?'

'Pat Sullivan. Aye, he does,' the woman replied, her eyes raking over them as she took in their poor condition. 'But he's not here at the moment. He's at work. You will have to come back later, after six thirty. He should be here by then, for it's dinner time.'

'Ma'am, we hate to trouble you, but could we wait for him?' John pressed. 'We have just arrived in the city and the children are all exhausted. Could we wait in Pat's rooms, do you think?'

' "Rooms", is it? I'll have you know that Mr Sullivan shares a room upstairs with three others. This is a men-only establishment.'

'We've been at sea for nearly eight weeks and the children need to rest a bit,' Mary said quietly. 'I promise you that we will be no trouble and won't be in your way.'

She could see the woman considering their situation.

'My husband and I came over on the ship from Galway, nearly ten years ago,' the landlady said, her tone softening. 'I still remember what it was like. I suppose that I could let you sit awhile in the dining room until Mr Sullivan returns home. But you and the children will have to leave then.'

The dreary dining room was home to a long table surrounded by fourteen chairs, and was already set for the evening meal. A sideboard containing bowls, serving platters and cutlery ran along the far side of the room, and a tall window looked out over the street.

Every member of the family was relieved to sit down but John stood at the window, watching the passers-by.

'Well, we can't stay here, so we need to find somewhere else to stay tonight,' Mary reminded him.

They did not want to be wandering the city streets of New York when darkness fell.

'I'm sure Pat will know of somewhere.'

Mary did not share her husband's faith in his brother's ability to procure lodgings for them.

'I think that we should go and look ourselves. We can see Pat later, or tomorrow.'

They were interrupted by the arrival of the landlady, who brought them a pot of soup, some bowls and spoons, and a plate of fresh soda bread.

'I'm sure you are all hungry,' she said kindly, distributing the bowls.

The children rushed around her as she ladled out portions of the thick meaty soup.

'Thank you, Mrs . . .'

Mary blushed with embarrassment, for she did not even know the good woman's name.

'It's Mrs Catherine Ryan.'

Mary could not believe the kindness of this stranger to them.

'Thank you,' she said tearfully, for it had been the longest while since such kindness had been shown to them.

Later, Mrs Ryan returned to remove the dishes and Mary took the opportunity to ask her if she knew of anywhere close by where they might find lodgings.

'Stay away from the Old Brewery,' she warned. 'It's a rookery and no place for children. Try down around Mulberry Bend or Cross Street. Number forty might have space. Or try the corner building near the tannery.'

Mary thanked her for her generosity and began to organize the children to get ready to leave.

'If you wish, you and Mr Sullivan may leave the children here with me a short while,' she offered. 'It will make it easier for you to go and search for rooms without such a brood.'

Mary was not sure about leaving the children with a stranger, but there was something about Mrs Ryan that made her feel she could trust her. Annie and Tim refused to stay with the landlady but the others remained in Little Water Street while John and Mary set off on their search.

There were no rooms anywhere they went, or if there were, they were not fit for a family.

They walked up and down the streets, knocking on doors. In desperation, Mary took out the card that the well-dressed woman at the wharf had given her. She realized it was for a boarding house on nearby Orange Street.

The owner shrugged. Mary was too late – her best rooms were already let.

'We would be happy with anything,' pleaded Mary.

Mrs Beatty hesitated, before beckoning for them to follow her down a set of steps to the rear of the house. The steps led to a room containing two old beds, a stained mattress stacked against a wall, and a few chairs. It was lit by a small window and, even though the day was warm, it still felt chilly.

'I provide rooms only and no meals,' she told them firmly.

'And this will cost a dollar a week. There is a tap and sink and shared water closet in the yard.'

Mary wrinkled her nose, for the stench from it was overpowering.

She suspected that what they were being shown was more of a storage room, but at least they and the children would fit here.

'Thank you, Mrs Beatty,' John said. 'My wife and I are grateful to you. We will take it.'

'It's grim,' he admitted as they walked back to collect the other children, 'but hopefully it will only be for a short time.'

They returned to the boarding house on Little Water Street to find Pat Sullivan deep in conversation with Nora, Sarah and Jude. He and John, the minute they saw each other, embraced tearfully.

'Brother, forgive me, but I never thought that I would see you again in this lifetime, let alone here in New York.'

'Nor I,' admitted John ruefully. 'But we had no choice. Mary and I were evicted from the home place and Wrixon Becher's men offered us paid passage to here.'

'Nora told me about what happened to Con.' Pat's voice broke. 'I asked her where her brother was and it's right cut me up to hear tell of his death on that ship! I'm so sorry for the both of you to lose your boy.'

Mary nodded tearfully as she saw the sympathy in his eyes.

'He was precious to us.'

'He was the finest boy ever,' added John, clasping his brother's shoulder.

John outlined the terrible events and tragedies that had befallen the family and their neighbours since Pat had left Skibbereen.

Pat's eyes filled with anger as John told him about the death of his uncle and aunt.

'I'm sorry, John. I know how much the place and the land meant to you. And poor Flor and Molly.'

Pat looked well, Mary thought. Compared to John, he was healthy, strong and muscular. If possible, he was even more handsome than ever, she decided, as she watched him covertly. He was full of talk of New York and this new land of opportunity, where a man could make his fortune. He explained how he had found work in a slaughterhouse at first.

'All that blood fair turned my stomach, for I had the job to clean it all up. Then I got hard labouring work on a house two blocks away. These days, I am working as a carpenter on a big new house. It's being constructed on a plot of land not half a mile away and will house plenty of families.'

'So there is work!'

'Plenty of it, but they work us hard. The foreman is a decent sort. I'll ask him if there is any work on offer.'

'But I know nothing of building and construction.'

'That's no matter. Like us all, you will soon learn.'

The other boarders had begun to return, so Mary took the children outside.

'We have found somewhere to stay,' she explained to them, as John and Pat joined them on their walk to Orange Street.

Mrs Beatty was not too pleased when she realized they had five children, not two.

'We are well used to sharing beds,' Mary said pleasantly as she led her family down the steps to the large dank room.

At least the landlady had provided them with a few blankets and a lamp. The following day they would go in search of a few more essential items they needed to purchase.

Pat had disappeared and returned shortly with two cans of milk, a few slices of salt beef and a loaf of a strange type of dark rye bread. He handed the items to John and pressed a few dollar bills into his hand.

'I'll pay you back once I start earning,' John promised his brother earnestly.

Annie and Nora were already half asleep, and Mary could barely keep her eyes open as John and Pat said goodnight, agreeing to meet again tomorrow.

As she lay in the darkness, Mary missed the rocking of the ship and the sound of the slapping water. As she listened instead to the strange and unfamiliar noises of New York City, she finally fell asleep.

Chapter 81

MARY OPENED HER EYES AS THE MORNING SUN CREPT INTO THE gloomy room. John lay asleep beside her and the children slept too. Tim's arm was flung across his head, while Jude snored lightly. Annie was curled up like a kitten beside Nora and Sarah. They were all tired and dirty, still wearing their soiled clothes from the long voyage.

She felt strangely weary as she stared at the damp-stained walls and grimy woodwork, the mouldy rug and mattresses. She tried not to give in to the disappointment she felt that after such an arduous journey they should end up in such a place, so different from their neat, tidy cottage and green fields. She was tempted to go back to sleep but there was much work to be done if they were to get used to New York and its ways.

She got up and went outside to the empty yard. She was delighted to see a large tin wash basin and that some obliging tenant had left a bar of carbolic soap beneath it. Quickly, Mary slipped back inside and lifted dresses, shirts, britches and jackets from the bodies of her sleeping family for washing and airing. Being poor was no shame, but being dirty was. She would not have her family sneered at or insulted!

She hung the laundered clothes to dry on the rope line that was strung across the narrow yard.

'Where is my shirt?' demanded John when he woke up.

'Mammy, my dress is gone!'

'They are washed and will be dry soon,' she assured them.

Despite the howls of protest, she washed herself and the children in the yard, scrubbing at their skin until it was pink, then combed through their wet hair to get rid of the lice and nits that had plagued everyone on board the *Lady Jane*. Finally satisfied that everyone looked decent and clean, she shared the remainder of the black rye bread and milk between them.

A few hours later, John set off in search of work.

'I hope you find something,' Mary said, kissing him lightly as she saw him on his way.

'Even though Pat put in a good word for me, they say they already have enough men employed at his place,' he sighed in disappointment, but he persisted in walking the district.

He enquired at the livery yards, abattoirs, and even the docks. He was glad to find work eventually at the nearby fish market, cleaning up and sweeping out the place.

'At least it's work, John,' she encouraged him when he told her the news.

The pay was low but Pat insisted on giving them a small loan to tide them over.

'You can give it all back to me when you get a better job,' he reassured his brother.

Mary purchased a bucket and a scrubbing brush, some baking soda and vinegar, and set to cleaning their place from top to bottom. Lord knows how long it had been since anyone had lifted a finger to clean it! She aired the mattresses and beat the rug. She washed away the grime and polished the glass in the small window.

'This place looks much better. If you keep this up, Mrs Beatty will want more rent,' John teased when he came back from work one day.

As she combed the markets and provision stores, she thought of the hunger back home. She could not escape a profound sense of guilt at the abundance of fresh meat and fish, butter, cheese and eggs, potatoes by the sackload, and vegetables, breads, cakes and spices available to buy. She longed to be able to cook a proper meal for her family, spend time preparing and making something John and the children would want to eat that would not sicken them or barely fill their stomachs.

However, Mrs Beatty refused to let her use the kitchen. Instead, they had to make do with cooking on a small fire they lit on an iron grate placed against the stone wall. Mary made the best of it, though. With her pot and a new pan and some cheap vegetables, a little lard, some offcuts of meat and a half-sack of flour and oats she had bought, she began to make more nourishing meals that little Annie and the children would eat.

The children played in the street with the other youngsters who lived in the neighbourhood. It wasn't long before they lost their pasty, gaunt look and began to regain their strength.

Mary found out about schooling from a neighbour. Jude, who had just turned thirteen, was considered too old but the rest of the children were enrolled at the old school building a few streets away. Tim was declared an excellent student, and Nora and Sarah, to her surprise, both took well to reading and began to learn all about the history and geography of this new country of theirs.

'They can teach *us*,' Mary said proudly.

Mary found those first days and weeks in New York a terrible trial. Although Pat was there to guide them as best he could, they remained outsiders, unused to city life. The crowded tenements, noise and pungent smells were overwhelming, for she missed home – the quiet of the fields and the fresh breeze blowing across their land.

Though their lodgings were now clean, the room remained damp and cold, and Catherine Ryan, who had been so kind to them on their arrival, was most helpful to her, warning her that soon the winter would come.

'Mary, I tell you, there is nothing as cold as New York in the winter. We'll soon be covered in snow and ice. 'Tis nothing like home and you'd best be prepared for it!'

'I need to get some material to make us warmer clothes,' she told John urgently.

She'd discovered a haberdashery that sold cheap offcut remnants of the exact material she wanted. With some money John had set aside, she bought what she needed and cut, sewed and made new warm dresses, shirts and coats for them all, to see them through the long winter days ahead.

Chapter 82

Skibbereen

'GOOD MORNING, FATHER,' CHORUSED THE SCHOOL CHILDREN loudly as they welcomed him.

Father Fitzpatrick smiled as he took in the desks packed with young pupils keen to learn and to receive the free meals supplied by the British Relief Association. Since the inception of its charity scheme for feeding children a few weeks ago, attendance at St Fachtna's School had never been so high, the place now crowded out. The Association's schools scheme ensured that nearly every hungry child in the district could not only get an education but also be fed.

A few of the children had protested and objected at first to the conditions that hands and faces had to be scrubbed clean, and hair had to be combed for lice and nits, but if the children wanted to avail themselves of the two free meals provided generously by the British Association every day in the school, they must abide by the rules. The scheme was a good one and though, at first, Father Fitzpatrick had wondered about its efficiency, the promise of a bowl of gruel in the morning and oatcakes later in the day enticed the hungry. Children from all over now flocked to school.

'It's a devil of a job, Father, trying to get them to let their faces and hands be washed every day,' confided the school master. 'And you should hear the roars from some of them when the poor assistants are trying to use the fine comb to de-louse their hair.'

'But it has made a difference?'

'Most certainly. How can a child be expected to learn when they have an empty belly?'

'Aye,' he nodded. 'The hope is that feeding and washing and cleaning the children will help curtail the spread of disease.'

The school and its classrooms had not been built to accommodate such huge numbers, but if the parents wanted the children to attend, he was happy for the school to oblige. It meant the burden of feeding so many mouths in a poor family was somewhat eased. No longer wan and pale-faced, the boys and girls, he hoped, could concentrate and learn.

As the priest walked through the town, he wondered how much longer they would have to endure such conditions. He remained tired and drained from the constant demands for his services. The young curate, who assisted him as best he could, looked of late to be exhausted too.

A few of the young men with whom he had studied and trained for the priesthood had already succumbed to the fever, which they had caught while performing their religious duties in their parishes. His friend Father James Coyle had died of typhus only a few weeks ago. A kind-hearted, gentle man, it had been a great loss.

Some days, he felt as if there must be an angel watching over him as he attended the sick and dying in the lanes and hovels of the town. His job was to bless and comfort them in their final hours on this good earth. He had come to realize that doing the Lord's work here in Skibbereen was what he had been called for, and that it was a true testimony of his faith.

'I have your meal ready,' declared Bridey when he returned home that evening.

The woman fussed over him like a mother hen, making sure that he ate enough and slept enough, and got a little peace to himself.

'If I don't look out for you, Father, who will?'

'Thank you, Bridey. Without your good care I would be lost,' he said, seeing her flush with pride as she returned to the kitchen.

Taking out his Bible, he began to read, finding great comfort in the familiar words . . .

Chapter 83

New York City
March 1848

THAT LONG, FREEZING FIRST WINTER IN NEW YORK WAS THE WORST, for John earned little and they had not even a proper fire or stove to warm them. In early spring, as the snow melted, a lad who worked on Pat's building, hulking bricks and materials, injured himself. He broke his shoulder and arm badly and was no longer fit for work.

'One man's bad luck is another's good luck!' observed Pat as he sent John to talk to the building foreman.

'He offered me the job,' John reported with delight after his brief interview. 'I start tomorrow.'

'I told you that Jerome Daly would change his tune mighty fast.' Pat laughed. 'And he's glad to hire you.'

In his new job, John disappeared early in the morning and returned home exhausted, but was glad to have found a position that paid decent wages.

'At least here we can afford to pay rent, buy food and some of the things we need,' he said proudly.

Pat also found a job for young Jude. The nearby printing factory was looking for an apprentice who was ready to learn and not afraid of hard work. Jude, in his own quiet way, was exactly what they wanted. He was turning into a fine young man and was very like Mary's late sister.

'Your mam would be proud of you,' she said, hugging him close.

Mary had struck up a growing friendship with Catherine Ryan, who would give her honest advice on where to go and what to do.

'I hear there are rooms coming up to rent in a house on Mulberry Street,' she tipped off Mary one day. 'The people renting them are moving out west.'

Immediately, Mary and John arranged to go and see them. The lodgings were on the second floor of a four-storey house and were made up of three rather cramped rooms, one of which was a kitchen with a small stove. In all, there were ten families living in the building.

'Oh, John, it's so much better than where we are,' Mary enthused, noting the way the sun streamed in through the windows, and the neat back yard with a water closet.

'It will cost us more,' John fretted, 'but to be honest, I don't know if I could face another winter where we are.'

The sun was warm in the sky when they packed up their few belongings and, with a small handcart, moved from the dank basement to their new rented home. Mrs Beatty watched from the door with a face like thunder, for she had been most put out when they had told her they were leaving.

'Mrs Sullivan, you might regret leaving this establishment,' she cajoled. 'As I may have two better rooms to let in a month or so.'

Mary certainly didn't have any regrets, though, and was in no way sad to say goodbye to Mrs Beatty's establishment on Orange Street.

'That old rip will soon find two other greenhorns off the ships to take our place!' shrugged John as they moved to Mulberry Street.

Annie, Nora and Sarah ran around their new home, delighted as Mary hung a curtain to divide into two the bedroom they were to share with the boys. There was a bed for them on one side, and a mattress on the other.

'Uncle Pat and I will make bunks for you boys when we can afford it,' promised John.

As she looked around their new home, Mary hoped that they and the children would find happiness there.

Each week, at Sunday mass at the Immigrants' Church, Mary prayed for Con. Not a day went by when she didn't think of and miss him. She asked the Lord to help her family get used to their new life and to look after the hungry and sick who were suffering back in Skibbereen. Afterwards, as the children ran and played and chased each other in the newly opened Madison Square Park, she and John walked arm in arm like two sweethearts.

Chapter 84

MARY STUDIED THE FIGURES SHE HAD WRITTEN DOWN, THEN totted them up again. John worked hard but, with their rent and food purchases, they were barely making ends meet. Putting on her coat, hat and boots, she made her way to Catherine Ryan's boarding house on Little Water Street and consulted with her about the prospect of finding dressmaking work.

'Some folks don't like hiring married women. That is the truth of it, but a family has to eat, I know. There are a few that might take you on, though keep away from Mena Stronge as she is meant to be a right old rip, and difficult to work for.'

Mary had taken out her sewing kit and gone from dressmaker to dressmaker and numerous garment factories in the district to offer her services, but with little luck.

'I'm sorry, Mrs Sullivan,' said dressmaker Betsy Smith, shaking her head, 'but I already have three women working for me.'

'I am a good worker with plenty of experience,' she pressed.

'I'm sorry, my dear. Why don't you try Mena Stronge on Pearl Street?'

Mary thanked Mrs Smith, but was nervous about approaching Mrs Stronge. However, needs must. Putting her pride away, she found herself on Pearl Street looking at the narrow shop window with a dress and a maid's uniform both on display. Taking her courage in hand, she pushed in the door and introduced herself to the tall woman presiding at the counter.

Mena Stronge's wavy hair was pulled back into a tight bun and she wore a neat, high-collared blue dress, which showed off her trim figure. She had enormous limpid, pale-blue eyes, which might lull a person into thinking she was perhaps a quiet type of woman, but once the conversation started, those eyes became wide and searching, for she was a highly intelligent and astute woman.

Mrs Stronge said little as Mary told her about working for Honora Barry.

'You seem to have made everything, from bridal dresses to fashionable styles and children's clothes, and done difficult alterations to patching and mending,' the woman said, somewhat sarcastically.

Mary blushed to hear her work described in such a fashion.

'Have you brought any samples of your work?'

Mary's hopes plummeted for a moment or two, before she thought to pass Mrs Stronge her plum-coloured winter coat and pointed out the finer details of the navy dress that she was wearing.

The woman examined the seams and hems, pin tucks and button holes meticulously.

'This is good work, Mrs Sullivan. Very good work,' she said admiringly.

'Thank you.'

'My business has a definite type of customer. I don't make wedding dresses or fine stylish gowns for women to wear. Mostly I service the needs of people who wish to have uniforms fitted and made for their staff.'

'Uniforms?'

'For house maids, nursery maids and cooks. Of late, I have been fortunate to make the uniforms for all the maids in two new hotels – one in Brooklyn and one over on Lafayette Street. There are big houses, wealthy people employing staff, who want their maids to look neat and tidy but also to have some kind of personal detail on their uniform to distinguish them from their neighbours'. I tell you, it's a growing business. That is, if you are interested in coming to work for me.'

'Mrs Stronge, I would very much like to work with you,' agreed Mary.

The other woman told her what her wages would be and explained that she would work for her for three full days a week at first.

'Then we can see what's what!'

Almost every day, maids came to the small shop on Pearl Street to be fitted for new uniform or to have an existing one repaired.

Every so often, Mary accompanied Mena as they travelled by coach to some grand house, where the maids were lined up to be fitted. Mary carefully wrote down measurements, names and details for Mena.

'Hold up your arms, please?' she asked a pretty girl from Kerry, as she ran the measuring tape over her.

Mary had started off fearful of Mena but, in time, came to respect the Belfast woman.

'My husband and son and I came over here nearly fifteen years ago,' Mena explained. 'He was working in the bank for nearly three years when he suddenly took ill. A week later he died of a bronchial attack, leaving me and my poor boy, Henry, here in New York without a soul to help us. What was I to do, return to Belfast or try to make a life here?'

Mary was filled with admiration for Mena's determination and business acumen. Bit by bit, she had built her business from scratch and, like Honora Barry, was a woman from whom she could learn much.

Chapter 85

MARY GOT TO KNOW THE MAIDS WHO WORKED IN MANY OF THE
big houses and mansions in St John's Park, Gramercy Park
and Washington Square, and she listened to their tittle-tattle
good-naturedly. They were most happy to have comfortable,
well-fitting uniforms, unlike the hand-me-downs and outfits
either too tight or too big that were used by the staff in some
other grand houses.

'I'm getting married in eight months' time,' confided Kitty
O'Kelly one day. 'And that will be the end of my uniform
days. What I will be wearing next June is a fine wedding dress
that I am saving for. Would you consider making it for me,
Mary?'

Mary had checked with her employer and Mena Stronge
had made it very plain that she had no interest in such work,
but had no objection to Mary taking it on. For Mary it was a
chance to sew something beautiful and delicate again, for the

pretty young Kerry woman, compared to the functional uniforms she usually spent most of her days making.

Over time, Mary developed quite a reputation in the Five Points for her dressmaking skills. She found herself making summer and winter dresses, outfits for weddings and funerals, and fine dresses for maids, housekeepers or cooks who, upon leaving their employment after long years of service to open boarding houses or eateries, wanted to be suitably attired.

It was good work and reminded her of Miss Barry's shop. Often, she found herself thinking of her friend the dressmaker, who had helped to make their survival and journey to America possible.

She worked hard and saved every dime and dollar she could, week after week, putting it into a savings bank.

Catherine's daughter, Lily, was getting married, and Mary was delighted when she asked her to make her dress. She was a pretty girl with the same thick dark hair and big brown eyes as her mother.

'I'm getting married in a month's time. It is only a simple affair, Mrs Sullivan, and I'm not one for fashion, but my mam told me that you will make me a special dress.'

'I'd be happy and honoured to.'

Mary smiled and did her best to put Lily at ease as she took out her measuring tape. The girl had a good waist and long legs. Taking out some samples of lace, tulle and pretty sprigged cottons, Mary showed them to her, and was not surprised when Lily chose the cotton. She suggested a high cinched waist, and encouraged Lily to consider adding a lace trim to the collar and cuffs.

'I can make them removable for easy washing and dressing the dress up or down.'

'We are to be wed at the Transfiguration Church,' Lily told Mary as they continued to chat. 'Mam is putting on a spread for us afterwards, back in the boarding house. If the day stays fine, she intends on putting two tables outside with summer daisies.'

'That sounds like a lovely day for you all,' Mary enthused.

'Michael Connolly is the man of my heart,' Lily confided, her face lighting up, 'and truth to tell, all I care about is that the two of us are married.'

'I felt the same as you when I was wed many years ago.' Mary smiled, remembering the day that she and John were married back in Cork. 'And it's still the same.'

Chapter 86

THE CITY COULD BE A LONESOME PLACE. EVEN THOUGH MARY WAS surrounded by the constant noise and sounds of the teeming, overcrowded neighbourhood with its packed tenements, abundant stores, back-lane saloons and brothels, and busy streets, she still, at times was heartsore and longed for the peace and quiet of the countryside. She missed their cottage in the sea of green fields and the stillness there. Her homesickness gnawed at her like a pain some days, as she knew that she would never set foot in her native land again.

When she thought of Con, she longed to hold him close and never let him go, to banish the memory of his death. It still grieved her so but she took comfort in the other five children and the joy they brought her, for she now considered Jude and Sarah very much her own children too.

Tim had taken to drawing and sketching. The school master said that he had a talent far beyond his years.

'Ma, I made you this,' he said proudly, handing her a sheet

of paper one day with a picture on it. 'It's our cottage. The way I remember it.'

Mary gasped. Although it was simply sketched and coloured, the cottage was exactly as she recalled.

'There's your vegetable patch, and the hen-house.'

Mary couldn't believe how their son had managed to capture with his pencils the place that meant so much to them.

'That's where Da had to fix the hole in the thatch, and there's where Patch used to lie in the sun.'

'Ah, Tim, this is the grandest present I ever got in my life,' she said, hugging him close.

'I wanted to always remember our home place,' he said softly.

John had studied it carefully, tears welling in his eyes.

Mary insisted on getting it framed, and made John hang it up for them all to see.

She and John both worked harder than they had ever expected. John continued to find work in construction, and proving himself a good carpenter he had been promoted quickly. On every street and piece of land, frame or brick building after building was being thrown up to house the city's growing population.

Nora often watched her sewing at home. One day, Mary took out a spare needle and began to show her daughter some simple stitches.

'That's the way, and try to keep the stitches even and the same size,' Mary urged her gently.

Nora chewed her lower lip, her hazel eyes filled with concentration as her fingers worked lightly. Mary could see her satisfaction when the neat square she had sewn was examined.

384

'Good work!' she said, praising her.

Sarah, on the other hand, like Kathleen, had no instinct for sewing. She pricked her fingers and tangled her threads and stitches terribly.

'I hate sewing, Auntie Mary!' she declared. 'I much prefer baking and cooking.'

A few weeks later, when Nora asked to be allowed to try to make a skirt, it came as no surprise.

Watching the children grow and settle in this new land made Mary accept that New York was their home now, and she must learn to get used to it.

Chapter 87

'BUSINESS IS GROWING IN THE CITY, MARY,' CONFIDED MENA. 'WHAT with all the big new fancy houses with staff, and grand hotels like the St Nicholas that are opening up. There are garment shops springing up all over, but as my work is custom made, I am thinking that I will soon need to find a bigger premises, away from the Five Points in a better area. The customers expect more of me than these two small rooms here in Pearl Street.'

'That is good news.' Mary smiled, pleased that Mrs Stronge was including her in whatever plans she was making.

'To be honest, I'll be sad to say goodbye to this place, but I have built a good business and reputation over the years, and I don't intend to lose either.'

'That wouldn't happen!'

'People can be fickle. They'll flock to whatever new fancy place or dress shop that opens, believe me!' She laughed. 'But

I've seen a suitable one on Centre Street, which needs a bit of work. It's got three larger rooms and if I can agree a fair rent with the landlord, I'll take it.'

'Three rooms? Then there will be lots of space!'

'Yes. As you know well, Mary, we are kept busy with so much work, but I was considering hiring a young apprentice. A suitable quiet girl.'

'My Nora is good at sewing and is a steady, honest girl,' she ventured, hoping she hadn't overstepped herself with Mena by mentioning her daughter.

'I intend on interviewing a few girls, so you send your Nora here to meet me. Mind you, I am not making any promises.'

Mary smiled. 'Of course.'

She'd far prefer her daughter to work for Mrs Stronge than one of the nearby garment shops, which employed large groups of women making clothes. Sweatshops – that's what people called them!

Nora was nervous about meeting Mena. Mary remembered how anxious she had been when she had first met the tall Belfast woman, but the one thing she had come to learn from working for her was that she was fair.

'Show her the few pieces you have made,' Mary encouraged her daughter. 'Your skirt and the blouse, and remember to tell Mrs Stronge that you want to learn.'

'I do, Mam. I really do,' said Nora, her pretty face the picture of eagerness as she set off to Pearl Street.

Mena had examined her work thoroughly and then made

her sew part of the hem of a dress, Nora told her mother when she returned home.

'I was scared but I did my best.'

Two days later, Nora was offered the apprenticeship, but would not start until they moved into Mena's new premises.

'She's a credit to you, Mary,' Mena told her. 'She is bright and polite, and will no doubt prove a good learner.'

'Thank you, Mrs Stronge. I am grateful to you for giving Nora the opportunity.'

'To tell the truth, Nora was head and shoulders better than the other girls. One, I suspect, had never even sewn a stitch in her life!'

Three weeks later, they moved into the new shop at the better end of Centre Street and, as Mena had predicted, the customers followed. As did many new clients – New York families that had come up in the world and could now afford staff.

Nora, to her delight, since leaving school was proving herself a good and willing worker, and got on well with the dressmaker, learning quickly from her.

A friend of Catherine's, who lived only a block away, had offered Sarah a position. She was in need of a kind, bright girl to help with cooking and caring for two small children.

'Lord knows you have plenty of experience of that,' agreed Mary when Sarah accepted the job gladly.

Jude was happy in his work and, to his delight, his wages as an inker had been increased.

'My poor da never got regular money. He was always full of plans but from what I remember never got a proper wage,' he admitted quietly. 'But I'm not like him, Auntie Mary, I want to stay where I am and work my way up.'

'Your mam and da would both be so proud of you, Jude,' she encouraged, hugging him tightly. 'I know they would.'

Tim and Annie both remained healthy and well, and were good students, thriving in school.

Sometimes when she walked down by the wharf and along the river, Mary would catch sight of the haunted look of fear and hope on the worn faces of weary men, women and children who were disembarking from ships that had crossed the Atlantic, or walking the city streets in their filthy rags. It still reminded her of when they had first arrived and how much their lives had changed.

However, she saw also the hope in the eyes of all those arriving month after month, not just from Ireland but from Germany too, hardworking people who lived nearby in the Kleindeutschland neighbourhood. It grieved her to see some of her fellow countrymen fall victim to despair and drink. The hunger had marked and scarred them, and homesickness consumed them as they often struggled to survive in the overcrowded Five Points.

'God help them,' she sighed. 'There is just too much sadness in them.'

Chapter 88

'MARY, PAT WANTS ME TO GO IN WITH HIM TO BUY A RUNDOWN frame building on Mott Street,' John told her nervously on his return from work.

'Are you gone cracked? We don't have the money for that,' she told him outright.

'Listen to me. Pat says it is a huge opportunity and that if we don't grab it, someone else will. The place is falling down but we can repair it and fix it up. In a year or two we can either rent it out or sell it.'

'We are paying rent and food. I'm telling you straight, John Sullivan, we have no spare money for such things,' she sighed, exasperated. 'Pat may have the money for it – he has no responsibilities – but we don't!'

'Pat says he'll put up a much larger share, but he wants me to be a part owner with him. We can use our savings and borrow the rest from the Emigrant Industrial Savings Bank.'

He badgered her over the next three days, wearing her down about the house and opportunity that he would miss out on.

'Oh . . . I don't know.' She gave in, exasperated. 'Tell Pat to come here and talk to us about it.'

'The worst that will happen, Mary, is that we improve the old building and sell it at a higher price than we paid for it,' explained Pat, his face serious. 'I promise you that we both will still have our proper jobs. We will do the renovations in the evenings and at weekends when we are free. We'll get a few of the men we know to give us a bit of a hand if need be.'

'But when will you have the time?' she asked with worry. 'You already work so hard.'

'You find time for extra dressmaking work,' John reminded her gently. 'It will be the same for me.'

She smiled. 'God knows we are both hard workers!'

Despite her reservations, Mary agreed reluctantly to John using their meagre savings to go in with his brother on the house. She prayed that he was not being foolish or wasteful.

The two brothers nearly killed themselves fixing up and repairing the house, month after month. John was so tired he would nearly fall asleep standing up.

By September, the work was finished and it was ready to be rented out.

'It's a lot better than Mrs Beatty's,' Mary had to admit when she went to see the finished Mott Street building.

The wood was freshly painted, which was basic, but the place was at least now dry and warm. They rented it quickly to

391

six families, who were glad to find rooms with a stove and proper outside water closet.

'Isn't it a bit crowded?' she asked, worried.

'We could have rented it out ten times over,' Pat reminded her dryly. 'Remember, it's the tenants who help us to repay the loan.'

Chapter 89

Skibbereen
March 1851

AS DAN DROVE FROM BALLYDEHOB INTO TOWN IT GRIEVED HIM TO
see field after field with tumbled cottages, their stones now
used to make low walls, and all the overgrown potato patches
covered with weeds and nettles, ferns and gorse, terrible
reminders of the hunger. Large areas of land all across the
Mizen had been cleared and now lay empty as family after
family had been evicted. Those people were now scattered to
the winds like birds across the Atlantic to Canada and North
America.

From reports he had read, the attrition rate on sea voyages
was a disgrace and many died on board. Coffin ships, some
called them. Even if they survived the journey, many died in
the quarantine hospitals, and for what? The herds of cattle and
sheep that now grazed these forlorn grassy fields! What a travesty, he thought as he urged his horse homewards.

*

He looked into the crib at his newborn daughter, Catherine. A perfect, healthy baby. He prayed that she would stay well.

'She looks like you, Dan,' Henrietta said with a smile. 'See that serious look on her little face, and the way she scrunches her nose?'

'She is a beauty like her mother.' He laughed, noting the pert little upturned nose of his daughter and perfect tiny rosebud lips.

The older children were all delighted with their new sister, especially three-year-old John, while one-and-a-half-year-old William was naturally a little jealous of the baby.

'Now, go run and play, children,' Henrietta urged them with a smile. 'Give your dada and me some peace.'

It did Dan good to see the family happy, and Henrietta was in her element with this latest baby to attend to. It had been a straightforward birth and Catherine seemed a good child so far.

He kissed his wife's head. She seemed surprised by his sudden show of affection.

'You and the children are everything to me,' he declared. 'You do know that?'

'Of course I do. We all do,' she said, reaching gently for his hand.

Dan took her in his arms and held her close. His wife was the one constant in his life. Her love gave him the strength and courage to carry on, even on the darkest of days.

'I love you, Hetty, and I always will.'

'Dan, I've loved you practically from the minute we were first introduced,' she teased, 'and I will love you till I am a very old lady.'

Satisfied, he held her close to his heart, where she always was.

Chapter 90

New York City
April 1853

MARY AND JOHN STROLLED PAST MR BARNUM'S AMERICAN MUSEUM on the corner of Broadway and Ann Street, with its exotic Siamese twins and strange and terrible wonders of the natural world. A place she longed to visit!

They stopped to admire the recently opened St Nicholas Hotel. It was magnificent and even more decadent than New York's renowned Astor Hotel.

'It cost a million dollars to build,' said John admiringly. 'There are six hundred rooms, but soon it will have one thousand.'

'It's beautiful,' murmured Mary.

She watched a little enviously as the crowds of wealthy women and gentlemen in their fine style passed through its tall, polished brass doors, noting the finer details of the ladies' dresses so that she could endeavour to copy them.

'Some day we will dine there,' promised John.

'We will never afford it,' Mary said with a laugh, as instead they walked on until they stopped at the corner of Broadway to buy oysters from the busy oyster cart.

'This country is different from Ireland, for here one man is as good as the next,' John said seriously, adding a shake of salt to his oysters. 'And one man's money is as good as another's! Once you work long and hard there is an opportunity, even for the likes of us.'

'And heaven knows we both work hard enough,' she said, squeezing his arm.

'Do you recall the narrow brick house down at the very far end of our street, with the broken windows?' asked John.

'Not very well. Is it the derelict one? 'Tis in a terrible state. A piece of shingle fell off it and nearly killed a poor messenger boy. It should be condemned.'

'Aye. Pat heard that the owner is moving away and selling it next month. I was wondering if we should consider trying to buy it.'

'You and Pat want to buy it?'

Mary sighed. She wasn't sure she wanted her husband borrowing more money or undertaking so much work again.

'No, it's nothing to do with Pat,' he protested. 'I was thinking that it might suit us to live in.'

'How can we possibly buy a home of our own?' she argued hotly. 'John Sullivan, you know well we don't have that type of money!'

'I admit it needs a whole heap of work, but Pat and I, and young Tim can do much of it, and Pat says the Emigrant Industrial Savings Bank might consider lending us the money.'

*

396

John sighed heavily as they inspected the inside of the ramshackle house on Mulberry Street. Its decrepit condition was far worse than Mary could have imagined.

'The floorboards are rotten and there is a big hole in the roof. The staircase has collapsed and half the windows are broken,' he admitted. 'I suppose that is why it is so cheap.'

Mary's heart sank with disappointment. A strong musty smell pervaded the property and one wall was running with damp. The yard was infested with cockroaches. It was a wreck of a place. No wonder it was lying abandoned and empty. She doubted there was any hope of salvaging such a place.

'However, there is more room than I expected,' declared John. 'I know that it will take months to make the building even habitable, but I believe it could make a decent home for us.'

'I'm not sure,' she admitted, 'that I'd ever want to live here.'

'Pat and Tim will give me a hand. With the right amount of work, I think that it will suit us and our needs. There is even a little room that you could use for your dressmaking.'

Mary could see how excited John was at the prospect of taking the old building and renovating it.

'It's an opportunity for us, Mary,' he pleaded. 'If the savings bank lends us the money, then it's a chance for us that we may not get again – to have a few rooms that we can call our own.'

Three months later, despite her reservations, John had borrowed from the Emigrant Industrial Savings Bank and the broken-down house was theirs.

Chapter 91

September 1854

MARY RAN HER FINGERS OVER THE NEW DRAPES, CUSHIONS AND counterpanes that she and Nora had made for the house on Mulberry Street. She and her daughters had scrubbed every last inch of the place. John, Tim and Jude had done much of the carpentry and repair work themselves. Pat too had helped with the rebuilding work and she was grateful not only for this but for everything he had done for them since they had first arrived in New York.

'Mam, look at our proper bedroom!' eleven-year-old Annie laughed as she jumped on the bed that she and Nora would share, while Tim and Jude were happy to no longer have to share with the girls. Instead, they would have the narrow room that overlooked the street.

The large kitchen was warm, with a fine new stove, and there was a smaller room that looked out on the yard that would serve as her sewing room. The top floor, with its two attic rooms, they would rent out.

She had never imagined that in time they would have a home of their own here in the city.

'I know that it's not in the best of neighbourhoods and still needs some repairs, but at least it is ours,' she said proudly.

'No one will ever take the roof from over the head of a Sullivan again,' pledged John firmly. 'Not while there is still life in us.'

'This place reminds me of a *meitheal* back home,' suggested Pat as he hammered some nails into the last step of the wooden staircase. 'Where everyone helps out, whatever way they can.'

Mary smiled, remembering when neighbours and friends gathered together to help bring in the harvest, mend a thatch roof, or repair a cottage damaged by gales or storms. Or even to give a hand to a young couple to build a simple cabin of their own. A *meitheal* always meant food and drink and hospitality.

Pat was right – so many had helped to turn this place into a home. She and John happily drew up a guest list for a house-warming, surprised by how many new friends they had made since they had first arrived in New York.

Catherine Ryan and her husband, James, insisted on bringing a large maple-glazed ham for the party, while Mena had made her a fine tablecloth and napkins. Lily Connolly and her new husband, Michael, brought along a porter cake, John's boss, Jerome Daly, arrived with a large bottle of *poitín*, and Sarah brought along a friend who worked with her.

'They never get proper home cooking, Auntie Mary,' confided Jude, who had invited two of the other apprentices who worked with him at the printer's.

Pat, much to their surprise, arrived, eyes shining, with a pretty, dark-haired young woman in tow.

'This is Ellen Cleary,' he said, introducing her. 'She works in the haberdashery shop near Broad Street.'

'I sell buttons and bows, mostly,' she said with a laugh.

'Welcome,' Mary said, smiling, delighted to meet the kind, blue-eyed girl who she suspected had stolen Pat's heart finally.

'I bought you this.' Pat laughed as he unwrapped a large slab of cooked corned beef in the kitchen. 'Try as I could, I couldn't find a hare to catch!'

'Mary and I thank you all for coming this evening and for your help in making this old house into a home,' John said to everyone, as all the guests cheered and clapped.

Smiling, they looked around them proudly at their family and friends, and everything this new life and hard work had brought them.

Later, with the house quiet and their friends gone, Mary and John sat out on the narrow back step together. The night was still warm and, as Mary gazed up at the starry sky and moon glowing over the city, she pondered the past. The calamity and sadness they had endured; the terrible hunger and crossing the wild Atlantic Ocean, where they had lost their beloved boy Con. She would never forget the ravaged streets of Skibbereen and all those dear to them who had been taken, and how she and John had been forced to leave their home place for ever.

Life had been so cruel, but somehow they had survived. Fate had surely brought them and their family here to this new life in New York.

Mary laid her face against John's. She still loved her husband as much as the day he had asked her to marry him. She had no idea where time would take them, but as long as they were together that was all that mattered to her.

They spoke little of the past. Instead, they looked to all that life here in this new land, America, would bring them and their children. Their heads and hearts were full of dreams and plans for the future, and the years together ahead of them . . .

ACKNOWLEDGEMENTS

I would like to thank the Skibbereen Heritage Centre where I did much of the research for the book.

Huge thanks are due to Philip O'Reagan of the centre for his invaluable assistance, his patience and kindness, and his insights into the life of Dr Dan Donovan and Skibbereen at the time of the Great Famine.

Thanks also to Margaret Murphy, Skibbereen Heritage Centre's genealogist, who helped me with Dr Donovan's family history.

Thanks to Father Patrick Hickey for meeting me. His book, *Famine in West Cork*, is a huge source of local information.

To the town of Skibbereen. Walking its streets and lanes, and seeing Abbeystrewery graveyard and the Old Steam Mill on Ilen Street where the soup kitchen once was, made it easier to write such a story.

Special thanks also to Professor Christine Kinealy for her absolute dedication to researching the period of the Great Hunger, and to the Great Hunger Institute at Quinnipiac University, Connecticut, US – a wonderful resource.

To Caroilin Callery of Strokestown Park House – the National Famine Museum – in Roscommon, for her huge commitment to creating even more awareness of the Great Irish Famine.

To my cousin Paddy Murphy for a piece of Skibbereen lore he shared with me.

My thanks go to my publishers, Transworld, and the team in both Ireland and London.

Special thanks to my editor, Fiona Murphy, for the enthusiasm and support she gave to me and the book during the long journey from page to print, and also to my London editor, Francesca Best. Huge thanks are also due to my copy-editor, Rebecca Wright, for her insightful suggestions and her patience working on such a big book, and to production editor Viv Thompson, Donna Hillyer, Josh Benn and Orla King.

To Fíodhna Ní Ghríofa in Dublin and Katie Cregg in London for their creative publicity campaigns, and huge thanks to Marianne Issa El-Khoury for her great cover design.

To my agent, Caroline Sheldon, for her constant support and friendship over the years, and to Rosie Buckman, my foreign rights agent.

To all the bookshops and booksellers, your support over the years is very much appreciated.

Thanks to all my writer friends for their encouragement and wisdom, especially Sarah Webb, Martina Devlin and Don Conroy.

My final thanks go to my wonderful family. My kind and patient husband, James, who has been by my side since I started this writing journey.

My children, Mandy, Laura, Fiona and James, and their partners, Michael Hearty, James Hodgins, Mike Fahy and Se Young An, and my grandchildren, Holly, Sam, Ben, Max, Evie, James, Alex and Harry.

Marita Conlon-McKenna is one of Ireland's favourite authors. Her books include the award-winning *Under the Hawthorn Tree*, which is set during Ireland's great famine. Widely translated and published, it is now considered an Irish classic. Her other books include bestsellers *The Magdalen* and *Rebel Sisters*.

She is a winner of the International Reading Association Award, USA and a former chairperson of Irish PEN.

Marita lives in Dublin with her husband and family.

REBEL SISTERS
Marita Conlon-McKenna

With the threat of the First World War looming, tension simmers under the surface of Ireland.

Bright, beautiful and intelligent, the Gifford sisters Grace, Muriel and Nellie kick against the conventions of their privileged, wealthy Anglo-Irish background and their mother Isabella's expectations.

As war erupts across Europe, the spirited sisters soon find themselves caught up in Ireland's struggle for freedom.

Muriel falls deeply in love with writer Thomas MacDonagh, artist Grace meets the enigmatic Joe Plunkett – both leaders of 'the Rising' – while Nellie joins 'The Citizen Army' and takes up arms to fight alongside Countess Markievicz in the rebellion.

On Easter Monday 1916, the Rising begins, and the world of the Gifford sisters and everyone they hold dear is torn apart in a fight that is destined for tragedy.

'Engrossing'
Irish Sunday Times

'Finally, women are being written back into the history of [Ireland's] awakening'
Irish Mail on Sunday

THE MAGDALEN
Marita Conlon-McKenna

The wide open spaces of Connemara, filled with nothing but sea and sky, are all lost to Esther Doyle when, betrayed by her lover, Conor, and rejected by her family, she is sent to join the 'fallen women' of the Holy Saints Convent in Dublin. Here, behind high granite walls, she works in the infamous Magdalen laundry whilst she awaits the birth of her baby.

At the mercy of the nuns, and working mostly in silence alongside the other 'Maggies', Esther spends her days in the steamy, sweatshop atmosphere of the laundry. It is a grim existence, but Esther has little choice. The convent is her only refuge, and its orphanage will provide shelter for her newborn child.

Yet despite the harsh reality of her life, Esther gains support from this isolated community of women. Learning through the experiences and the mistakes of the other 'Maggies', she begins to recognize her own strengths and determines to survive. She recognizes, too, that it will take every ounce of courage to realize her dream of a new life for her and her child beyond the grey walls of the Holy Saints Convent.

'This book pulls no punches . . . Marita Conlon-McKenna is breaking new ground with *The Magdalen*'
Image magazine